THE BLUE
ROAN CHILD

THE BLUE ROAN CHILD

JAMIESON FINDLAY

SCHOLASTIC INC.

New York   Toronto   London   Auckland   Sydney
Mexico City   New Delhi   Hong Kong   Buenos Aires

Originally published in 2002 by Doubleday Canada, a division of Random House of Canada Limited.

Published in the United Kingdom in 2004 by The Chicken House, 2 Palmer Street, Frome, Somerset BA11 1DS.

ISBN 0-439-62753-2

12 11 10 9 8 7 6 5 4 3 2 1   4 5 6 7 8 9/0

Printed in the U.S.A.   40

First Scholastic paperback printing, September 2004

Book design by Elizabeth B. Parisi
Map illustration by Malcolm Cullen

To my Mother and Father

contents

NOTE FROM THE AUTHOR

The preferred pronunciation of "Syeira" is "Sigh-AIR-uh."
The quoted lines on page 221 are from Chaucer's
"The Squire's Tale." I have partially modernized them
using several current translations.

Mayhap a Horse will bee No Solid Color, but Roan'd, which is, Mixt and Ingrain'd like the Blended Dawne, who is a Cordiall of Sun and Shadow. Thus a Blue Roan hath a Black Coate, with White Haires Threaded in; He is Gray Duske with a Scruple of Indigo, and Clear Twilight showing through a Cloudy Squall, and so is a Rare Thing, with a Brave Temper most times. . . .

And to the Question, What is an Efficacious Charme for the Roans, to keep away Cholick and Fevers (and Witches if there bee Such in the Parisshe), the True Answer is: a Sprigge of Growing Laylock [lilac] above the Stalle, or a bit of Antler Carved Out, or a Shell, or any thing Living or Hollow, that might hold a Dreame or Memorie. . . .

—from an old Hayselean horse manual

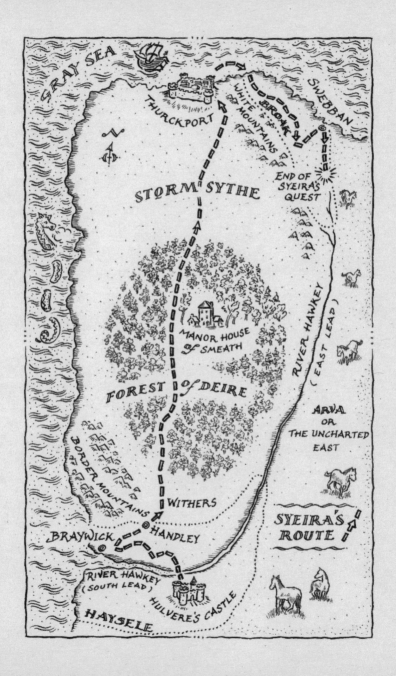

ESCAPE

Nobody knew much about Syeira except that she had been born in the river stable, among old horses and the ghosts of horses. Her mother had died when she was little, and her father might have been the wind for all that people could remember of him. She was small for her age — whatever her age was — and skinny, too; but otherwise she was no different from the dozen other children who worked in the stables of King Hulvere. She slept in a loft and dreamed often of her mother, whom she remembered as a warm blond voice, with skin that smelled slightly of hay.

To spend every day in the king's stables might seem like paradise to some, and so it was — for members of the royal family. They didn't have to do any of the chores. But for a stable orphan like Syeira it meant working all day and much of the night. She mucked out stalls, hauled water, fetched straw, repaired bridles, groomed and fed the horses, stoked fires, and swept the stone floors around the torch pits. Some nights she slept no more than the horses, which was about four hours. Still, the stables were the only home she'd ever had, and they were at least warm and safe. The main stable was very old, with great oak beams and a huge fireplace at one end. Here the king kept his stud stallions and broodmares and chargers-in-training. Rich people came from the far corners of the land to buy these horses, for King Hulvere — ruler of a small country called Haysele, land of horses and horse-sensitives — was a famous horse breeder. There was also a stable beside the jousting fields, about a mile from the castle. It was called the Stable of the Lists and housed the king's own cavalry.

Finally there was the rundown stable near the river, where Syeira had been born.

People of importance rarely visited this river stable, for it was a fair walk from the castle and held no animals of value. It was actually a home for horses that had come to the end of their careers. Here you could find old draft horses as imperturbable as oak trees, bow-backed mares who had foaled many times, and war horses who had grown tired of war. On the walls was a wonderful array of old tack — huge leather collars for the draft horses, armored hoods for the chargers (chamfrains, they were called), and blinders and spurs and the heavy, high-backed war saddles. You had the feeling, while walking through this stable, that great horses had lived out their days here and still lingered in spirit.

If you are unlucky enough to be an orphan, it helps to grow up among horses. Horses take life as it comes. Like holy hermits or milk-fed babies, they are without ambition or regret. It is true that they sometimes breathe on people, but this is nearly always pleasant for the people. The breath of horses is as mild as weak mead. If you took a sun-baked melon — large but slightly underripe — and cut it open with a single stroke, you might get something like the breath of horses. Of course, Hulvere kept some bad-tempered chargers, horses whose breath carried a hot note of menace; but the river stable had none of these. The horses Syeira had grown up with were unfailingly calm. When she was very small she used to run between their legs and clamber roughly onto their backs. This was the early morning of her life: the smell of hay and the light of her mother's hair and the quiet sentinel presence of horses.

But her strongest memory was not of horses at all. It was of a tiny yellow bird, a bird quick as a spark from the blacksmith's anvil. Even now she could hear its vivid song — a kind of filigree of the air that shone in her mind like a horse brass. No one else in the stables remembered it, but she was sure she hadn't made it up. She liked to lie in a loft of the river stable and imagine it darting through the hay-scented shadows. Probably the old horses would remember it, if she could only ask them. But horses only spoke in her dreams, or in the tales the blacksmith told; and this hard truth always brought her wearily out of her loft and back to the main stables, where the ordinary horses were waiting for a brush and a feed.

Of all the king's stock, Syeira's favorites were the Arva horses. They were wild horses from the hilly lands of Arva, which lay to the east of King Hulvere's realm. The king's handlers had got there by water, sailing up the River Hawkey in their special horse transports called *taride*. No ordinary horse handlers could have come within a mile of these animals, but Hulvere's men were not an ordinary lot. They had hunting hawks to worry the horses and large nets to trap them, and they could hiss like snakes and howl like wolves when they really wanted to terrorize their prey. As a result they had managed, with much effort, to capture a mare and her two yearling colts. But before long they had remembered why the horsemen of the old days had left the Arva horses alone. During the loading of the horses the mare had shattered a man's leg with a single kick and almost staved in the side of the ship. (The *taride*, being equipped with oars as well as sails, could be brought close to almost any shore.) On the voyage home, the captives had thrashed and bucked and neighed. Even when brought ashore, sick and dizzy from five days on the river, they had managed to nearly bite the finger off a groom.

Excellent, said the king when he heard about this; he was always looking for aggressive horses for his charger line. And when he saw these ones in a paddock, he wasn't disappointed. The mare was more than a horse: She was a landscape. She flowed like a tall grass field or an avalanche, and her hock joints were like the roots of trees. Her colts were just like her, except smaller, and with longer legs. It is very unusual for a horse to have healthy twins, but these colts were as quick and supple as rapiers. They always stood with their long legs slightly apart, quivering a bit.

They walked as if they could breathe through their skin. Black as peat they were, and their mother was blue roan — that is, the color of a storm cloud. All of them had shaggy manes that came down in two locks between their eyes. They were flawless in every way except that the mare didn't seem to run as well as her colts. After studying her stride the king put this down to an old injury in her back left leg. Still, she was fast enough to carry a knight into battle. Most big horses lack stamina, but the wild horses of the East had always been both large and strong-winded — perfect for chargers. Arva devils, thought the king, you'll make me richer than I deserve to be.

But after a while even he had to admit they were hopeless. They refused to let a man near them, let alone on them. They also refused to be quiet. At first the grooms would leave them out in a paddock at night — it was too much trouble to bring them in — but their neighing carried a long way, and nobody could get any sleep. Eventually they were moved to the far back of the river stable, well away from the castle. There they chewed the railings of the stalls and glowered with their green-flecked eyes.

And there nobody would visit them except Syeira. At that time she was helping with Hulvere's spring foals and would often go to the river stable still carrying the foal smell, which she knew was the least threatening smell to wild horses. The mare would sniff at her warily over the stall, and Syeira would sniff back. She never went too close to the Arva captives. At most she would toss apples and carrots into their stalls, or tip fresh water into the runnels that led to their troughs. Even then she would move very slowly, making soft sounds in her throat. She knew that these horses, like the old horses nearby, disliked the *busyness* of humans — the shouting and gesturing and organizing. Syeira was never busy in the river stable. She knew something about the group soul that surrounds certain horses, a soul that can tear like a membrane at a clumsy touch, and she knew how to move without disturbing it.

ᑕᗷᑋᘙᗢ

One summer's day a great lord and a scourge — Ran of Stormsythe — arrived to buy horses. He was ruler of a huge empire to the north, and almost every year he paid a visit to Hulvere, sailing his splendid *taride* down the coast and up the River Hawkey. Then all of Haysele felt as if it had a fever coming on. People told many stories about Ran — that he personally trained his horses to draw and quarter prisoners, that he often bled himself of "weak" blood, that he had dreamed nothing but nightmares since the age of ten. Hulvere believed them all, from the look in Ran's eyes. But during these visits he did his best to put the stories from his mind. He had to deal with Ran in such a way that the warlord would leave his country alone, as he had done for almost a generation. As long as Haysele provided Ran with superb horses and horse expertise, it remained free — wary and often uneasy, but free.

For weeks leading up to Ran's arrival, all the stable hands had been kept busy ensuring that the horses were in top showing form. When he finally arrived, they were run off their feet; the warlord wanted to see *every* horse in the stables. (Rumor had it that he was facing a rebellion in the northeast and needed lots of chargers quickly.) Sometimes Syeira actually slept standing up, leaning against a horse or a stall door; and no matter how hard she worked she was often cuffed by the harried grooms. Never for a moment was she able to escape to the river stable. Most of the showing was done at the Stable of the Lists, and she dared not step away from there.

At last Ran sailed away one morning under a brisk wind, carrying a hundred prize horses in his holds, and a sigh of relief went up from the castle. Everyone took that day to rest. Syeira herself, gray as a cinder from overwork, fell asleep in the main stable. When she finally slipped groggily from her loft, night had long since come. She didn't have to put anything on, for she always slept in her cow-skin jerkin and thongs. For a moment she stood still, taking in the changed shadows, and then made her way toward the main door of the stable. The ghost of her mother was there in her small, serious face and in the listening way she moved. People used to say that mother and daughter were as alike as two tones of a horse's bell. Syeira's hair wasn't quite as blond — more like the color of dirty flax — and her eyes were a light feathered brown rather than a kindled green, but these differences were too small to be generally noticed. And anyway, sometimes it was hard to tell *what* color Syeira was. The dirt would harden on her like a dusky enamel, so that she looked darker than she actually was.

The blacksmith, as usual, was telling his stories around the forge. From the way he stood, darting and swooping his hand before him, Syeira knew he was speaking of winged horses. He claimed to have seen one himself, as a boy — just a white speck in the sky, and moving as fast as a diving falcon. (The grooms had always assured him that it *was* a falcon.) The listening faces followed his hand raptly, trying to imagine a *horse* racing through the blue air. Syeira generally liked to sit and listen with the others, but tonight she had no wish to join the circle. She just wanted to escape to the river stable.

Outside, the night was quiet except for the distant strains of music from the castle, which, now that Ran was gone, was alive with merriment. Syeira went around the great keep of the castle, through a patchy meadow, and past the wooden hut that housed the hunting birds.

Out in the darkness, beyond the hayricks and crumbling stone fences, was the hillside where her mother had been buried. That had been half a dozen years ago, or a lifetime. People said that her mother had fallen from a loft onto a stone floor. Syeira wasn't sure how old she'd been — some said five, others six. (Precise age only mattered with horses, not stable children.) Once, she had overheard two old women talking about it in the main stable; one of them said she couldn't get over how blond the dead woman had been. Blond as the noonday sun, were her words. Syeira never visited the grave. In her dreams, her mother was still alive, which was why she dreamed so much, and why she stayed away from the grave. Sometimes when she woke in the morning her mother's smell was still in her mind — a smell like honey mixed with sunlight, with a bit of hay around the edges. She found it hard to hold on to the scent. All the workaday smells of the castle pushed it out, and she would have to wait until night to get it back. She never told anybody about this, but a few of the stable hands might have understood. Horse people know what a single scent can do.

As she came up to the old stable, the marshy smell of the river wafted over her. Inside, the light was dim. Because of the risk of fire the stable was never lit by more than several candle lamps, which were housed in arbors of stone called torch pits. In one such pit against the far wall, two old grooms sat slumped and happy, drinking homemade beer. They were talking so loudly that they didn't hear Syeira come in. She glided to her left, down the first row of stalls, and then turned toward the back. She wanted to see the Arva horses first.

The other horses, the old regulars, greeted her with soft neighs, but she barely noticed them. She was wondering what had happened to the stable itself. One stall door had been wrenched off its hinges and now stood at an angle. Another bore the familiar half-moon gouge of a horse's unshod hoof. A sense of foreboding gripped her, and she hurried to the back. There her worst fears were realized: The Arva horses were gone.

She stood there in dismay, gazing at the empty stalls. Why on earth would Ran have taken these horses? Anybody could have seen that they would kill a man if given half a chance. She went right up to the three stalls and gazed in — something she had never dared do when they were occupied. *But maybe*, she reflected, *Ran had taken them exactly because they* would *kill a man*. He was just that kind of horseman. Maybe he planned to leave them with other horses in some far-off paddock, figuring that they would breed eventually and produce a savage charger line. Or maybe he intended to break them, even if it meant killing them. Whatever the reason, he had obviously decided they were worth the trouble of transporting.

And he certainly must have had trouble. He had probably used whips and maybe even torches to get them out. (Nobody in Haysele would have used torches on a horse, which is why the stable hands had had such a problem moving the Arva captives.) She had heard nothing about it, but then, only Ran's handlers had been involved. The warlord had the run of the castle when he was here, and he would generally load the chosen horses himself — using his own methods.

Syeira was standing there dejectedly, hoping the horses hadn't been hurt, when she heard a sound behind her. She turned. At the end of the aisle, just where the greasy lamplight gave way to shadows, she could make out a horse in a small, high stall. Its dark head was just visible above the stall door. She moved closer and with a start of joy recognized the Arva mare.

"Choo," she whispered soothingly. The horse made no movement, but its eyes gleamed like a cat's. She could hear its wheezy breathing and smell its heavy sweat, a bit like damp oakum.

The mare was in a narrow stall that had been designed for unruly horses. The sides were solid oak and the back was the stone wall of the stable. Not even the Arva mare could have kicked her way out. It also had two doors — a heavy iron-reinforced one and another, just as heavy but slightly higher, about six feet in front. The two doors made sure that there was always a barrier between the horse and a handler. A man could open the first door, throw in some hay to the horse, and still remain out of reach. The stall had come in very handy for Ran's men. They had put the mare in here first and then, safe from the mother's wrath, had taken the colts away.

Syeira was now closer to the mare than she had ever been. *So Ran didn't take you*, she thought. *He probably didn't like that leg of yours. . . .*

The mare's breathing sounded noisily in Syeira's ears. *You need a drink*, she thought. There was no drinking trough in this stall; she would have to get a bucket. Looking around, she spied a water barrel farther down the aisle, with a bucket beside it. Quickly she stole over and dipped the bucket in.

"Easy, easy," she whispered, as she returned to the stall. She didn't like the way the mare was being so quiet. Setting the bucket down, she put one foot on a cross-joist in the stall door and stepped up. Still the mare didn't move. Syeira remained poised on one foot, waiting to spring away if the horse so much as twitched. Now she could see dark patches of blood on the horse's coat. She also smelled the thing she most detested in the world — singed horsehair.

"They *did* use torches," she whispered angrily.

The gloom around her seemed charged, like that of a seance or an owl-haunted wood. Standing on the door, she caught the whiff of burning torches and turned sharply, expecting to see somebody coming. But there was only the darkness and the mare breathing. Its eyes were larger than a lion's. Syeira leaned toward it over the stall door.

"If I give you a drink, will you behave?"

The mare pawed once and exhaled with the sharp, plosive sound that stable hands know so well. Its ears were back, but not all the way back.

"All right," said Syeira nervously. "I'll take that as a yes."

She let herself down again and turned her attention to the door. It had two large slide bolts, one under the other, each secured with a pin and chain. She worked them free and then, taking a deep breath, she stepped inside the stall. The horse turned its head slightly to watch her. Syeira felt its breath on her face, warm as a sunny autumn. The mare slid its huge neck over the inner door, and she held up the bucket with both hands. She was so close to the horse that she could see the vein that ran down its nose.

"I'm glad he left you," she whispered.

The mare raised its head, and again Syeira caught the smoky whiff of torches. The sensation was so strong that she looked about her wildly. Was somebody hiding nearby? The only light was the candle lamp thirty feet away. Syeira turned back to the horse, nervous as before.

She will never see her colts again, thought the girl. *Does she know that? Does she* feel *it?*

The mare moved its nose toward Syeira, and suddenly the girl gasped. For a second, for the length of a single heartbeat only, she *smelled* the colts — smelled them as they would be in Arva at sunrise, smelled the buckwheaty scent of their coats, still damp from the dew. She stared, seeing nothing. The darkness came close and then drew back.

"What . . . was *that*?" she asked hoarsely.

She moved closer to the mare. Astonishment had been stricken out of her by something even more intense. In her mind she still smelled the colts, as wild and fresh as newly turned sod in a mountain meadow. She knew then beyond any human telling how the mare loved its children, and how it would die many times over to get them back.

"Your colts . . . ," she began, but that was all she could manage.

Her shaking hands moved to the bolts on the door; she had made a decision without thinking about it.

"I'll get you out," she whispered. "Don't kill me."

The chain of the first bolt was knotted, and she had to pick away at it feverishly. All the time she could feel the breath of the horse on her neck. The second bolt squeaked as she drew it open, and she gritted her teeth in apprehension; but no sound came from the front of the stable.

Moving to the side, she swung the door open.

She realized then how rash she'd been: The horse could have bolted or turned savage. But it only stepped out, tense yet quiet, and sniffed the air. Syeira didn't want to take hold of the horse. She simply moved along the haystrewn aisle toward the back door, and the mare followed. The girl was terrified that the grooms would sense the moving horse — people who have worked in stables seem to have that ability — but the mare glided like the shadow of a cloud. Fortunately the surrounding stalls were empty, since the Arva horses, being a bad influence, were kept apart from the others.

At the back door Syeira put out a hand to the horse. From the darkness came a low threatening snort, and Syeira withdrew her hand. "All right," she whispered. "All right." The mare waited there in the gloom, and Syeira knew it wanted her to leave first.

"I'm going," she said and stepped out into the soft summer air. There was nobody in sight. This was the tail end of the castle grounds, and it was usually deserted, even during the day. The river was weedier here than farther up, where the harbor was, and only the stable boys ever fished here. The beginnings of a trail were just visible in front of her, wandering down through the pasture to the river. She turned back to the door. The horse was gingerly easing its girth through the opening.

"You can't go out by the castle gates," whispered Syeira; she was babbling away as if the horse understood her. "You'll have to swim across the river. There's a road on the other side."

The mare, ignoring Syeira, had already started toward the river with its usual fluid, high-stepping walk. Despite its size it carried almost no suggestion of weight, any more than a well-made sloop does. It moved as if buoyed by the air. Syeira followed at a run, and in a minute they had reached a shabby little beach draped with weeds.

"You must hurry," said Syeira, slightly out of breath. "Ran set sail this morning. He might stop in Braywick for hay and water, but then it's the ocean, and —"

She stopped. Why was she going on like this? The mare couldn't understand her. It couldn't know that its colts were in a ship; it couldn't know where they had gone.

But the horse knew one thing — that men and torches lay in one direction, and escape in another. It stepped toward the water, blowing and tossing its head. In a second Syeira was beside it.

"I'll come with you," she said. "I'll help you."

The mare paid her no attention. Like a lot of horses, it had to get up the nerve to enter deep black water. It laid a forefoot down in the water, snorted, and then laid down the other. Syeira was now up to her knees in the river.

"I'll help you get your colts back," she said desperately. "You need me. You can't undo bolts and steal keys and sneak into ships and . . . You *need* me."

The mare was plunging forward like a stone tower toppling into the sea. Syeira slipped in silently, swam a few quick strokes, and grasped the long mane that floated on the water like kelp. The horse was now swimming freely. Syeira expected it to twist and bite her, but it was too busy keeping its head above the water. Beneath her, she could feel the mare's powerful muscles working. In the midst of her fears she felt a ripple of hope and elation. *I can help her*, she thought. *She needs me.* Slowly she was drawn behind and slightly to the side of the mare, so that they made a single wake in the enormous night. To the end of her life, to the last dream of old age, she would always remember these two wild smells — the Arva horse, the muddy river — and how they had carried her out of a lonely childhood.

For in Syeira's country they remember these things. On certain Hayselean nights, the scents of the world are as clear as voices heard across water.

2

THE HACKLER

The king had been right: The Arva horses had unusual stamina. Despite its long ordeal in the stable, the mare cut a strong and steady furrow through the moonlit water, its head nodding in rhythm with its powerful strokes. In the darkness of the opposite shore it shook itself like a dog. Syeira came close, putting a hand on its flank. It made a noise of disgust but didn't rear up. *She wants me to get on*, thought the girl. For a moment she stood there, gathering courage; and then, as lightly as she could, she pulled herself up onto the wet horse. She felt a tremor go through the mare, but it only moved ahead and up the steep path to the road. Crouched low against the mare's neck, Syeira could smell horse and river as well as some mild summer flower from beside the path.

At the road she applied the slightest pressure with her leg, and the mare, taking the cue as well as any palfrey, set off westward at a strong canter. Syeira had never been so high up on a horse; she felt as if she were riding an outcrop.

All night they rode by the moon, and when the sun rose they found themselves in a country of rolling fields and meadows. The people of Haysele had been farmers for many generations, and most of the sharp edges of their land had been worn away by the plow. The grass was a deep, water-rich green, the wheat was a soft tawny, and here and there in the valleys you could see a fine rose mist of poppies. There were only a few trees. Most of these were large oaks or the beautiful wych elms, with their foliage like the spume of a breaking wave. Very often they could be found right in the middle of a field, for the country people respected big trees and generally plowed around them. Between the fields were unplowed ridges, called bors by the farmers, which over the years had accumulated bright ribbons of cornflower and bluebell. There was meadowsweet, too, and as the morning wore on its rich scent filled the air. Blackbirds sang from the hedgerows and butterflies feinted through the meadows. It was a perfect day for riding.

But Syeira had little chance to enjoy it. Every passerby made her uneasy. She was sure they would all talk about the mare, and sooner or later the talk was bound to reach the king's stables. After a while she began to direct the horse down bridle paths and across pastureland, to avoid people. On the whole they were successful in this, but the roundabout route slowed them down, and occasionally Syeira made mistakes. Several times they went down a path only to find that it led nowhere, and the mare would snort in irritation as they backtracked.

It was the strangest thing in the world, to be riding the mare. Syeira could *feel* its distaste. Had the horse acted on its instinct, she knew, it would have thrown her twenty feet. But it followed her slightest movement as well as any trained horse. *She knows I can help her*, thought Syeira. She began to realize that the mare was smart, smart in the way that *she* was; only it didn't think like her. It thought in *smells*. And somehow — she was sure she hadn't imagined this — it could *breathe* its thoughts into her head. She felt as if she had stepped into one of the blacksmith's tales.

And all the while she was wondering if they had any chance of catching Lord Ran. In less than three days he would be at Braywick, where the River Hawkey emptied into the ocean. He'd almost certainly get there before they did: The river ran straight west while the bridle paths meandered. Syeira could only pray that he would stop for a while in the port town. A horse-laden *taride* went through hay and pure spring water very quickly, and he just might decide to stock up before his ocean voyage.

But what if she and the mare arrived to find the ships gone?

When night fell they rested briefly and then rode by the moon. They finally slept under a clumpy ash tree, but Syeira continued to ride in her dreams, feeling the hot sun on her arms and the sweating horse beneath her. Just before dawn she was nudged awake by the mare. She sat up dazedly. Around her the meadows were a deep motionless blue and streaked with mist. The mare stood over her, a huge breathing shadow.

"I have to give you a name," said Syeira, as she pulled herself up.

Like everybody in Haysele, she believed that a name was a kind of talisman, and that to be lucky a horse had to have the right name — the *true* name. But nothing came to mind right then. She wasn't sure she could come up with a name that would fit this horse. She reached down to touch the mare's neck and suddenly felt a small surge of happiness. For the first time since her mother had died, she was no longer alone. She remembered what the grooms had said about wild horses: that the mares of a herd always adopted an orphaned foal. Well, she had been adopted — not just by the mare, but by the whole herd of Arva horses. Their fight was now her fight, and she and the mare would wage it together.

That day was very much like the first one, green and lemon-bright and heavy with the smell of meadowsweet. Around noon they came upon a fat farmer sitting by the side of the path. He had evidently been repairing a low stone fence behind him and was now in the middle of an enormous lunch. Beside him on the grass were two loaves of bread, a half-eaten chicken, cold dumplings, several kinds of cheese, and an earthenware bottle. By then Syeira was as hungry as she had ever been in her life. She didn't think she could get the mare to stop, but oddly enough the horse slowed of its own accord.

"Ho!" exclaimed the farmer. "Where'd you get that horse, didi?"

"Didi" was country slang for gypsy girl. It was not generally considered a term of respect.

"She's . . . my father's," said Syeira, answering the first thing that came into her head.

The farmer took a slow bite of a drumstick. "Your *father's*," he echoed, with oily skepticism.

"Yes," continued Syeira, "and I'm taking her home now, but I still have a long way to go, and I haven't had anything to eat for two days — two days *and* two nights — and I was wondering —"

"No," said the farmer.

Syeira blinked. "I was only going to ask —"

"I said *no*," repeated the farmer. "And I'll say it louder, case you got any of your sibs skelpin' about: You *can't* have any of my hard-earned scran."

"But you have so much of it," Syeira protested.

"That I do, fresh," replied the farmer. "But you see, I'm nowise 'clined to share it with you. You and your cousins already been a bit too free with my soss. Stole the bread the missus put out to cool t'other day; and what happened to my second-best bridle what was hangin' on the byre?"

"I don't know," said Syeira angrily. "*I* didn't take it."

"Maybe not," returned the other, "but I'll warrant you nicked that horse, and that's a good sight more serious." He stood up and took a step toward the mare. "By my steers and ganders, that's one brawm mare. You're not ridin' one of the king's horses, are you, didi?"

Suddenly the mare reared up, snorting. Syeira had to clutch at the horse's mane to keep from falling off.

"Easy, lady!" exclaimed the man, stumbling backward. Like most farmers in Haysele, he considered himself a match for any horse, but he had never met one so large and savage-looking. The mare took a step toward him, still snorting, and he hastily decided that he valued his health more than his pride. In a blink he was up the trail-side bank and over the fence. Throughout all this Syeira had kept one eye on the food, and when she saw that the farmer was out of the way, she swung a leg over and slipped to the ground. As she landed she bent her knees slightly, for it was a long drop.

"Dall and danker you for a thief, didi!" yelled the man, as Syeira scooped up the largest loaf of bread.

"Don't call me didi!" hissed the girl, and scrambled back up onto the mare. At once the horse wheeled and galloped down the path. With one hand clutching the bread and the other the mare's mane, Syeira barely managed to keep her seat.

Later, as she sat eating the bread under a tree, Syeira said indignantly, "He thought I was a *gypsy*."

The mare didn't look at the girl, but its whole manner said, "Hurry up, didi."

By the end of the third day they were both feeling the effects of their relentless pace. Syeira was sunburned, hungry, and dazed from lack of sleep, while the mare had long since lost its easy, tireless canter. Its back leg was bothering it, and some of its cuts were starting to fester. Syeira had treated them as best she could with spring water and herbs, but the sweat and dirt were preventing them from healing properly.

Now, however, the girl had something else to worry about. They should have hit Braywick by then. She knew they had lost ground by taking the back routes, but they couldn't have lost that much. Had she made a mistake? She had tried to head generally westward along the bridle paths she knew, keeping north of the main road and away from people. But late last night they had passed out of familiar country, and since then she had been traveling by instinct. She wished that this day, of all days, hadn't been cloudy. With a sunrise she would have been able to check their direction.

And so twilight found them both weary and silent, trotting along a path that edged a remote strip of pasture. Several times Syeira glanced up at the gray-black sky. *No moon tonight*, she thought. Riding these back trails would be risky, with all their rabbit holes. They should really try to get back to the main road, for on a moonless night like this it was bound to be deserted. But she wasn't sure how to get there. *Maybe we can just ask the way*, she thought unhappily. At this point she considered it worth the risk — especially if there was the possibility of getting something to eat. But they were now in the less-populated parts of Haysele, and they hadn't seen any farmhouses for some time.

"We're not . . . too far from Braywick," said Syeira. "Another few hours, maybe." By now she often spoke her thoughts aloud to the horse.

The horse increased its pace. *She knows I'm lost*, thought Syeira. Turning in her seat, she scanned the countryside, and from across the field to the south came a flicker of light.

Thoughtlessly she pulled on the horse's mane. Without breaking its stride the mare gave a leisurely half-buck — just enough to send Syeira off, but not enough to loosen her grip on the mane. For a second the girl dangled across the horse's flank like a broken girth strap. By the time she had pulled herself back on, the mare had come to a stop and stood looking straight ahead.

"I'm *sorry*," spluttered Syeira.

The mare turned, in the shuffling way of horses, to look out across the field. Syeira tried to hold her anger in check. *I'm doing my best*, she thought, but she didn't say it out loud. Instead she said in a tempered voice, "At least let's see what the light is."

The mare was thinking — or rather smelling. After a moment it began to canter southward along a bor. They came to the edge of the field and paused behind a large oak, looking out across some rough pasture to the light, which flickered from within a thicket of trees. Now they could hear a faint crackling.

"It's a campfire," Syeira whispered. "Maybe it's gypsies."

She really didn't want to ride into a circle of gypsies; she'd heard the stories about them. The king's grooms never allowed the traveling folk near the stables, and with good reason: Years earlier a gypsy horseman, brimful with talent and mischief, had appeared in their midst and showed them up rather badly. Ever since then, they could be counted on for stories of how the gypsies kidnapped children, mistreated horses, caused the milk to turn sour, and so on.

The mare may have sensed the girl's uneasiness, but it paid her no attention. It moved forward, stepping cautiously over the dark ground. Before long the delicious odor of stew reached Syeira. A small figure moved into the flickering light and stirred a pot over the fire. *At least there's only one of them*, she thought.

They were forty feet away when the figure, a man, turned. "Hish!" he said, briskly but without alarm. "Who's there?"

The mare stopped. Syeira swallowed and said clearly, "My name is Syeira, and . . . er . . . this is my horse."

The man had moved stiffly to the edge of the firelight. "Aye," he said. "I couldn't miss that horse if I was blind. Where'd you be going this night, traveler?"

He was no gypsy, that was clear. He was small, not much larger than Syeira herself, with bowed legs and a slight hump to his back. Even in the dim light of the fire, Syeira could see that he had a very wrinkled face. But he gazed at them with alert fearless eyes, standing bent but sturdy like one of those tiny pines that grow on mountainsides. Behind him the fire snapped softly.

"Well, I want to go to Braywick," said Syeira, "but I'm not sure of the way. Is it far, do you know?"

She was dreading the answer, but at his next words she closed her eyes in relief.

"Not far t'all," he said. "A few hours' jog. But I hope you don' wunna ride there now, daughter. It's risky for your horse, on such a thick night."

"I know," replied Syeira, "but we have to get there quickly, because . . . well, my mare has a foal in stable, you see, and she hates to be away from it too long, and . . . we just have to get there tonight."

All the while Syeira had been speaking, the man had been gazing at the mare, his head to one side, as if he were listening. "Yea," he said. "From her breathing, I'd say she's been running for days." He moved a few steps closer, peering. "And is that slites I see on her chest?"

The mare gave an ominous snort, and Syeira spoke up quickly: "Sir, my horse is very nervy around strangers, and . . . could you please just tell us the way?"

But the little man shook his head. "Nay," he said. "I canna do that."

"Why not?" asked Syeira in dismay.

" 'Cause I canna let you ride a horse in that condition, tha's why not," replied the man. "She's woltered out bad, and prob'ly smarting from them wunds."

"That wasn't *me*," began Syeira — she didn't want anybody to think she would ever mistreat a horse — but then stopped.

"Well, whosoever it mighta been," said the man, now fishing in a sack that hung from his belt, "it's no way to treat a horse." After a moment he drew out a small white bag. "If she's nervy, then *you* put it on," he said, and tossed it up to her.

"What's this?" asked Syeira, catching the bag.

"Shanks' Balm," replied the little man. "A power o' good for cuts 'n' 'brasions."

Syeira saw that she was dealing with an old horseman who probably thought he knew everything about horses. She just had to humor him.

"Well, thank you," she said. She put the bag to her nose but couldn't smell anything. "Um — what's in it?"

The little man gave a half smile. "Now, daughter, I wunna be near much of a hackler if I gave out my secrets."

"Hackler!" exclaimed Syeira. "You're a hackler?"

There was excitement, and some relief, in her voice. A hackler was what the country folk called a master horseman. Such people moved from town to town, farm to farm, doing the really difficult and delicate horse work. They knew how to train the most ill-tempered three-year-old for the plow, or what to give a pregnant mare to make it foal well, or how to take out a horse's tooth with a saddler's hook. They made up a small and very select fraternity, one which guarded its secrets closely. Hacklers were the knights of the countryside: In the Hayselean songs they were always outwitting dragons, taming demon stallions, or winning the hand of a princess by curing her beloved mare of stomach problems.

"Aye, a hackler," said the little man. "Will Shanks is my name. At your service — and your horse's. Now I suggest you sit down by the fire and have a bite o' stew, and then we can do for your mare."

Syeira shook her head. "We *must* get to —"

The man held up his hand. "Naw then, I heard you the first time. If you're set on getting home tonight I can show you a better route by the crick. Not so many holes for the lady to fall in. But right now she needs a rest and something for them slites; and I'll wager you could take some stew. So first things first."

"Just two minutes," Syeira whispered into the ear of the mare and then slipped to the ground. Will Shanks watched her keenly.

"No saddle or bridle," he observed. "Practicing for the circus, daughter?"

"She . . . doesn't like a saddle or bridle," said Syeira.

"Hmm. And don' like to be tied nather, I see. A horse with opinions. I've known a few like that mysel'." For a moment Will Shanks looked as if he was going to ask more questions, but then he evidently changed his mind. "First, the stew," he said decisively and began spooning some out for Syeira, who had taken a seat on a nearby stump. Now, close to the fire, she could see him better. He wore a patched tunic, an old wool shirt, and breeches. He had a tuft of hair on the crown of his head, and two tufts over his ears, but that was all. On his forearm Syeira could see a horse-head tattoo — the sign of the hackler.

"Have a tass o' this, now," he said, handing Syeira a battered earthenware mug filled with a strange-tasting tea. She made a face. "Bratwort," he announced. "It's good for you." He sat down himself, rather creakily, on another stump. "So your family is in Braywick, daughter?" he asked.

"Er — yes," replied Syeira, her eyes on her plate.

"Ah," said the man, "so is mine. Maybe you know 'em? Old Forby and his brother Skidder from Oakley Farm. And Felice from the miller's place — neck like a queen, she has, but sides like a mason. And young Lone Lightstocking from the Coombs. A calm, sweetful gentleman with the plow, is Lone. Which is very odd, 'cause his mauther was Viking Ada, the most contrary old swanker ever to try and bite my ear and kick me in the tinderbox. And talking of contrary —"

"I don't think I know them," said Syeira nervously.

"Well, tha's not surprising," replied the little man mildly. "It's horses I'm speaking of, daughter, horses. They're the only family I ever had." He fished in his bag and brought out a large, knobby pipe. "I've helped 'em get born and trained 'em and looked after 'em when they were sick, them and their bairns and their grand-bairns. And not just in Braywick — all over the country." He put his pipe in his mouth but then took it out again, his eye on the mare, who was fidgeting nearby. "What ails you, jane?" he said. "My, that horse is kittlish."

"I think she just wants to get going," said Syeira. "Are you on your way to Braywick, too, Will?"

"Nay, t' other wise," replied the man. "I've just come from

Braywick this morn. Got a ride in John Hobelar's wagon, bless him."

Syeira had stopped eating. "Tell me," she said eagerly, "have you seen or heard tell of Lord Ran's ships?"

"Aye," replied the little man, who was watching the horse intently. "The whole countryside knows when Ran passes. But wha's your interest in that old weasel, girl?"

"Please, are his ships in Braywick?" pressed Syeira.

The man's gaze moved from the mare to the girl. "Nay," he said. "Set sail for Stormsythe this morn."

Syeira stared at the man, mouth open, and then shifted her eyes to the mare. The horse must have sensed something in Syeira's reaction, for it came close, agitated, snorting like a bull. Syeira stood up, and Will turned around on his stump. The mare seemed to be heading for him: It came within two feet of the fire and stood there, its eyes fierce as flowing lava. The night had grown small around them.

"Wha's this?" said the hackler.

"She knows," said Syeira fearfully. "Somehow she *knows*."

The mare suddenly stamped hard, and both humans felt the ground tremble. Syeira's plate, which she had set down on the stump, fell off into the dirt. The girl was now well behind the fire. She would have gone up a tree right then, but she guessed that Will's climbing days were long past, and she couldn't leave him to face the mare himself.

"Get behind that tree, Will," said Syeira, trying to keep the panic out of her voice.

Amazingly, maddeningly, Will would not. He stood up very slowly, watching for the muscle twitches in the horse that would signal a kick or a plunge. "Wha's the matter, lady?" he said. The mare, still snorting, lowered its head as if to charge. Syeira closed her eyes: She had once seen a man trampled to death by a mad stallion and never wanted to see it again. When she opened them again, horse and hackler still faced each other — but the man had actually taken a step closer. A strange look had come into the eyes of Will Shanks.

"You left something out of your story, daughter," he said in an awed voice. "She a'n't got one foal. She got *two*." He glanced at Syeira, who had inched closer.

"You smelled them, too?" she asked quickly.

"Aye," breathed the hackler. "Two colts as quick and sparksome as you could wish. A *scent picture*, tha's what it was." He turned back to the mare, still wonder-struck. "You're one of the ancient horses. I thought you was long gone, you."

Maybe the mare could sense a change in Will; maybe it could smell when fear and apprehension gave way to a different emotion. In any case, some of the fury went out of its eyes, though it didn't back up a step.

"One of the ancient horses?" prompted Syeira, but Will didn't respond. He seemed intent on stilling his breathing, which had grown a bit wheezy.

"Tell me your *real* story, daughter," he said, after a moment.

"I can't," said Syeira. "She'll know. She picks things up, I don't know how —"

"'Tis your movements and breathing she listens to," returned Will. "And your voice. All horses can do that, but I'll wager she's better than most. Just speak your bit nice and calm, and don' wave your hands about."

As calmly as she could, Syeira told him the story. "And I didn't get us to Braywick in time," she concluded, "because I couldn't see the sun, and I couldn't tell if we were going right, but I tried — I *tried*."

This was probably not the right thing to say: At Syeira's tone the mare began to grow uneasy again. But Will said quietly: "Hold, now. Even if you'da caught the ships, girl, you couldna saved her bairns. Ran didn't even dock at Braywick; they brung out water and hay for him in a barge. He had a fine fast wind and wanted to hang on to it. You two woulda had to swim out to his ship, kick a hole in it, cut through the ropes, and then swim away faster'n his arrows. And I doubt that even *she* coulda done that."

He stooped stiffly to retrieve his pipe, which had been lying on the ground the whole time.

"But I'll warrant her bairns haven't given up hope," continued the little man, rubbing off the mouthpiece of his pipe. "And nather should you."

"But what can we do now?" asked Syeira. "They're on their way to Stormsythe."

"Then you must go to Stormsythe," replied Will.

Syeira stared at him. Already she had traveled farther from home than ever before; to her Stormsythe was as distant as the fabled land of Perremuda. All at once she felt small and fluttery-weak, like a butterfly setting out against a strong wind.

"There is a route through the Forest of Deire," continued Will. " 'Tis long, and it goes through some grim country; but it avoids the border barons, and it'll take you all the way to Ran's seat by the Gray Sea. I traveled it mysel', when I was younger."

"But . . . how long will it take?" asked Syeira.

"Well," said the hackler slowly, "that depends. The ocean is faster, tha's for sure. Ran'll prob'ly get there in a few weeks, and —"

"A few weeks!" exclaimed Syeira. "The colts will be —" She checked her tone with a glance at the mare. "— almost dead," she finished, as casually as she could.

Will shook his head. "I wunna worry about 'em. Ran may be a tyrant, but he looks after his horses at sea. After all, he pays good coin for 'em. Puts slings under 'em, you know, so they don' get sick from their own weight. Let's hope the colts are smart and just go along with it. If they do, they'll get to Ran's stables in good fettle."

He glanced at Syeira. "And I'd say the lady's going to need *you* to get 'em out. A girl's going to be a lot more handy there than a *championne* like her. But it won't be easy, I say that to your nose."

"Will you show us the road?" said Syeira faintly.

"I will," replied the hackler, "but tomorrow. You're both soccered to your very bones. You need rest." He paused, looking at the mare. "And I wonder if she'll be kind enough to take some of my balm. It does wonders, and it a'n't just me who says that."

"I don't think I'd try," said Syeira.

Will, however, had already picked up the white bag (it had been lying beside Syeira's stump) and opened it. Inside was a bit of wrapping which smelled faintly of rosemary. This he also undid to reveal a clump of greenish substance, and without the protective wrapping the odors could get free. Syeira smelled something minty. The mare sneezed and shook her mane, but she seemed to like the smell.

"Tha's right, ma'am," said Will, smiling. "From Arva. I gathered it mysel', when I was there. The worts make good treatments." He moved a step closer to the mare. "So you're one of the old horses of Arva. The original tribe. The king's handlers must be dearly skilled, to catch you."

"The grooms said she *let* herself get caught," interjected Syeira. "They had her colts."

"Ah, yes," said the hackler. "Can you believe it, there was a time when I woulda tried that dodge mysel'?" He rubbed some of the balm on his fingers. "Now, you know these worts, ma'am. May I?"

The mare only snorted, but Will Shanks took this as a yes and tentatively began to rub the balm onto its forequarters. Syeira held her breath. To her relief the mare submitted, though with ears held slightly back — the equivalent of a human gritting his teeth.

"So you've been to Arva, Will?" said Syeira.

Will nodded. "You'll find a fair strew of hacklers in the western parts. Gypsies, too — we trade secrets, you know. A lot of us hacklers go there when we're just starting out, and then, when we feel we're getting close to the end, we take a last journey back." He grew serious for a moment, then gave a chuckle. "But now, I ne'er thought I'd be putting my own humble and reasonably priced balm on an Arva horse. And smelling them colts — it was like my thoughts came alive inside my head. A'n't that a contrivance, them scent pictures?"

"How can she *do* that?" asked Syeira.

Will shrugged. "Maybe all horses can do it, in some wise. You know how horses touch noses, when they meet? They're smelling one another, but per'aps they're also breathing pictures into each other's heads. Could be they do it with us humans, too, only we canna catch the smells. Our brains a'n't good for that no more. But I think maybe the Arva horses shape the smells to find the old places in our heads." He moved to the mare's shoulder and began rubbing some balm on her sores. "Sometimes, I'll wager, she don' even know she's doing it. Whatever is in her mind, she breathes out. Through her nose, of course — horses only breathe through their noses."

"So I can read her mind," said Syeira, pleased.

"You could put it that way," said Will. "But you hafta be right near to her, since the thoughts are carried on her breath. It's a kind of close, quiet talking what was meant for the old world. The world afore words, afore language." He looked around at Syeira. "The first mare, Arwin, mother of all the horses — she talked like that, they say. Talked like that to eagles and mice and trees."

Syeira's eyes lit up. "Arwin," she said, looking at the mare. "*That's* her name. I was waiting for a good name."

Will Shanks chuckled again. "Nothing puny about that name. What do you think, lady?"

Arwin seemed indifferent to the humans and their chatter. She was starting to feel the fatigue of the journey, and stood with her head down, her skin twitching occasionally under Will's hand. She knew that something had changed, that her quest had taken a different direction, but she didn't know why. She would just have to stick with the girl. From Syeira's movements and expressions and changes in breathing, the mare tried to figure out what was happening in this strange, violent, speeded-up world of humans. That may have been why, in fact, she had chosen the girl. To a horse it is always the small ones who tell the most.

Syeira slept soundly that night for the first time in several days, wrapped in a spare cloak of Will's. When she opened her eyes next morning, the sun was high and the fire was crackling. She lay in the cloak, still half asleep, watching Will stir the pot. "Naw, daughter," said the little man, when he caught her gaze, "it's only dribs and drabs for breakfast, but you're welcome to it. Here's a cup o' bratwort to start." Syeira sat up, an imprint of grass on her cheek, and sleepily took the proffered mug. After the tea came some stale bread and a hunk of infamously hard Hayselean cheese, about which one country song said, "It turns aside all but the dragon's teeth."

It was late morning by the time they set off. Astride the mare, Syeira wore the hackler's extra cloak, and tied around her waist was one of Will's cloth bags containing a good supply of the Arva balm. Will walked alongside, bent-backed but cheerful; he had declined a ride. "It'd take me too long to get up there," he had said. "And if I did, I'd never get down." Fortunately they didn't have far to go. They went across pastures and down bridle paths, and once cut a wide circle around a tiny farmhouse — the only one they encountered. Shortly before noon, they came to a small dirt road heading northeast. Now the Border Mountains were clearly in sight. They looked like tiny, motionless waves, etched in blue and white against the horizon.

"Do we have to go over the mountains?" asked Syeira apprehensively.

"Nay," said Will. "All the passes are guarded by Ran's seneschals. You'll go the forest way, east of the mountains." He squinted down the road. "Listen now: Follow this road for a good three days and you'll come to the town of Handley. There's plenty happening there now, with the Festival of High Summer and all, but I'd not a'vise you to linger much. Too many gossips there. Once you're through the place, get on the road going north — it's the one what's not been used much. Follow that for a day or two and you'll soon find yourself in the borderlands, the Withers. A'n't much there — just wind and rain — so you'll be safe enough. After a while you'll be among large trees. Tha's not the Forest of Deire. When you're among *enormous* trees, *tha's* the forest."

"I don't suppose there's a path through it," said Syeira.

"No path," affirmed the old man. "Only creepers and vines and thorns to make you mad. They say the winds off the ocean bring in seeds from all over the world, and so you get worts of every ilk there. You'll have to find your own way through, keeping your eyes and ears open — there's wolves and catamounts aplenty, just to let you know — and always keeping straight north. Heed the sun and the stars, and when you're not sure of the direction, cede to your mare. If you've been heading north all the while, then I suspect she'll keep going that way. This horse catches on fast."

"And what's after the forest?" asked Syeira.

"Then comes Stormsythe," said Will. "Once you're out of the forest, you won't have no problem. All the roads lead to Thurckport, the capital of Stormsythe. Tha's where Ran's stables are. After that, you're on your own."

"Stormsythe," murmured Syeira. The very name was cold iron against her soul. "What's it like?"

"A strange place," Will replied. "Sharp-edged and strange. The people accept the empire because it gives 'em wealth. But they've given up something for it, something vital. A lot of 'em look the same, I noticed." He shook his head. "I'll tell you one thing: I ne'er seen so many damaged horses as in Stormsythe."

"All our best horses end up there," Syeira remarked sadly. "To fight and die in Ran's campaigns."

Will gave a weary nod. "Aye, 'twould be a wonderful justice if the steeds rose up against him. Tha's how it works in the old tales: When the horses o' men are tyrannized by their masters, they call on their fellows from the wild places — kelpies from the mountain lakes, and winged horses from the upper sky, and —"

"Arva horses from Arva," put in Syeira.

Will smiled. "Now that would make a beautiful *new* old tale." He continued to gaze into the distance. "But no empire lasts forever, and one day Ran will overreach himsel'. There are signs even now that things a'n't so settled as he might like. I've heard talk of a rebellion in the northeast, in Broak. Do you know the place, girl? Sits right on the shoulder of Stormsythe. Used to be a fine rumgumptious country of its own, till Ran took it over. Seems that the more sensitive citizens there have taken to sabotage and lightning raids, to ease their painful memories. We can only wish 'em luck, from down here."

Arwin stamped once, eager to be off, but Syeira dismounted and stood beside the mare.

"Will you come with us, Will?" she said.

He shook his head. "Nay, chobbin, I'm too crampled up with the years. I'd just slow you down. But I've something for you."

From his bag he drew out another small pouch, this time a black one, and untied the drawstring. He had just begun to unwrap the packet inside when Arwin suddenly snorted and threw back her head.

"Hish!" said Will. "I've forgot how powerful it is. Sorry, ma'am."

"What is it?" asked Syeira.

The little man chuckled. "It *is* vile," he said. "I really shunna be giving it to you, but I think you'll need all the help you can get. It's devil's scratch."

"Devil's scratch?" repeated Syeira. She was watching Arwin, who was pawing and shaking her head.

"Aye," said Will, retying the bag. "A hackler is supposed to have all these spells, to get a horse to do things, but they're mostly just different sorts of scratch. And this is one o' the best — or the worst. You and I canna smell it, but the horses can, and they hate it. Rub a bit o' this on your brow and arms, and the wickedest stallion won't come near you. Fact, you could walk into a cavalry charge and not even lose your hat. The horses would be shying and jibbing like rabbits afore a stoat. I don' use it much mysel' — generally just to get to some mares without being bothered by the chief." He hefted the bag. "But I'm thinking you might find it very handy for the low work in Ran's stables. With this stuff you can cause some lovely grand schisms — even if you *are* pretty small."

"But, Will," said Syeira, her eyes still on Arwin, "*she's* not running away."

"No," agreed Will. "But she knows it's just a mixture; she saw me take it out. Ordinary horses don' know what it is. It smells like the worst thing they could imagine — something alive but rotting. For us humans it would be like waking up to see some ghastly grinning trollibags from the old tales standing next to your bed, smelling like he just come from the grave —"

"We *could* use that," exclaimed Syeira, excited to think that she now held in her hands one of the hacklers' famous secrets.

The little man handed two bags to her — the black one and another gray one. "You'll need this stuff, too," he said. "It's the damper. You put it over the scratch and it'll take away the smell right quick."

"But you need the scratch yourself," objected Syeira.

"Nay, I've saved a bit for myself. I'm not retired yet." He stepped back. "I canna make you a hackler, daughter; only life can do that. But you've got a good start with this scratch — and with this horse. Many a hackler would give his childhood to go on the quest you're going on." He paused, looking a bit uncomfortable. "Well, I guess that's it." He stuck out his hand, and Syeira shook it solemnly and carefully, as if she were working the handle of an old pump.

"And remember," said Will, "take it easy for the first while." He cocked an eye at the mare's back leg. "I noticed she has an old slite there."

"It only bothers her when she's really tired," said Syeira. She got up on the mare's back. "If she knew what you've done for us, Will, she'd thank you, I know."

The hackler smiled. "Well, you see, I can understand a bit what she's going through, because . . . I've had no end of grief from my own bairns. My four-legged bairns, I mean." He shielded his eyes from the sun. "Don' forget the balm, now. Every night and morn."

"I won't forget," replied Syeira. "Good-bye, Will." She had to turn in her seat to say it, for Arwin was already trotting ahead. At the first curve Syeira turned again to wave. Will Shanks waved back — looking, she thought, more bent than before. After that they rode in silence, except for an occasional sneeze from Arwin.

"I bet you can still smell that scratch, can't you?" said Syeira solicitously.

It occurred to her that the mare could have told her exactly what was in the scratch — or rather, breathed a picture of it into her head. But she really didn't want to know. She had once seen a trollibags in a nightmare and had no wish to smell one.

3

ZEPHYRA

They did not hurry on the road, but neither did they take their time. The colts were always in Arwin's mind, and though she was now more careful about her injuries, she nonetheless kept up a steady pace. They trotted and rested, trotted and rested, and slowly their strength returned. Arwin, of course, rode to suit herself. Perhaps she felt that a girl needed no more sleep than a horse, and Syeira got into the habit of snoozing on the mare's back as they trotted along.

Still, the girl was happy. The open road was something new for her. At night her sleep was all grass and rustlings and the moist earth beneath her, alive as a heart. The stars would drift out of their holes and sound clear as chimes. The moths would labor by in pale blurs. Awake or asleep she would hold close the bag of scratch, for it was her one weapon and amulet against the dangers ahead. During the long days she would sit on the mare's back and talk. She talked about ghosts, nightmares, winged horses (did they really exist?), *sea* horses, the disgusting habits of Hulvere's grooms, and her mother's skill with horses. This was her favorite topic. Once, she told Arwin, she had watched her mother pull a foal out of a mare that would die minutes later. She didn't remember much about it, but she did remember how slippery the baby had been, and how he had snorted minutely, like somebody breathing through a reed. She could have done the same rescue job today, she told Arwin; she was practiced enough. What she didn't say was how the foal tried to stand but couldn't; and how it lay on the straw for several days, peering around with its half-shut eyes, looking for something, always looking. For years she had felt exactly like that foal.

After too much talk Arwin would shake her head impatiently, and the girl would grow quiet. A human voice became to the mare, after a while, like the yapping of a dog.

Syeira knew they were getting closer to Handley, for they were seeing more people on the road. One evening, just before sundown, they came upon a farmer and his big dray horse. Arwin moved to the edge of the road to go around them, rubbing up against the brambles. The farmer saluted amiably, and the dray made an inquisitive sound in his throat. Most likely he was attracted by the wonderful minty balm on Arwin's coat.

"Evenin', neighbors," said the farmer, but Syeira — remembering Will's advice — just gave a quick nod and put her head down.

They trotted ahead in the warm antique light of early evening. On their left was a long twisting hill that stretched for several miles. On their right was a scraggly fence, made of intertwined hazel branches. The road followed the contours of the hill, which meant that generally they could see just a short way in front of them. More importantly, since the wind was at their back, Arwin could only *smell* a short way in front of her.

They turned a corner, and sitting at the side of the road was a short, henlike woman in a dress that looked like it had been made out of potato sacking. Her face was red and tear-stained, and her eyes were the same color as the muddy shallows of the Hawkey. Seeing the horse, she scrambled to her feet.

"No!" she exclaimed. "Is it you, Carina?"

She stepped onto the road, her eyes never moving from the mare. "By the star-candled welkin, it *is* you!"

Arwin snorted and immediately began to look for a way around; but the road, very narrow and bordered by fence and hill, gave her no escape. The woman turned her red face upward and held out her hands. "Carina!" she said. "You know me! Why do you run?"

Arwin took a step forward, perhaps hoping the woman would move aside, but the stranger did not budge.

"What!" exclaimed the woman. "You would trample me? After all I've done for you?"

"Who are you?" asked Syeira.

The woman seemed to notice the girl for the first time. "Who am I, child?" she echoed. "Only the humble she who saved the life of your magnificent horse. And now I'm a weed to be trampled by that same slate-eyed queen!"

She and Arwin faced each other, both of them blowing now. Arwin was turning her nose this way and that, as if bothered by flies, and stamping in place. But she didn't force her way ahead, and Syeira guessed that she did indeed know the stranger.

"Hear me, Carina," puffed the woman. "I say to you that old debts have come due. Do you remember how I set you free that night, cut the halter that might as well have been iron? Well, now it's *me* who's in trouble."

Syeira knew she had to do something: The longer they stayed there, the more irritated the horse would get. She couldn't help being curious about the woman and thought that Arwin might tolerate her as a rider — as long as they kept moving forward.

"We can give you a ride," the girl offered quickly, "if you're going toward Handley. But hurry."

"A ride?" said the stranger nervously. "Well, I'm out of training, but —"

Arwin gave an impatient snort, and Syeira said, "Quick! Up behind me." The woman put a hand on the horse's flank, and with much tugging from Syeira she managed to clamber up.

Before she was properly on, though, Arwin took off at a good clip.

"Help! Help!" cried the woman.

Syeira turned in her seat, put one hand on the woman's back, and hauled her closer. "Hold on to me," she instructed. The woman clutched Syeira's waist but could not bring herself up to a sitting position. They remained that way for several miles while Arwin trotted along.

"Ow, ow, ow," wailed the woman. Because of the way she was sitting (or rather lying) on the horse, she was bumped by every movement. "Tell her to stop galloping!" she cried, to the small of Syeira's back.

"Just hold on," called Syeira encouragingly. She didn't tell the woman that Arwin wasn't even close to galloping.

They rode for a good half hour, and when they finally halted, it was twilight. Syeira dismounted first and then helped the woman down while Arwin quivered and stamped. "By my corns and bunions," gasped the woman, "you still ride like a demon, Carina. My kidneys have been shaken right down to my ankles. Let me sit down. Oh, what a day, what a day. Do you know, I don't think I *can* sit down — my backbone has come right out of its socket. Anan!"

Now Syeira was able to get a good look at the woman. Her face was the shade of a crab apple. She had a neat, dimpled chin that would have been pretty had it not been set in a second, much more expansive, chin. She wore no jewelry, but a beautiful embroidered pouch hung from the piece of twine that served as her belt. Her hair came out in a kind of spray and had been so teased and hennaed that it resembled the frayed ends of a thick shipboard rope. It was about the same color, too.

"Yes, I'm not too proud to ask for help, Carina," continued the stranger. "And I needn't add that I can help you in return: I've got soothing liniments and healing plasters and calming ti-sanes. But they're in my wagon, and my wagon has been stolen — and there's my whole calamity!"

Syeira was silent, wondering. The woman kept addressing the mare, as if the latter understood her.

"Well, it's too late to do anything tonight," sighed the stranger. "I suggest we make a fire — I still have my tinders, thank the welkin. We can do it by the knoll over there. Then we'll hear each other's stories. Surely you can stop long enough for *that*, Carina."

By moonrise they had built a small fire behind the knoll. Arwin stood cropping a bit of grass while the woman, who had introduced herself as Zephyra, chatted with Syeira and gave the girl her first taste of pipe smoking. The two had already eaten the bread and sausage that Syeira had been given earlier by an old farmwife.

"Arwin," said Zephyra reflectively, as Syeira's eyes watered madly from the smoke she had just inhaled. "So that's what you call her, eh, child? Mother of all the horses. Well, it suits you, Carina. Very dignified. I called her Carina, girl, which means 'deer.' But she doesn't really look like a deer any longer, do you, Carina? She's still got the blue in her coat, though, and the green in her eye. I couldn't miss that."

"How do you know my horse?" asked Syeira.

Zephyra raised her eyebrows at "*my* horse," but she replied calmly, "Well, that's a long story, child. Carina knows most of it already, and I'm sure she'll correct me if my memory fails." She drew a moment on her pipe. "I suppose the first thing you should know about me is my trade. I'm an herbalist. I make medicines from plants — love potions for those who need love, and purges for those who need purging, and sweet juleps for the bruised and benumbed heart, and mortars for marriages that have grown cracked or grieved with time." She held up her pipe and squinted at it. "At any rate, that's what I can do *today*. But my story goes back ten years, to when I was less versatile and more vulnerable to the whims of the market. At that time I fell in with a swanking heathen of a man — a man who so thicks up my blood with loathing, when I think of him now, that I can barely walk."

"Who?"

"I'll tell you who," said Zephyra portentously, puffing on her pipe. Syeira waited. Against the midnight blue of the sky she could see the tiny pipistrelle bats, jagging over the meadows.

Arwin stamped once, as if to say, "Get on with it," and Zephyra exhaled her words in a trembling veil of smoke: "Black-lock Davy. The horse dealer."

Syeira said she had never heard of him. Zephyra told her she was lucky.

"A rogue gypsy, he was," continued the woman. "Wandering the land with his cart and his cant, and cheating even the Hayselean farmers, who know a thing or two about horses. We met at a fair in East Haysele. Just like the lovers in the songs, faugh! I was going through hard times, I don't mind telling you. Hadn't sold a thing in weeks — everybody is so plaguey sane and fit in those parts. Well, Davy comes up to my wagon all smooth and suent and polite. We talk about horse medicines for a while, but I knew he was just sizing me up. Then he says, 'I need a 'prentice, sister, and you look quick and mannerly.' I had to laugh. A *'prentice*. I knew perfectly well he needed a dickey; otherwise he wasn't going to sell so much as a mule in Haysele.

"You're wondering what a dickey is, child. It's the clean white shirtfront that makes a horse dealer presentable. He may be slimy as a banana slug underneath, but if he's wearing his dickey — stiff and starchy, with maybe a bit of lace on the edges — then people might do business with him. That's what Davy needed. He looked like a sharking bravo, and he knew it. Probably looked like a sharking bravo even before he was weaned. Me, I had a nice matron's cheek and no scars. Who would *you* buy a horse from?"

She sighed. "Well, I won't prolong the prologue. I became his dickey. I had to eat, didn't I? I put my wares in his wagon and we began traveling the country. We had the stock out behind, roped nice and loose, and in front we had an aging stallion that Davy could never sell. Name of Joseph Patrick Swaggerman. Good old Joe! He's been the stalwart in my life, but we'll get to that in its place. Anyway, we'd be bumping along in the old gypsy wagon, and Joe would be humming contentedly out front, and Davy would be swearing at him for going after butterflies, and on a sunny day it could be nice, I have to admit. Behind me in the cart I would hear the bottles clinking in Davy's chest of horse medicines. What a box of tricks that was! There was paste of the waylick berry: Mix it with water and you'd get every pigment from cremello to deep chestnut — perfect for painting stolen horses. And Davy's special moonscatter: a bit of that on a horse's forehead and the animal would shine like a firefly. Good for attracting children and gullibles." Zephyra leaned forward. "And most important of all, in a black squat bottle at the bottom of the chest — the Sleight."

"What was that?" asked Syeira, who was getting interested.

Zephyra gave a wry smile. "I never did learn exactly what it was. Humans couldn't smell it unless they put it on their skin and sniffed close. Whatever it was, though, horses were mad for it. Davy could sprinkle a few drops on his handkerchief and then pretend to blow his nose, and every horse around would be sneezing with delight and straining at its tether. Darksome gypsy magic, that's what it was."

"I bet Will Shanks would know what was in it," said Syeira.

"Will Shanks?"

"He's a hackler we met."

Syeira expected Zephyra to be impressed by this, but she just said, "Well, maybe so and maybe no. Davy had the wise more than any hackler I've known. It was he who got the crowds to come, though I did the actual selling. He had a monkey, a wiry little thing with long grabby fingers, and he'd get it to do acrobatics on one of the ponies. Before long he'd have a bunch of kids around him. The mothers would come to get the kids, and of course Davy would be a sugarbreeches to the mothers — he *could* be a sugarbreeches even with his scars, the cur. Then he'd get out his birds. He had a nightingale and a finch and a tiny green lad, and they'd all been taught the gypsy scale of music. Soon as twilight fell, he'd start singing gypsy songs, with the birds cheeping and trilling along with him. Then you'd never know he was the biggest pirate ever to file down the teeth of a nag. I think he forgot himself then, the way a wolf does during an eclipse: The night took him so far inside his own skin that he began to howl in a different voice. And the birds would be like twinkling lights inside his song, and moving around them you'd see the shadowy folk of the ballads — blades and beauties, crones and fiddlers, and animals like the horse of honey and the horse of cloves. They were his favorites, those two. I remember that ballad he used to sing:

> *Two brawm coursers came riding at a run*
> *Riding like the moon and riding like the sun;*
> *One was honey to the roots of her hair*
> *The other was spiced like the midnight air . . ."*

It was then that something very strange happened. Zephyra's song — the pitch, the rhythm — must have stirred up Arwin's thoughts. As the horse breathed out, Syeira — who was sitting closest — suddenly caught a fleeting scent. It was a bit like what the bees smell when they fly over a hill one morning and find a whole field of ripe goldenrod. It was a bit like what the sailors smell when they come near the Eastern Isles, where the very mists of the dawn are scented with vanilla and nutmeg. Syeira thought there might be something in it that would make a really good pie. It was the most delicious thing she had ever smelled, light as a thought, yet large as the life before her; but somehow it filled her with longing. She didn't know she had missed it until now.

And she knew what it was, sure as she knew the smell of

spring. It was the Sleight of Blacklock Davy. Arwin must have smelled it herself, years ago, and was now *remembering* it.

Syeira looked at Zephyra, her eyes alight, but the woman apparently hadn't smelled anything herself. "Davy and his songs, yes," she continued, shaking her head. "Well, I told myself I would leave him, but whenever I made hints in that direction he'd grow ugly. I knew all his secrets, you see. Since the man had a fair hammer of a fist, I decided just to bide and be quiet. We had gone through Haysele then and were traveling in Broak. I'm sure you've heard of the place. A bit unsettled now, I gather, but back then it was just another hardworking little country in harness to Ran. Full of shipbuilders and sword makers and men with wheel grease in their beards. Anyway, we were riding by the River Hawkey one fine day, with the Arva grasslands all green and wavy on the other side, and I happened to see something lying on the shore. I thought it might be a deer, but it wasn't the right color. Davy saw what I was looking at, and of course he had to stop the cart to investigate.

"We went down through some big oak trees, and when we got close to the animal, we saw it was a horse — a filly. And what a state the creature was in! Lying on her side in the mud, and caked in blood and foam. She seemed to be odd-colored, streaked all over with black, but when we got closer, we saw it was *flies*. Absolutely covered in flies she was, and so woltered out she couldn't even raise her head. She just blinked at us through those awful streaks of black.

"So Davy comes close to her, quite close, and then all of a sudden he staggers and backs away. I didn't figure out what had happened until later. The filly — young Carina, I guess I don't need to tell you — had breathed a curse at him."

"A curse?" repeated Syeira.

"Well, something nasty," replied the woman. "The poor thing couldn't bite or run; all she could do was breathe. And I'm sure

Davy got some fine fiery stench right then. Maybe she put an entire dead whale inside his head, one that had been rotting for days. Or maybe a nice little stew — skunk oil and stink beetles and the four hearts of the hagfish. Or maybe just a great big cesspool. Whatever it was, he backed up fast."

Syeira laughed. Zephyra glanced fondly at Arwin and resumed:

"For a while he just gawked, like one of the country georgies he was always making fun of. But then he got to work, and when Davy got to work, he didn't fool around. First, he ran back to get something from his medicine chest. I don't know what it was, but he rubbed it on Carina's nostrils — keeping well behind her, so he wouldn't breathe in any more curses — and she was asleep in a second. Then we walked all around her and saw her back leg, with the torn tendon. Davy said it was wolves. Said she must have swum across the river to get away. He was talking in a daze, as if he had taken some of that physic himself.

"So we got out the old linen tent, and worked it under the filly from the back, and tied it loosely around her to make a dragstretcher. I would have sworn you were dead, Carina, except that I could see your chest going up and down under the tent. Then we got Joe Swaggerman down there and tied him to the guylines. We picked all the stones out of the way and got Joe pulling, and Davy and I puffed and sweated, to move Carina along nice and gentle. We got her to a shady spot and lit some herb bundles to keep the flies off. Then Davy cleaned her up from nose to tail. He put on so much balm that she looked like a ghost. And he never stopped saying, 'So it's true about them Arva horses!' His eyes had that glint I knew well. He had found a beautiful horse out of the old tales, helpless and injured, and he was just thinking of how much gold he could make out of her."

Syeira drew in her breath through her teeth, as she might have done on finding a dead rat in her old sleeping loft.

Zephyra shrugged. "That was Davy. The man had a saint's touch with injured horses, but a heart of wormwood. Well, he put a halter on Carina and crosstied her, loosely, between two trees. When the physic wore off, Davy was there watching. We both were. Carina managed to get to her feet — he'd left enough slack for that — but essentially she was helpless. The crossties stretched from either side of her head and kept her more or less in place.

"When Davy saw this, he grinned in his awful way and said we'd stay there for a while. So we brought the wagon off the road and began setting up camp. Now and then Davy would call to the filly, 'Wonder foal! How do you fare? Say hello to the lofty man who rescued you.' But Carina would not say hello to the lofty man. She tested the ropes and found them hopelessly strong. Found, too, that her sore leg wouldn't tolerate much thrashing. So she took to endless neighing, in the manner of Arva horses. Kept it up for days. Turned *me* into a sleepless wreck, but Davy just laughed. Eventually Carina wore herself down and would just stand silent and smoldering, like a root fire. I could have easily slipped away from Davy during this time, but I couldn't leave such a beautiful filly with such a canker. All we could do was wait, Carina and I. At least her leg eventually got better by itself."

Zephyra began refilling her pipe. "In the meantime, word got around that we were there, and some of Lord Ran's soldiers came by to look over the stock. They were an evil bunch. The whole countryside was afraid of them — except Davy, of course. He would give them tips on choosing a charger. One day, he's going on about how he knows horses and their ailments, and a captain says to him, 'Well, gypsy, do you know thrush?' And Davy says, 'Georgie, I know thrush like the bottom of my pocket.' 'Glad to hear it,' says the captain, all weasel-eyed — I could see he was getting tired of Davy's flummery. He says, 'We got five chargers down with thrush so bad they can't walk.' 'I'll take a look at 'em,' says Davy. He took me with him, of course, because by then he didn't trust me with Carina. We had a look at the chargers, and their feet looked pretty ugly to me, but there never was a case of hoof disease that Davy couldn't cure. This one took him five days. After that, to get in good with them, he showed the captain how to make liquor out of moss. Soon he was damn near an officer without commission.

"Well, one moonlit night he and the captain were drinking near the wagon. I was as far away from them as I could get, picking toadscap near the river, but I could hear them laughing and carrying on. I got to thinking how Carina was doing, so I began creeping over to her tie-up. Once I looked up through the trees to see them both sitting around the fire. The birds were in their cages, singing away, and Davy — drunker than I'd ever seen him — was sitting with his crossbow between his knees. The captain was wobbling and belching right beside him. At the other edge of the firelight I could see the monkey. Davy had got the creature to put an apple on its head; he was going to try a bit of target practice.

"I couldn't resist watching for a second. It was amazing how Davy could get animals to trust him. The monkey was gibbering and twitching and looking extremely vulnerable — for a pickpocket. When Davy raised the crossbow, I guess it decided it didn't trust the man *that* much, and darted away. Davy cursed and let fly the arrow, and I heard the creature give a yelp of fright. Then it was gone into the darkness. The captain started laughing, and pretty soon they were both roaring and spluttering and hawking. This was more entertaining than shooting a monkey, you see — watching each other laugh." She snorted.

"Well, I had no wish to join the entertainment, so I dodged along to where Carina was tied. There was still a lot of noise coming from the fire circle, and I could hear the faint *whick* of crossbow arrows as they shot at trees. I pulled up some grass for Carina — who ignored me, as usual — and then went back down to the river. Luckily, the marksmen stayed where they were: I guess they were enjoying each other's company. I picked some more plants, and washed them, and looked at the moon; and at long last the noise from the fire circle faded.

"I moved up the slope toward Carina, listening. The night was swollen up beautifully with dew and stars and animal mutterings. And there was another sound, like two fat oxen complaining of indigestion. Finally, I thought. It was Davy and the captain snoring. I figured I'd be able to relax now for a while, but just then a movement caught my eye. Davy's nightingale was beside me in a tree, shaking its wings, as if it had water on them. Then I saw the finch dart into some bushes nearby, followed by the green lad. Davy must have left their cages open.

"They were all acting a bit funny, those birds, preening and fluffing. Carina was kittlish, too, I could see. Something was going on, something only the animals could sense. I started up toward the wagon, and just then I saw all eight of the stock horses coming down the hill toward us. The birds took off in alarm, and I don't blame them. I've never seen horses so charged and breathy. Like a line of dark surf, they were — not spooked, but hot and eager. As they went around me I could see the picket line trailing from Joe Swaggerman. They'd been staked in earlier that evening — Davy always strung them along a picket line and clipped the end onto Joe — but somebody must have worked the rope off the stake.

"I turned back to Carina, and that's when I saw the monkey. It was high in a tree, its eyes glittering, and I thought at first it was some big night bird. But it gave a monkey gibber and dropped something — something that shattered on the stones. 'What was that?' I said out loud. I was starting to get a bit spooked myself.

"Carina was sniffing the air as if it was her last breath. I thought of the glass thing that the monkey had dropped, and that's when I understood. The monkey must have stolen the bottle of Sleight and sprinkled the birds with the stuff. Then it had released both birds and horses. The horses had no desire but to follow the beautiful streamers of smell that trailed behind the birds. By morning, Davy's stock would be scattered all over the land — and the monkey would have got its revenge.

"I was sure Davy would have been awakened by the commotion, but I guess his horrid brew had knocked him right out. Of course I was frightened. When the gypsy woke up to find no horses, no birds, and no Sleight . . . Well, you can guess the end of my story. I cut the halter off Carina, then grabbed on to her and wouldn't let go. She didn't throw me off, either; I guess she understood I had just saved her life. Anyway, we rode all night southward, back along the Hawkey. At one point it narrowed enough to allow Carina to swim across, and so we parted company. I wouldn't say it was an affectionate parting, but somehow I knew I would see you again, Carina."

She smiled at Syeira.

"So that's the story of your horse and me," she said. "Eventually I managed to work my way back to central Haysele. Thought I might be safe there. Davy had never liked those parts; I gather he'd once been chased out of the castle neighborhood by some of Hulvere's hands. No doubt there had been a woman involved — that was the usual source of his tribulations. Davy never said much about it, but sometimes when he got drunk he would glower and moon and curse Hulvere's men most picturesquely. At any rate, the ill will served me kindly right then. I scraped together some new wares and took up my trade again. After a good long while I began to range out of the central parts. I lived in constant fear of meeting Davy one dark night, but I never heard anything more of the old stain." She relit her pipe. "But you know, it's funny how the past is always just around the corner. Who do you think I happened to spy one day at a horse fair, talking to butterflies? Joseph Patrick Swaggerman, that's who. He'd gone through many owners since Davy's time, and the farmer who had him was ready to get rid of him. I picked up an old cart, along with Joseph P., at the same fair. And we've all been together since then, and doing fine — until this morning." She paused, looking curiously at Syeira. "Now what's *your* story, girl?"

"Well," said Syeira cautiously, "Arwin was imprisoned in my stable and we escaped."

Zephyra looked impressed. "*Your* stable?"

"The king's stable," Syeira said reluctantly. "They'd captured her in Arva. I set her loose. We've come along the Handley road because . . . er . . . we were afraid of being seen along the river."

"Well, I'm going to Handley, too," said Zephyra. "Why don't we go together?"

"But King Hulvere has soldiers in Handley," objected Syeira.

Zephyra shook her head vigorously. "No soldiers there; no need. Nothing ever happens there. The sole authority is that smelly little mongrel the Sheriff. It was *he* who stole my wagon." Her look changed to one of outrage. "Came all the way out along this road to ferret around. No doubt he promised a share of the booty to whoever gave him a lift. First he comes to me, all puffed up with his own importance, and says, 'On your way to the Fair, mother? What have you in the cart?' So I tell him, very respectfully. He listens, then says, in an ugly voice, '*Love* potions.' Yes, I say, and proven effective, too. Well, he mutters a bit and then shuffles away, and I think that's the end of it. I started off again in my cart, but we hadn't gone half a mile when I saw a patch of pink at the far edge of a field. Shrimpbrow it was — wonderful for the liver, child. So I left Joe at the road and went out with my apron. I'd been out there less than ten minutes when I heard some neighing and creaking. I looked back to the cart, and there was the Sheriff sitting in the driver's seat and whipping poor Joe! I could hear the cracks right across the meadow. I yelled and came running, but the little toad was using his whip so hard that Joe was almost out of sight by the time I reached the road." Zephyra was near to tears. "And now look at the state I'm in. By the time I get to Handley the Fair will be over. Who knows what will have happened to Joe by then?"

Syeira felt uncomfortable. She didn't want to leave Zephyra in a lurch — after all, the woman *had* set Arwin free years ago — but she hated to lose time in Handley.

"The thing is," said Syeira, "we're on our way to —"

She hesitated. She wasn't sure she wanted to reveal her entire quest to Zephyra. The woman was watching her intently.

"I've never asked for help in my life, dear," she said. "But I *must* get into Handley. And if it's just me who confronts the Sheriff, he'll only laugh. But if I have some muscle behind me . . ." She looked at Arwin.

"All right, all right," said Syeira. "We have to start early, though — before dawn. Arwin will get restless if we don't."

Zephyra winced. "Before dawn. Well, so be it. I have to get back into training, anyway."

They actually got up at least two hours before dawn. They had no choice: Arwin nudged them both awake. Getting Zephyra onto the horse was as laborious as before. The mare stood with her tail flicking impatiently, like a lion, while Syeira pushed (rather ineffectually) and the woman wriggled on in stages. Eventually they were trotting silently through the moist darkness of early morning. Zephyra didn't say much at first, but after a while she had woken up enough to tell Syeira about Joe Swaggerman.

"He talks to me just as Carina does," she affirmed. "I have a special way with animals, you see. We herbalists can conjure up what is sometimes called the Halo of Knowing, in which . . . Well, it's a bit difficult to explain to the layman. Let's just say I've run

with the wolves and leaped with the salmon and dived with the
whales and whispered to horses. And yes, Joe has told me all his
adventures since leaving Davy. Of course, they're mainly *smells*.
He followed Davy's birds for days, convinced they were going to
take him to paradise. Then somebody found him and put him to
work turning a miller's wheel. Isn't that the way of the world?
After that he traveled pretty well all over Haysele. He was sold
to a bargeman, and then to a circus, and after that . . ."

Syeira soon found herself nodding. As she dozed, the meadows
turned from black to pearly gray to a cool, shadowless green; and
long before Zephyra ran out of things to say, they were in Handley.

For most of the year, Handley slept the ancient sinless sleep
of the Hayselean countryside. Only during the Festival of High
Summer did it come alive. Then the commons — the patchy field
in the middle of town — became a city of stalls and booths. The
barber shaved men under the sign of the striped pole; the bee-
keeper sold honey and beeswax candles under the sign of the hive;
and under the sign of the quill pen, the caricaturist put the heads
of farmers on their horses. The smells thronged like spirits —
mead, hot bread, fire-cooked potato, freshly sheared wool, spiced
apple, toffee, garlic, leather, dog, goat. People could see a fire-
eater, soot-blackened under the eyes, swallow a torch; they could
watch a fletcher fit a crossbow bolt with leather feathers; they
could buy a pure white hen or a pure black one. The only thing
Syeira didn't see, walking through the crowd with Zephyra and
Arwin, was soldiers. Zephyra had been right: Handley was such
a sleepy little town that the authorities rarely bothered with it.

They had been on the commons not five minutes when
Zephyra hissed, "That's him!"

Syeira followed Zephyra's outstretched finger. Through the
river of people they could just make out a small, bent man sitting
on the edge of a cart. His head was very large and bald, with a
circlet of hair that looked like a dead twining plant. His jaw was

slightly out of kilter with the rest of his face, as if somebody had punched it sideways. Over his small frame he wore a tattered mail shirt, to which was attached a large blue ribbon. He seemed a small, uninviting island in the crowd; no passersby stopped to talk to him. But this didn't stop him from talking constantly to *them*.

"Let's go," said Zephyra grimly. "That little hairball."

She began to force her way through the crowd, with Syeira and Arwin close behind. The man looked them over as they approached, but never paused in his patter.

"Now then, Gervase," he said, addressing a young farmer who had just set down a bag beside him, "I trust that's all peppercorns in there, and no clay balls mixed in." He shifted his gaze to a large woman nearby. "A fine day, Mistress Pelcher!" he called. "Hope you sell lots of soap. Watch the jokes about the king, though." Then, producing a pastry, he said, "Well, I've earned my batterjack," and bit into it with relish.

Zephyra, with the others in tow, now planted herself before him.

"So, we meet again," she said, her eyes flashing.

"We do?" replied the man blandly, his mouth full. He avoided Zephyra's gaze. "I don't recollect ever meeting you, auntie, nor your niece, nor your *championne* there." Now, up close to him, Syeira noticed he had a disagreeable smell — harsh and turpentiney.

"You weasel!" shouted Zephyra. "Where is my cart? Where is my *horse*?"

She would have flown at the man if Syeira hadn't taken hold of her. As for the Sheriff, he dropped his pastry and scrabbled for his sword, which had been resting on the cart beside him. It was a two-handed sword that would have been enormous had it not been broken a foot from the hilt. Now he brought it up defensively in front of him. The broken blade had been wrapped in heavy linen, presumably to prevent accidents.

"That's right!" he said sternly. "They're the property of the town now. You're talking to the Sheriff of the Fair, Mistress Trollwife. See this ribbon? It means I can confiscate the tackle of shadowtraders, gold dowsers, casuists, and all other enemies of the Weal Publique —"

"Weal Publique!" spat Zephyra. "I'll give *you* a Weal Publique that you'll wear to your grave. How did a pestilence like you get to be Sheriff?"

Gervase the pepper seller now joined the conversation. "His pater was Sheriff afore 'im," he said listlessly. "'Tis the way it works here." From his tone it sounded as if the tradition was starting to wear thin.

"That's right," said the Sheriff, still holding tightly to his sword. "My guv'nor held the office, and his guv'nor preceding him, and now it's *me*. Folks come from far and wide to the Festival of High Summer, and they don't want to be cheated by witches and brazen britches who hawk their sham hair tonics and beauty creams and" — here he flushed angrily — "*love* potions!"

For once Zephyra just seethed silently, like a wasp. Syeira, who kept one restraining hand on the woman's arm, said, "But you didn't need to take her horse and cart. She's just an old woman."

The Sheriff grinned to see the effect of this defense on Zephyra. "She don't look that old to me, little squit," he said. "Just ravaged. Probably led a dissipated life. As for that horse, he was nearly dead, anyway. It's a crime to keep a horse like that. He's better off at the knacker's."

"The knacker's!" yelled Zephyra. "You gave Joe to the knacker?"

Arwin, who disliked crowds and clamor at the best of times, now snorted and shook herself all over. Several onlookers backed up a step. Others were showing signs of impatience — not with Zephyra, but with the Sheriff.

"Now, Sheriff," said Gervase wearily, "can't we have our Fair quiet and peaceable, just for once?"

"Gervase Hobyn," declared the Sheriff, "you don't know this woman. She's a criminal. Preys on the weak and the ill-favored."

"She don't look dangerous," said a woman. "And what's this about potions?"

"Potions for *love*," Syeira replied, still holding on to Zephyra. The crowd was now murmuring sympathetically, saying things like, "Give the woman back 'er goods, Sheriff," and, "Got anything for warts, auntie?" Zephyra turned to the bystanders.

"Gentles," she said clearly, "I have specifics for warts, rheumatism, gout, toothache, thin blood, thin hair, dog bite, bee sting, goat's breath, insomnia, indecision, jealousy, and leprosy — along with sworn testimonials regarding their efficacy and worth. All my galenicals have been tested on myself and my horse, who is the most precious friend I have, thirty years old and still hale. At least he *was*. Your Sheriff stole him from me — *stole* him — and gave him to the knacker!"

At this the crowd's disapproval grew so strong that the Sheriff had to relent. Clearly he held on to his authority by the thinnest of threads.

"Oh, all right!" he scowled. "I try to keep the peace and this is the thanks I get. Very well, McFrump, I'll take you to your poxy horse. I must say you two go well together."

"And if anything's happened to Joe . . . ," said Zephyra ominously.

"*Nothing's* happened to your Joe!" snapped the Sheriff. He stuck his sword into his belt — upside down, since the hilt was longer than the blade — and began making his way through the crowd. Zephyra and Syeira followed closely, with Arwin moving like a restless sea at their side. "But I can't guarantee the knacker will let you have him," the Sheriff called over his shoulder. "The knacker's his own man. He doesn't bow to the crowd, let me tell you."

They made their way across the commons and down one narrow street after another. The Sheriff mumbled to himself constantly, but the only words they could catch were "the guv'nor." At length, near the edge of town, they reached a small dirty house, which they guessed was the knacker's. The grass, Syeira noticed, was all dead around the entrance.

The knacker has more or less disappeared from the world, but in Haysele at this time he was a necessary (if unloved) member of society. He was the man who slaughtered old horses — horses that were far gone in age and ailments — and made glue and animal feed out of the carcasses. From the look of things, this knacker was also a tanner, as they often were. Tanned hides hung outside on a line, and beside the entrance was an instrument for scraping the flesh off hides. Stacked up by the doorstep were strips of oak bark, used to make tannin for turning the hides into leather. Everywhere Syeira looked she could see large, shallow vats, brimming with the brown, bark-flecked tannin. Indeed, the knacker's yard was too small to contain them all. There were two on either side of the gate to the yard, and another one beside the doorstep.

"Well," said the Sheriff, "here we are. Home, be it ever so humble."

"Home!" said Zephyra sharply. "*Your* home?"

"Surprise!" said the man unpleasantly. "*I'm* the knacker. Yes, I do all the thankless tasks in this town."

Arwin was snorting and pawing in disgust; the unpleasant odors massed here like insects on a rotting log.

"Now I know why you smell the way you do," remarked Zephyra. All of a sudden, gazing off into the backyard, she cried, "Joe!"

From the far corner of the knacker's yard, a dun stallion was trotting slowly toward them. Syeira could tell by the way he was moving that he was old. Up close she could see just how old he was, with his gray muzzle, rubbery lips, and sunken teeth.

Nickering feebly, he stuck his head over the fence that surrounded the yard. Zephyra hugged his neck. "Joe! Thank the welkin you're still alive. And there's my wagon!"

Zephyra's wagon, which looked as rickety as her horse, was just visible in the far corner of the yard. Some bottles and clothes lay in a heap beside it.

"You've been pawing through my things, you wretch," said Zephyra angrily.

"They're the property of the town," shot back the Sheriff. "And *I'm* the town while the Fair is on."

Zephyra shook the padlocked wooden gate before her. "Open this gate," she commanded, and added in a low voice, "Smelly."

This was too much for the Sheriff. "Pardon me, Mother Scarebabe," he said in cold fury. "Maybe I do smell bad, but that's because I make an honest living. What do you do? You make *love potions*."

"If you're asking for one," said Zephyra tightly, "I'll have to see if I have anything prodigiously potent. In the meantime, open this gate."

"Don't tell me what to do!" said the Sheriff furiously.

Zephyra, her patience gone, made a grab at the man. For several seconds they grappled and clawed and cursed. But Zephyra had the advantage in weight, and probably also in righteous anger. The man's foot slipped, Zephyra seized her chance, and the Sheriff tumbled into one of the tannin vats beside the gate. Syeira could do nothing: She had her hands full with Arwin, who was now thoroughly agitated. Suddenly the mare took a step forward, reared up, and brought her full weight down on the fence. The wood splintered like matchsticks. Zephyra wasted no time; in a second she had stepped through the opening, dodging Arwin as she went. "Easy now, Joe," she called to her horse, who was cowering behind the wagon. "Yes, I know. Fortunately she's on our side. You just relax, and we'll be out of here in a wink."

The Sheriff had not been hurt by the fall, for he now splashed to his feet, bits of bark sticking to his hair. He stood there shin-deep in the water, quivering with rage and frustration.

"Vandals!" he yelled. "You've destroyed my property!"

Then, to Syeira's surprise, he began to weep. Arwin, still snorting, put her ears back at him.

"You're just lucky," sobbed the man, "that I don't believe in using a sword on women or children. Or *horses*." He noticed that the ribbon was gone from his jerkin and bent down to fish it out of the vat. "That's why I'm the . . . *Sheriff*," he said, coughing out the words. "I do the honorable thing. My guv'nor always said to me, he said, 'Garf, my son, we don't always get the gifts we want in this world, but we can always do the . . . *honorable* thing.'" He stepped out of the vat and, slumping down to the ground, tried to pin the ribbon back onto his jerkin. He was still weeping like a child.

The storytellers of Haysele say that horses and humans were once siblings within the same womb, and so carry a distant memory of a shared bloodstream. Maybe this is why the old horses in the river stable never kicked the young Syeira, even when she pulled their tails and ears. They sensed that they were linked by something hidden and vital, like an artery tree. In a lot of ways Syeira resembled the horses she had grown up with. Now she turned from Arwin and took a step toward the man.

"I'm sorry about your fence," she said.

"Sorry!" spat the man. "I bet you're sorry. You're cackling like the other one. Witches, that's what you are."

"No, we're not," said Syeira, but just then Zephyra stuck her head out of the cart and exclaimed, "I'm going to skin that man and patch my wagon with him. He's gone through all my things and everything is a shambles!"

Arwin seemed to have calmed down somewhat, so Syeira left her and ran over to Zephyra's cart. As she hopped up, the woman said, "See if you can untangle that," and handed the horse traces to the girl. The two of them crouched just behind the driver's seat, with the canopy — a patchwork of canvas and linen — hanging damply above them. Zephyra began picking up some clothes that were strewn on the floor of the wagon. "Some of these might fit you," she said, holding up a garment. "Perhaps tonight, after the Fair, you can try some of them on."

"I don't think we'll be here tonight," said Syeira.

"What!" Zephyra cried. "You're not leaving already?"

Syeira kept her eyes on the tangle of reins. "Arwin doesn't like being around humans."

Zephyra sighed. "Ah, well, I suppose she has a good reason for that. But consider, now. Wouldn't you like to stay with me? I lead a pretty exciting life, as you can see."

Syeira shook her head. "I can't, Zephyra. Arwin needs me."

"*Needs* you?" Zephyra glanced sharply at the girl. "Ah, there's more to this than meets the eye; I knew that at the beginning. I could ask why you're here in north Haysele rather than on your way to Arva, but I won't pry." She sighed again and took the leads from Syeira. "Well, let's get Joe hooked up."

When Joe had been harnessed and the cart was ready to go, Syeira cleared away the damaged fence so that Zephyra could drive through the opening. Joe strained at the cart and brought it creakily out of the yard. The Sheriff was now leaning against his fence, a picture of sour exhaustion.

"I hope, sir," Zephyra called from the driver's seat, "now that my property has been restored, that there will be no bad feelings between you and me. We both have vocations to pursue, useful vocations —"

"Shh, Zephyra," said Syeira. She'd had an idea. Taking out the bag of Arva balm, she detached a good chunk and tossed it to the Sheriff.

"Here," she said. "That's from Zephyra."

"What?" exclaimed Zephyra, but Syeira pressed ahead before the woman could get a word out. "It's one of her balms," she said quickly. "For horses, but people like it, too."

"For horses," repeated the man, slowly and peevishly. "Why would I want something for *horses*?"

Joe was suddenly very interested in the Sheriff. He began to lead the cart on an angle toward the man. "Come on, Joe," said Zephyra, pulling on the reins. The Sheriff raised his eyes and regarded the old stallion curiously. Probably no horse had ever willingly approached him.

"Just put some on your forehead and arms," Syeira instructed. "It will cover up — I mean, you'll smell nice. Right, Zephyra?" She jumped off the cart and stood beside Arwin. "Good-bye," she called, turning to face them.

Zephyra, alarmed, stood up in her seat. "Wait! The end of the adventure already? Oh, hold a moment, dear, so I can give you some essentials for the road."

Syeira waited while the woman disappeared into her wagon. The only sounds were those of Zephyra rummaging and Joe loudly sniffing the Sheriff. The man looked suspicious but not hostile; the balm must have smelled pleasant even to him.

"You know," said Zephyra, emerging with an armful of things, "in all the fairy tales, the wise woman gives the heroine gifts like magic slippers, geese that can tow the stars across the sky, and so on. Well, I'm afraid I've got a lot less tinsel in my cart, and a lot more homeweave. You can't work very long as an herbalist without having the fairy tales leached right out of you." She held up a small apothecary's bottle. "What's this? Oh, yes — *Medic Synonyma*. A little something left over from the Bards and Romancers Festival. Might come in handy, in a small way. Child, do you ever have difficulty finding the exact word? Well, just mix a bit of this in your tea and think of a word. Immediately a tree-ful of synonyms will bloom in your mind! Synonyms, dear —

words that mean the same thing, or roughly the same thing. You just pick a word from the tree, and immediately the meaning will be there in your —"

Arwin gave her mane an impatient shake, and Zephyra said, "Oh, all right, Carina. It's just that I'm very proud of my *Synonyma*, because . . . well, it *works*. I've a testimonial from both a poet and a man who writes leases all day, and I didn't even have to pay them for it. Not much, anyway." She began sorting through the other items she had brought out. "But let me see. A knife — you'll need that. And here's some stonewafer and cheese. And a good strong satchel, since you have no saddlebags. What else, now?"

Soon Syeira had the satchel strung over her shoulder, containing a large chunk of cheese, the hard Hayselean bread, and several kinds of "revivifying" tea. The tea was inside a waterproof spice pouch; Zephyra seemed to consider it the most important. The knife Syeira wore at her belt. The *Medic Synonyma* had also made its way into the satchel. "You can have some fun with it," said Zephyra in a low voice. "Never mind what Carina thinks."

"And now, give us a hug, child," concluded the woman, enfolding the girl in her arms. "I can't help thinking of the good times we could have had. And Joe likes your smell. He says he knows you from somewhere, isn't that funny? But maybe he's just getting old. We've both lived a lot since we left Davy." She drew back, her eyes misty. "And by the way, if you ever run into that winking pagan, slip him a hit of arsenic for me. Horses will thank you. Women will thank you. The gypsies themselves may even thank you, since Davy's reputation covers them like soot wherever they go. I'm sure they must sometimes wonder if they've got more kin to an adder than to that rash of a man."

4

THE FOREST OF MEMORIES

B read, cheese, a knife, and a potion that apparently gives you words all shaped and notched, ready to fit any keyhole of the world — these are useful to stable raiders as well as to poets. Syeira was glad to have them and a satchel to put them in. The first evening out from Handley, she spread the things on a dry patch and looked them over. She was mildly curious about the *Medic Synonyma*, but right then she was more interested in food and weapons. She had some of the bread and cheese, and after testing the edge of the knife, she decided to cut her hair. For several minutes she sat cross-legged in silence, biting her lip in concentration, alternately looking at the ground or the sky as she carved away.

"There," she said, pleased, when she had finished. She didn't know it, but she had given herself a haircut that was as jagged as a jack-o'-lantern's smile. She stood up to brush the hair from her lap, then bent down again to pick up a handful. For a moment she studied it in her serious way.

"What do I smell like?" she wondered aloud, holding the hair to her nose. She liked to think she smelled just like her mother.

"Joe Swaggerman knew my smell," she continued, glancing over at Arwin. "He knew me from somewhere."

Arwin didn't look up from her grazing. Syeira tried a horse's nicker, but still Arwin ignored her. "Listen," called the girl, and for a full minute went through her repertoire of whinnies, snorts, and neighs. It had no effect.

"I might as well be talking to *myself*," said Syeira. She put the things back into the satchel, then spread out her cloak and lay down. For a while she thought about all the horses she had seen in her life, but she couldn't remember Joseph Patrick Swaggerman. *Well*, she thought sleepily, *he probably got me mixed up with someone else.*

Overhead the clouds dispersed, and the lanes of the night opened up. She was slipping back over the years to the river stable, where she usually went in her sleep. Her mother's smell was in her mind, like sunlight working on honey. . . . If you put a bit of fresh honey in a crack of old applewood and let the sun work on it, the honey might turn into a pure white butterfly. *That's* what her mother smelled like: honey and sunlight and a hint of applewood. . . . A thought came to her then: Maybe it was her *mother* Joe Swaggerman had met before, and not her. Yes, that made sense: Hundreds of horses came and went through the castle grounds — farmers' horses, tradesmen's horses, minstrels' horses — and her mother always talked to as many as she could. Joe must have visited the castle years ago. She wondered what had brought him there. . . . The night creatures coughed and churred around her as she drifted away from her thoughts. Her breathing became a noiseless ebb and flow. Into her dreams the little yellow bird flashed once, like a whispered name, and was gone.

All night long, the stars swirled above her, caught in eddies of the turning earth. She awoke just once, in the cool darkness before dawn. She saw that the sky had changed. The constellations were those of next season. She didn't know it, but her patch of the earth was now facing a different part of the cosmos. For a while she lay looking at the out-of-season stars, thinking about the little yellow bird. Her mother's bird, she knew. She remembered how she had looked for it after the burial. Nobody could tell her where it had gone. It was just that kind of bird, they said. It came and went like a gypsy. It was as free as one of these stars.

Still —

"He could have come back," she said, turning over. "He could have come back just *once*."

⤫⤫⤫

They were in the Withers now and saw nobody but a few peat farmers. After a few days the country began to change. Shrubs and small trees appeared. Syeira could *feel* the forest coming. The trees began to appear in islands, and she got the impression they were joining gnarled hands under the ground, getting ready for some great upheaval. One sunny day they crested a small rise and saw a sparkling stream ahead. On the other side of the stream, trees thick as castle turrets towered a hundred feet high. The Withers had erupted into ramparts of bark and foliage.

Arwin splashed through the stream and entered the forest.

At once they were enveloped in a moist, lettuce green light. Around them the trees exhaled deeply and variously, like a family of whales. Only about half the trunks actually looked like tree trunks. The rest were still, silent explosions of leaves and bark and moss. Some were like huge clumps of bread dough that had risen and then hardened, acquiring grotesque sags and folds. Some were like parcels of enormous bones, wrapped together with creepers and thorns. Some were flaked like mica, mottled like a moth's wing, or bubbled and crusted like a toad's back. Most of them were far enough apart to allow a horse to get through, but here and there the smaller trees came together in a savage intimacy. There were trees growing under trees, trees growing through trees, and trees quietly peeling off their skin and splicing it onto other trees.

Very little light reached the forest floor, so undergrowth was sparse. Arwin's hooves fell mainly on thick moss, decaying logs, and a few ferns. But here and there, in the small islands of sunshine, they would see strange flowers — flowers the color of raspberry sherbet, or tangerines, or the winter sky at dusk. Syeira would have liked to stop so she could look at them, but she didn't want to distract Arwin. The horse was alert and preoccupied as never before.

"I wonder what you're smelling, Arwin," said the girl.

It wasn't long before she knew. The mare was in such a heightened state that almost everything she smelled was reflected back (though in a weaker form) when she breathed out. Here in the forest she couldn't *help* thinking aloud. When they did stop, Syeira got into the habit of dismounting and standing in front of the horse in order to catch these strange figments. With their noses almost touching, they seemed to be a single mind, a single breath. Syeira would stand with eyes closed, one hand on the mare's cheek, as the wisps of scent moved between them.

First there were the pollens, filling the air like a fine misty rain. To Arwin they were like a thousand tiny voices, some sharp as onions, some soft as lavender. The mare had never encountered so many and kept snorting to clear her sinuses. Then there were the animal smells: badger and flying squirrel; a young deer that had lately passed and left a faint tawny afterscent; and by a small stream, the remains of a fish left by an otter. The big forest slugs, over half a foot long, would leave their own slimy trails of scent. Once Arwin caught the whiff of a rabbit, and then felt the smell actually change in her head — like a clear flame that suddenly becomes smoky — as the rabbit caught *her* scent and darted away in fright. Every once in a while a press of young tree smells would waft up from under her hooves, for she often trampled seedlings as she moved. Herbs, too, sent up a kind of tickling plainchant from the ground. She smelled rue, sage, basil, thyme, marjoram, wild garlic, rosemary, mint, fennel, and even saffron. Will Shanks had been right: This forest had acquired seeds from all around the world.

As dusk descended on the forest, the smells changed.

Bats came out and painted the night with their moist, leathery slipstreams. Arwin could actually hear them, too: They sent out tiny sparks of sound, halfway between a bird's squeak and an insect's click. When several of them swooped at a moth, the sparks came out in a cascade, sounding like a box of pins being tipped onto a wooden floor.

The mare became particularly alert when night fell. Syeira, who often sat up in her cloak and peered nervously into the darkness, caught little of what Arwin caught. On the first night, the mare sensed a big owl in a nearby tree and knew it had been hunting. After a while she heard it regurgitate a pellet of fur and bones and then smelled the thin spurt of odor as the pellet fell in the darkness. She smelled weasels, too, and a huge forest rat, and a tiny wildcat no bigger than a stable tabby. All night she stood between sleeping and waking. She didn't like this forest. It had evil growths, smells that kept out of her way but were always there, faint as scratching mice. At least, though, she smelled no wolves. When morning came, the whole forest began to take on a different odor as sunlight seeped into the greenery. In mid-morning Arwin caught the day-old scent of a bear but guessed from the smell that it ate mainly berries and grubs.

Soon the trees became more gnarled, and everything was covered with thick moss. The air was warm and censed like the air inside an apple barrel. Water dripped endlessly off the leaves, and beneath the forest floor, hidden by skunk cabbage and huge piles of decaying logs, small rivulets trickled softly in the green silence. Arwin sometimes had to bull her way through vegetation, sending up clouds of decayed matter that made both horse and girl sneeze.

Syeira felt sure this part of the woods had never seen people. This was the forest before the stories, before witches and wood-cutters and lost children. The twilight had a certain ancient purity, like the immensity behind the evening star. The smells were such as might have been smelled by Arwin's namesake, the mother of all horses, when she lay in her nest so long ago. There were layers of smells, smells nested within smells, smells reaching out in huge expanding halos to the sun. But there were no smells of hay or houses or horses. For the first time, Syeira began to miss Haysele.

One morning they came to something they hadn't seen previously in the forest — a patch of berries. An enormous tree had fallen not long before, creating a small glade and allowing the berries to take root. The light here was a clean citrus light, not the leaf-tinted bleedthrough of the thick forest. Clear water gathered in a depression. Arwin, her flanks streaked with sweat and bits of bark, lowered her head to drink. Syeira slipped off the horse's back, sinking up to her ankles in moss.

"I wonder if those berries are all right to eat," she said.

She moved toward the edge of the glade. Directly before her, towering over the berry patch, was the loamy wall created by the root structure of the fallen tree. Clumps of dirt dangled from rootlets like Christmas tree ornaments. She heard around her the rustling of the tiny birds that they'd seen throughout the forest, birds that spent more time in the undergrowth than in the trees. She put out a hand to the berries. At that moment she heard a rustle inside the patch, and she peered in, trying to see the bird.

But it wasn't a bird. A silvery face — a bearded face — blinked out at her.

Syeira gave a cry, and Arwin raised her head.

"There's someone in there!" gasped the girl, stumbling backward.

The berry patch rustled again. "That's me," it said nervously.

Arwin was clearly startled by the voice; in a second she was standing beside Syeira, ears forward and body tense. They both watched as out stepped a skinny man with a flowing silvery beard. He seemed to be part human and part plant: Bulbs and tubers dangled from his belt, shoots and flower heads protruded from a sack on his back, and tiny starlike lichens dotted his tunic. His hair was so thick and matted with dirt that he seemed to be wearing a large beret. He had a skin bottle at his side and carried an oak walking stick. A pair of wire spectacles dangled from a string around his neck. His eyes moved nervously from the horse to the girl.

"Er," he said, "could you remind me who you are?"

Syeira blinked. "Remind you? I've never met you before."

"Oh!" said the man, looking relieved. "That explains it. Well, that's easily remedied. I am Sir Gemynd O'Smeagreson Smeath, Scion of Saxe O'Smeagreson Smeath, and Last Knight of the Weald of Deire."

"How long have you been in there?" asked Syeira warily; she was amazed that Arwin hadn't smelled the man.

"In where?" he said vaguely.

"In the berry patch."

"Oh, the berry patch," said the man, but he didn't turn around, and it wasn't clear that he knew what she was talking about. "Not too long, I don't think. Between two minutes and two days. Under a week, certainly." He added hastily, "I didn't overhear anything."

"Didn't you smell him, Arwin?" asked Syeira, turning to the horse.

"Oh, I don't smell like a man," said the stranger, with quiet pride. "I smell like a fungus. The Wight of Malai toadstool, to be exact. When prepared correctly and eaten regularly, it will permeate your blood and sweat so that you lose your human scent. Helps you avoid wolves and bears."

He doesn't look *dangerous*, thought Syeira. "Do you live in this forest?" she asked.

"Of course," replied the man. "I am a Smeath." Since this obviously meant nothing to her, he said, "And you two? You have the look of transients and temporary denizens."

"We're going to Thurckport," said Syeira shortly.

"No!" exclaimed the man. "Right through the forest? That's dangerous, that is."

"We've managed so far," said Syeira. In her opinion she had the best guide in the world.

"Child," said the man in agitation, "I tell you truly that this forest is treacherous beyond the knowledge of men or horses. It is Sir Gemynd O'Smeagreson Smeath who speaks, partisan of the trees and brother to the good lichens. The plants here are as willful as ghosts. You're coming to the worst part, too. Corpse flowers everywhere — you'll go mad from the smell. And one of you is bound to eat the Black Samaritan. A tasty and nourishing plant — as long as you consume it during the right phase of the moon. Eat it at the wrong phase, and it will start to eat *you*, from the inside out. And look up there. Gory Mumble." He pointed almost straight overhead to a small reddish climbing plant.

"What does *it* do?" asked Syeira.

At the sound of her voice, Sir Gemynd O'Smeagreson Smeath gave a start and lowered his eyes. His blank gaze showed no recognition; it was as if he had suddenly come across them.

"Oh, hello," he said uneasily.

The man looked so lost that Syeira said, "Are you all right, Sir Gemynd?"

He stared at her. "You know my name."

"You just told it to me," said Syeira, puzzled.

The man raised his spectacles — the lenses of which, Syeira noticed, were covered with a faint green film.

"Ah," he said. "So we're not . . . old acquaintances?"

"No," replied Syeira, now completely bewildered.

"Well, *that's* all right," said the man, but he looked sad and shaken. "I had better tell you," he continued laboriously, "who I was. Who I *am*, too. And then you can tell me who you are. And then, if we forget, we can . . . *remind* each other."

"I think that's a good plan," said Syeira.

❦

They heard his story at the edge of the glade, where a relatively dry log provided a seat. Syeira learned very quickly not to ask any questions. When Sir Gemynd was distracted, he forgot not only where he was in his story but even that he had been telling a story at all. This was his sad affliction — he forgot things as soon as he turned his attention from them. Strangely enough, while he could not form new memories, his old memories were extremely vivid. The reason for this became clear before long.

"I am," he said, "the last surviving son of the House of Smeath. Our ancestral home is in the northern part of the forest, a week's ride from Thurckport. My father was a valiant knight, always crusading for causes just, and nearly just. Saxe O'Smeagreson Smeath was his name — Saxe the Axe. Beside him fought my younger brother, Wystan, and sometimes even my mother, the fair Dorelia. I usually stayed home. I was hopeless on the battle-field. At least they didn't force me to be their squire, for which I was always grateful." He sighed. "I was supposed to guard the manor while they were away, but mainly I collected plants. I've always collected plants. My father used to say to me: 'You can collect plants when you're old. Now, when you're young, is the time for fighting!' But I guess I was born old.

"Well, tragedy struck before I was twenty. My father and brother were both killed in battle. My poor mother went mad, trying to avenge them. I think she eventually sailed off to the East, to be either a mercenary or a hermitess. After two years of searching for her, I gave up and returned to Stormsythe. I found our manor abandoned by the servants, who were always nervous about living alone in the forest." For a moment Syeira thought he had lost his place, but he continued sadly: "As heir to my father's land and title, I really should have stayed there. But I couldn't bear to live in the empty house, with the memories rustling like a dry wind over an empty lakebed. So I gathered up a few things and went to live in the forest.

"How long have I been in the woods? Long enough to see oak seeds become strong young trees. Long enough to see the Hoary Honeyjet bloom twice. And all these years I have lived only for plants. Many times I have nearly poisoned myself, trying some extract or another, but I was always careless with my own life — what did I have to live for, anyway? — and so have learned a great deal."

Arwin exhaled and twitched her ears toward the humans. Syeira smiled. It was as if the horse were asking how close they were to the end of the story.

"I say in all modesty that an entire monastery could not contain my knowledge of plants," continued Sir Gemynd. "Neither would the holy men welcome my knowledge, for much of it concerns those plants that cause gaudies and phantasms of the mind." He paused. "The visions I've seen! The worlds I've explored! I cannot tell you about the beauties and horrors I have experienced, for there are no words for them. No — but there are words for *this*."

For the last few minutes he had been fingering the skin bottle at his belt, and now he detached it and held it up before Syeira. "Extract of the plant known as Pale Madeleine," he said. "What does it give one, you ask? Something beyond even the power of angels to bestow. It gives one the past."

He uncorked the bottle and sniffed. "I was curious about it right from the time I saw it. First I tested a bit of the leaf on my lips and tongue. It tasted sour but pleasant — no burning or numbness — so I made some tea from it and had a small cup. I didn't notice any particular effects except that, walking through the forest afterward, I was reminded of things from my youth. A bird's call, for example, so clear and sharp, was to me like a string of runes in the air. I had loved runes as a boy. In that birdsong I saw the silvery glyphs from my childhood and felt again the slight ache in my arm that I would get from carving them out. The next day I tried a bit more of the extract. The coals of memory began to glow as if under a bellows. I tried to collect specimens, as I usually did, but the whole forest was filled with the past. An aspen would quiver with the voices of the dead. A seed case no bigger than a pea would turn out to hold a tiny shriveled memory, one that bloomed again when I held it in my hand." Sir Gemynd's eyes were now feverishly bright. "Oh, it hurt me, that plant hurt me, but soon I found I could not live without it.

"At night the memories would seep into my dreams, and I would find myself walking through the wonderful pageant of the past. I smelled again the roast venison in our great fireplace; I heard the minstrels tuning their lutes; I saw my beautiful mother in her gown, as bright as coral. And I felt my body young and strong, for I was a boy again. I grew wild with joy. Out of the house I rushed, to the tree where my brother and I had hung a rope; and I swung on it, laughing, until my arms ached. My father came out and said gruffly, 'Well! Maybe this boy will make a warrior after all.' This made me laugh even harder. He didn't know that his boy was actually old enough to be *his* father."

He shook his head. "All day long, after I woke from my dreams, the memories would rage like bonfires. So did the pinings and regrets, but at night I could lay these to rest. For didn't I have my youth back? Wasn't I the dramaturge of the night, able to rewrite the pageant as I wanted, correcting all the flaws? Soon my life was one fervid dream. A few hours a day were spent collecting Pale Madeleine; the rest of the time I was adventuring among the beloved dead." He sighed. "You will say I was weak, of course. But who wouldn't want their past back? Who wouldn't call back the lost voices? I know now that everything we have experienced is still inside us. That is the strange power of the Madeleine: It not only polishes our treasured memories to a holy sheen but unearths the buried ones — all the half-decayed sensations from our earliest years, the images of our fathers as young men and our mothers as young women —"

"Oh!" exclaimed Syeira, jumping up in her excitement. "Can it really do that?"

Arwin suddenly shook her mane, and both humans gave a start. After a moment Syeira said, more soberly, "But it must be a strange kind of memory potion. You forgot who I was the minute after we met."

Sir Gemynd looked uneasy. "Well . . . I've never been very good with names."

"You didn't forget my name," said Syeira. "You forgot *me*."

At once she regretted this: The man suddenly looked devastated, as if all the tragedies of his life had been brought home to him. He glanced around, at the horse and the girl, and said feebly: "It's true. I forget. It's all gray around me, gray behind me, nothing but gray . . . Sometimes I seem to have been born a minute ago. I don't know what I did yesterday, or last year, or ten years ago. Maybe I didn't do anything. I only know what I did when I was young."

There was a silence. Syeira racked her brain for something encouraging to say. "But you haven't forgotten the plants of the forest," she pointed out. "Like the Black What's-his-name."

The man sighed. "Yes, well, I've been in the forest for so long I've become part plant myself. I know all their tricks."

"Could you be our guide?" said the girl suddenly. "Could you take us to the other end of the forest?" Up till a few minutes ago she would never have accepted help from anybody — even someone who knew the forest as well as Sir Gemynd. But she had become very interested in the Pale Madeleine.

At this suggestion the sadness seemed to dissipate in the man's eyes. "I should be glad to," he said. "I am a Smeath, after all. Which way are you heading?"

"North," Syeira replied patiently. "We want to go to Thurckport."

"Hmm," said Sir Gemynd. "In that case we will pass my ancestral home, which I haven't seen for . . . well, a long time." His brow furrowed with anxiety.

"But you *do* remember how to get to it?" asked Syeira.

"Rest assured on that, ma'am," said Sir Gemynd eagerly. "I explored the forest thoroughly when I was a youth. You're lucky to have found me. May I suggest we start immediately, before it gets too hot. I'll just have a quick drink before we go." He took a swallow from the skin bottle, returned it to its place on his belt, and got to his feet. Now, however, he was looking at her with a puzzled, anxious air.

"Er," he said, "could you remind me who you are?"

Despite Sir Gemynd's affliction, they made good progress. He knew where to go to avoid the corpse flowers, and though Arwin got slightly nauseous — she could smell them from far off — Syeira did not notice them at all. He often collected nuts and roots for them to eat, and pointed out the dangerous plants. (The smell of Gory Mumble, Syeira found out, somehow affected the nervous system so that the victim would begin mumbling and never stop. Whatever the afflicted person tried to say, it would turn into a mumble; and he would *keep* mumbling until only the bees would tolerate his company. Fortunately, though, this only happened after long exposure to the plant.) Syeira found that Sir Gemynd could retain things as long as his attention was anchored. She got into the habit of talking to him almost constantly so that he kept them and their destination in mind.

Now and then they would come to an encampment beside the path — the remains of a fire, a blackened pot, scraps of clothing, and so on. At first Syeira was alarmed by these encampments, for Sir Gemynd said he knew nothing about them. But she soon realized that they had been made by the man himself. After setting up camp in one place he would wander away and forget about it — and then make another camp. This was confirmed when, at one of the encampments, they found his old tinderbox. Sir Gemynd's eyes grew bright at this: He said he'd had the box from the time he was eight. "I couldn't think what had happened to it," he added.

The first night they slept at an encampment. They boiled and ate several tasty potato-like tubers; Arwin had some, too. Then darkness came and made them quiet. Syeira had a bit of a shock when she saw what looked like red-hot embers floating down from the trees, but Sir Gemynd explained they were phosphorescent seeds from a harmless climbing plant. "Dire lights, we used to call them," he said. "On the ground they quickly lose their glow. See, those ones are already gone." They watched the dire lights for a while, and then the two humans lay down on their cloaks.

"Well, good night, friends," said Sir Gemynd. "Whoever you are."

In this way they traveled ever deeper into the forest. It was hard going for a horse the size of Arwin. Her only consolation was that she didn't have to worry about wolves and bears; these animals found it hard going, too, and stayed on the outer reaches of the forest. By day they labored sweatily through brambles, around stumps, and over logs; by night they ate an astonishing variety of nuts, fruit, and boiled vegetables. Then Sir Gemynd would talk about his childhood and sip from the skin bottle. Syeira was puzzled as to why he could remember the bottle and yet forget everything else. She eventually concluded that the potion must be an *old* memory and so remained as strong as his memories of childhood.

One day, passing through a shadowy patch of cedars, Sir Gemynd stopped and pointed. "There," he said.

At the edge of the path was a small, thick-stemmed plant with whitish flowers.

"Pale Madeleine," said Sir Gemynd. His tone grew pensive. "Have I told you about it?"

"Yes, yes," said Syeira. She was fascinated. "Did you just boil it?"

"Just boiled it," confirmed Sir Gemynd. "After the first time I mixed in a bit of willow extract, since I found that in its pure form it caused side effects — fevers and headaches, mainly. But it really needs no preparation and no distillation. You could eat it raw if you wanted to."

Arwin was keen to get moving; she always grew impatient when the two humans stopped to chat. They began their slow march again. Syeira noticed that Pale Madeleine was common in that part of the forest. Presently they came to a great spruce tree that had fallen across their path; at its base Syeira could see more of the plant. Sir Gemynd walked along the spruce, his hand on the trunk, and peered into the undergrowth. In a few seconds he and Arwin had pushed their way through. Syeira was alone. Quickly she bent down, pulled up a handful of Pale Madeleine, and stuffed it into her satchel.

⤙◈⤚

Sir Gemynd had become increasingly tense as they approached his ancestral home and talked more than ever about the old days.

"We had a stable," he said, that night around the fire, "built by my grandfather long before I was born. Of course we had a Bayard tree: My grandfather planted it right inside the main entrance."

"A tree?" said Syeira. "Inside the stable?"

Sir Gemynd nodded. "For good luck. Horses like the smell of the blossoms, and it needs very little light or water. We had all sorts of beautiful things in that stable. The most precious was a charm — a little mobile. Three tiny horses, hanging on chains as fine as a spider web. When a breeze blew through the main door, the horses would turn and move with a tinkling sound, as if they were galloping in midair. There was nothing like it in the world, but to the man who made it, I'm sure it was just a trifle."

"Who made it?" said Syeira.

"The greatest craftsman in these lands," replied Sir Gemynd. "The Stablecharm Man."

Syeira had heard the name before, in connection with one or another of the blacksmith's tales.

"You know his story?" continued Sir Gemynd. "Used to be an ordinary mechanical in Broak, they say — a clockmaker. Then he got to making these charms, and people loved them, so he gave up clocks. That's when he stopped being a mechanical and became something of a magician — and a healer. He came to know my father slightly, just around the time my brother was made a knight and everybody was very proud." He was silent a minute, looking out into the darkness, then said, "The Stablecharm Man gave his gifts only to those who'd lost something."

He raised the skin bottle to his lips. Syeira, who by now understood what the potion was doing to him, said, "I don't think you need any more of that, Sir Gemynd. You seem to be remembering fine. But go on. You were speaking about the Stablecharm Man."

"Ah, yes," answered Sir Gemynd. He'd obviously forgotten exactly what he'd said, however, and so he moved on to a related topic — a strategy he often used to save himself embarrassment.

"I made a charm myself," he said, "when I was sixteen. The stable had *its* charm, and I wanted one for the house. By then I'd learned some forest runes, the runes that woodcutters and vergers use to protect their lodgings. One night, when my family was gone to battle, I carved the runes over the fireplace. A runic poem in rock is a powerful charm, you see. Strong as the rock itself.

The only runes I knew were those that protected against forest scourges — wolves and weeds, vermin and caterpillars — but I put them down, thinking that at least the house would never fall victim to the forest. The last lines, I remember, went like this:

> By the light of the moon, by the starry flock
> I cut these words into the rock;
> So may they banish the blight and decay
> And keep the scythe of the world at bay."

He shook his head sadly. "Well, there are no runes against the scythe of the world, as I found out. But at least I know the House of Smeath will always stand fast against the forest. Mold and woodrot and beetles cannot touch it. It will forever be the house of my youth."

It was strange how Sir Gemynd's mind worked. Throughout the night, Syeira could hear him muttering and sighing; and when he woke up in the morning, the first thing he said was, "The house of my youth."

"You'll see it soon, Sir Gemynd," said Syeira, reminding him briefly — as she did every morning — who they were and where they were going. While he made a fire, she went out to wash at a nearby stream. Once out of sight, she removed the Pale Madeleine from her satchel. Her heart was beating as she slit open the stalks with Zephyra's knife. They oozed a milky substance, like dandelions. She found that the stem had a tough fibrous center, but that the outer sections were soft and edible. She cut out a few pieces and ate them like rhubarb, trying not to crunch. The forest watched her indifferently through the violet light of dawn. After a few minutes, fearful that the others would start to miss her, she put the Madeleine in her satchel and made her way back to camp.

The day was like all the others before it. Syeira was beginning to tire of constantly trying to keep Sir Gemynd in the picture. She plodded on behind the other two and sneaked some Madeleine whenever she could. So far she had noticed no effects from it. *Maybe it only works if you've got mushrooms in your blood*, she thought irritably. When they stopped for the evening, all of them were worn and silent. Sir Gemynd began laying a fire and Arwin pawed through rotting logs to find something edible. Syeira stood quiet, listening to the birds around her. Their song was as cool as spring water, and she took a few steps away, trying to find them in the undergrowth.

"Nuthatches," said Sir Gemynd, raising his head.

"They're just over here," said Syeira. She went over a log and around a patch of thorns, and after a minute or two came to a stand of large but relatively young cedars. Each tree stood steadfast and distinct, gigantically calm in the twilight. *Like horses*, Syeira thought. She remembered lying on a clean bed of hay — behind the drinking trough it was, in the river stable — and looking *up* at horses, at the groove that divided their chests, at the flanks taut and rounded as a filled sail. On their bellies she could see the wanderings of veins, which stood out against the fine hair like stray laces caught under a tight bodice. She would lie there for hours, talking to herself and the horses. Sometimes she would whisper her name over and over — *Sigh-air-uh* — until she was sure the horses were as light-headed as she was. It was a curious name. People had told her it wasn't a common Hayselean name. It had a bit of the sky in it, she liked to think, and maybe a bit of the open road. . . .

Now she stood still, absorbing the silence of the cedar grove. She felt at ease here. From fifty feet away she heard Sir Gemynd talking to himself. One of the nuthatches flew to another tree, and it seemed to be trailing a small golden shadow. Suddenly a door opened there in the forest, and she saw for an instant the yellow bird of her mother's, darting through hay-flavored murk. She gave a cry and ran forward. The nuthatch was barely visible against the muddy gray bark of the cedar. It chirped — a brown, jagged chirp, not at all like the yellow bird's. The golden shadow had vanished; the door had closed. Syeira felt stricken and bewildered, as if someone had pressed a pin deep into her heart and withdrawn it so quickly there was no blood.

She remembered Sir Gemynd's eyes. The same wound was there, the hair-thin puncture that grew bigger with every breath.

Feeling suddenly tired, she turned and made her way back to camp.

Syeira would have gone right by the stable, so buried in undergrowth was it; but Sir Gemynd had been watching closely all afternoon. Through the trees he picked out the stone horse's head, now pocked and lichen-covered, that rested just above the door. They labored toward it through the greenery. Syeira walked with her head turned away and her eyes almost shut, as people do when they expect to be hit any moment by recoiling branches. Strangely, the stable was intact; two small windows beside the entrance were still unbroken. With trembling hands Sir Gemynd pulled open the doors. Old stone and timber smells wafted out. They stepped inside, relishing the space, the freedom from the undergrowth. The light was the color of clear cider.

"The tree," said Syeira in wonder.

Beside the door was the Bayard tree that Sir Gemynd had spoken of. It must have got enough light from the small windows (plus the chinks that every old stable has) and enough moisture from the air. It was about twelve feet tall and still had its blossoms, which were a very pale blue. The almost transparent bark clung to the trunk moistly, like a sweat-drenched shirt. The foliage had a feathery and somewhat wayward shape, as if someone had punctured a pillow and pulled it through the air.

"It's amazing that it's still alive," observed Syeira.

"It has light and water," said Sir Gemynd. The roof had leaked a bit; they could see water stains running down the walls. "And after all," he added, turning toward the center of the building, "the stable has a charm."

Syeira followed his gaze. From the door frame over the tack room, turning slowly in the amber light, hung the mobile. It had a very thin, elongated S form that, when seen from the side, faintly resembled a horse's head. The girl went close to it. From three points on the S hung little horses no bigger than grasshoppers — one gold, one black, and one tawny. The colors hadn't faded. Syeira blew on them, and the horses turned and danced lightly.

"No one stole it," she remarked. She looked inside the tack room; harnesses and saddles still hung on the walls. "Nobody has been here."

Sir Gemynd nodded. "Woodcutters and soldiers know that the deep forest is dangerous. This is too far in for them. Even robbers don't come here." He glanced around once more and took a breath.

Syeira waited; Sir Gemynd had that clouded, uneasy look that he often had. At length she said, "Should we go to your house now?"

"My house," said Sir Gemynd. "Of course."

Once again they wrestled through the undergrowth, alert for noxious plants. Syeira had a vague sense of the house's shape through the trees. Soon they could see the high dormer windows and the blurred line of the roof. The gate posts — two crouching griffins — might have been small trees, so smothered in greenery were they. Syeira felt cobblestones under her feet. Finally they saw the knocker on the front door — a lion's head with a ring through its mouth. Sir Gemynd was a bit unsettled to see the huge double doors hanging askew, pulled off their hinges by vines and creepers. Without a word he began clearing away vines with his stick. Syeira helped him. At length they managed to wrench one of the doors open, and the two stepped into the main hall.

Sir Gemynd gasped.

The forest had come in wherever it could. Waves of ivy ran up the walls; vines smooth and thorny hung from the domed ceiling; wild grapes encircled the carved banisters of the stairway. The roof had fallen in at several places and the high lattice windows — all of them broken — admitted sunshine as well as huge tree limbs. One of these limbs had a line of large branches shooting up from it; the effect was that of a thicket of trees in midair. Water dripped down the walls and onto the moss-covered carpets. From somewhere close came the smell of rotten fruit and the buzz of insects. Sir Gemynd stood with his mouth open, turning around and around.

"No," he breathed. "No."

They moved through the house, Sir Gemynd leading like a man in a dream. No corner remained untouched by the forest. In the drawing room stood half a dozen plush chairs whose seats were now a mass of mushrooms. Over the entrance to the dining hall was the stuffed head of a magnificent stag; between its antlers, on a gauzy bed of cobwebs, lay twigs and leaves and the remains of a caterpillar nest. In a small alcove stood a harpsichord, its beautiful berry-stain finish darkened by mold. Syeira touched one of the keys, and a cloud of mildew rose.

Sir Gemynd walked slowly, his lips moving. "What happened?" he mumbled. "My poem . . . The runes . . ."

Syeira followed him into the scullery, where the great fireplace stood. The gray stone was dotted with aureoles of lichen, but the expanse just above the grate was clear. Sir Gemynd ran his hands over it. No runes could be seen.

He turned to Syeira with an agonized look. "Where is my poem?"

"Are you sure you carved it here?" asked Syeira.

"Yes, yes," said Sir Gemynd frantically. "It couldn't have faded, it was carved right into the rock. Where is it?"

Behind them Syeira could hear Arwin moving in the main hall. She wished the horse were here beside her.

"Where is my charm?" Sir Gemynd demanded loudly of the house, of the forest, of the powers in the woods. A few rooms away from them, Arwin stopped moving.

Syeira had her eyes on the potion at the man's belt. "I think I know," she said slowly.

Sir Gemynd stared at her, his eyes wild.

"You carved it with help from the Pale Madeleine," said Syeira.

The man took a step closer to her. "What do you mean?"

"Don't you remember what you told us?" replied the girl. "Oh, no — I guess you don't remember. You said you dreamed about when you were a boy, and then you did a lot of things that you wanted to do. You changed things. You set things *right*. And that's when you must have carved this poem."

"No!" shouted Sir Gemynd. "I carved it when I was sixteen. I remember!"

Syeira looked away uneasily. "Well, it doesn't matter. You're home now. You can fix up your house and —"

"The cook came in," said Sir Gemynd, trying to keep calm. "The cook came in while I was carving, and said, 'Eh, Master Gemynd, what would you be carving now?' She was one of the few servants who actually liked living in the forest. I remember *that*."

It was then that Arwin appeared at the entrance to the scullery. She was too big to get inside, and just stood gazing in. She looked like one of the forest powers herself, all streaked with sap and dried fruit pulp. Her scars were like small white accents on her chest. She was extravagantly out of place in that kitchen: Seeing her there was like seeing a narwhal in the village pond.

"Didn't I tell you about it?" asked Sir Gemynd weakly, look-ing from the horse to the girl. "They were on the battlefield, my family. Every one of them. And I thought about them all day, how they might not come back, and how I would be alone . . ."

Suddenly he sank down on his knees in front of the fireplace, shivering as if in freezing wind.

"No, it's true!" he said faintly. "I see it now. It *was* the Madeleine."

He continued to shake, and the thin, splintered sound that came from him made Syeira crouch down by his side. It seemed as if the tears were flowing *inside* him, flowing narrowly through him as water flows through a plant; but no tears showed in his eyes. The flower heads in his sack nodded gently as he trembled. He coughed and got his breath.

"Look at me," he said in a ravaged voice. "By my own hand I have become less than a skeleton, less than a husk." He creaked very slowly to his feet, helped by Syeira. "I was wiser as a child, for I knew that the things that have happened to us are gone. They're *gone*. A simple truth, but it was burned out of me by the Pale Madeleine."

From his belt he detached the skin bottle. "I thought this was my salvation," he said, holding it up. "In truth, it was my slayer."

And unstopping the cork, he tilted the contents onto the floor.

For a moment there was silence, broken only by the wheez-ing of Sir Gemynd. A breeze blew outside, and somewhere in the house leaves rustled.

"It'll be night soon," said Syeira anxiously. She wondered how much of this Sir Gemynd would remember, and whether they would go through a similar scene in a short while. For now, though, he seemed to have kept it all in his mind. He looked around at the scullery, at the mold-stained walls, and nodded sadly to himself.

"In the old days," he said, "I could have shown you great

hospitality. You, madam horse, would have enjoyed hot mash and a rubdown; and you, daughter, would have had a bath of pure spring water and a feather bed. But now all I can offer you is a stable."

"I like stables for sleeping," said Syeira, but she was looking at the ground, where the filmy white Madeleine was slowly soaking into the stones.

❧

In the dead of night, something woke Syeira from dark and jumbled dreams. She lay on the ground, every nerve strained. It was pitch-black inside the stable, but through a window she could see the midnight blue of the sky and a few stars. She wondered why she was so hot; when she had gone to sleep, the stable had seemed wonderfully cool. Sir Gemynd was snoring weakly not far away. Arwin, she knew, was lying in the far corner of the stable, sleeping the wakeful sleep of a wild horse.

And then she heard it again, the sound that had woken her — a woman's sobbing. It came from outside.

She was on her feet at once, so quietly that Arwin did not stir. The Bayard tree was whitish in the darkness. Stealthily she moved to the stable door, and again, faint but unmistakable, came the sobbing.

She knew it from somewhere.

The stable door was closed. Syeira lifted the latch as silently as she could and stepped outside. The summer moon was large and lightly veined, like the wings of a butterfly.

Again came the sobbing, and with a stab Syeira recognized the voice. "Mother!" she cried.

She darted along the side of the stable, clawing and scrabbling at branches. "Mother!" she called frantically. The undergrowth eventually became too thick for her, and she turned and stumbled toward the house. Her progress was better in this direction, for they had already broken a trail there. She fell through the front doors, slipping on wet moss and banging her shoulder on the door frame.

"Mother!" she yelled.

The house echoed emptily around her. She stood still, her breath coming out in gasps.

"Mother!" she called again. "Where are you?"

Only silence answered her, the moist living silence of growing things. Syeira turned to see Arwin standing just outside the doorway.

"My mother is here, Arwin," gasped the girl. "Help me find her!" Her face was shiny with tears.

From the direction of the stable came Sir Gemynd's anxious voice; the commotion had woken him. Arwin shook her mane, perturbed. The girl seemed to sense something that she herself could not hear, smell, or see. All of a sudden Syeira darted forward, slipping right under the horse's belly and into the yard. There she ran straight into Sir Gemynd and knocked him flat.

"Who's that?" he wheezed.

"Sir Gemynd," said Syeira desperately, picking herself up. "My mother is here. Help me find her. She needs me."

"Of course," mumbled Sir Gemynd. He was completely bewildered, since he had woken to a voice he did not know and a horse that seemed as big as the night. Syeira was already off again, thrashing and snaking through the darkness. Arwin was now beside the old man who, looking up, thought it best to remain where he was.

"Who are *you*?" he asked. Arwin only snorted and moved along the path.

Syeira's unhealthy energy took a while to spend itself. Sir Gemynd did his best to follow and calm her — he knew from looking around that he was on his old land, and so had a duty to help her — but he couldn't keep up with the girl. Eventually she collapsed by the stable door, bruised, cut, and crying inconsolably. Then the same scene from that afternoon was played out again, but with the roles reversed. Sir Gemynd crouched beside the girl, who shivered and wept on the ground. "There, there, daughter," was all he could say. Arwin stood silent and uneasy a few paces away; she could smell the girl's fever from where she was. Syeira's sobs gradually dwindled. Finally, exhausted by her wild search, she fell into a restless sleep. It was then that Arwin went close and, lowering her nose, touched the girl gently — just as she might have done with one of her colts.

In the morning Syeira's intensity had given way to listlessness. Her eyes were dull, her face pale behind the dirt. She wordlessly accepted food from Sir Gemynd — boiled wild carrots and herbal tea — and sat all morning wrapped in her cloak, looking like a battered sparrow that had just survived a storm. She didn't speak to Arwin, who remained a good forty feet away, cropping grass where she could find it.

"Can you pick me some more Pale Madeleine, Sir Gemynd?" said Syeira, when he brought her a second cup of tea.

"Pale Madeleine!" exclaimed Sir Gemynd nervously. He didn't remember anything from the previous night, but Pale Madeleine was one thing he *did* know about. Already he had picked up enough clues to suggest that the girl had consumed some Madeleine and should have no more. He got up and began wandering vaguely toward the house. When Arwin found him half an hour later, he had in his bag not Madeleine but a large quantity of berries — the same kind of berries he'd hidden among almost two weeks previously.

"Portia berries!" he announced, when Arwin brought him back to Syeira. "They're a bit sour but good for jam."

Syeira sighed. "I wanted Pale Madeleine," she said. But she took the berries, anyway; they were as sour as he had said.

The day passed slowly. Arwin kept an eye on both the girl

and the man, silently retrieving Sir Gemynd when he went off on his own. If she was impatient to get going, she didn't show it. Syeira did not hear any more sobbing that night, but she again slept fitfully. Just as the darkness began to lighten, she sat up suddenly. Arwin was alert at once. Syeira looked out the window, seeming to breathe in the coming dawn. She remembered the river stable at night, and how the little yellow bird would roost somewhere in the darkness, singing quietly to itself. Now its song streamed into her mind and made her think of the gypsy Blacklock Davy and *his* songbirds. She could imagine the songs that they would sing — songs with lots of moonlight in them. Sad airs, slow airs, airs of loss and longing. After a moment she lay down again: She had suddenly thought of her mother crying in the darkness. She was very quiet, but Arwin could smell the tears on her face. The girl wrapped herself in her cloak and remained awake until morning.

That day, though still subdued, Syeira went with Sir Gemynd to explore the house further. For the next hour they cleared away debris and scraped mold off the furniture. Syeira was more productive than Sir Gemynd, for the man would often find a plant that interested him and ignore the cleaning.

"There are some extraordinary specimens here," he would say.

Syeira was standing before a writing desk that held a long-dry ink pot, which now contained a plant like a small sea urchin. "Sir Gemynd," she said, turning to him, "if you wrote things down, you wouldn't forget them."

"Hmm," said Sir Gemynd, who had his eyes two inches away from a patch of mold.

The girl began pulling out the drawers of the writing desk. "Is there any parchment here?" she asked.

There was no parchment, but there was something just as good — the papery bark from a small dead tree outside. Sir Gemynd stripped off several lengths of it with Syeira's knife. He said the juice of Portia berries would make an excellent ink, and while Syeira mashed the berries he made a fire. At length the ink was ready, and Sir Gemynd spread out his bark and dipped a reed into the pot. "Midsummer, at the Manor of Smeath," he said, scratching away on the bark. Syeira watched him with interest and envy; she had never been taught to read or write.

"Well," he said, "what should I write?"

"Write first of all that you never remember anything," said Syeira.

Sir Gemynd did this, dipping his pen several times into the berry juice.

"And now write how you met me two weeks ago," said Syeira.

While Syeira recounted the events of the past two weeks, Sir Gemynd put them down in runes. The story was entirely new to him, of course. He became grave when Syeira began talking about the Pale Madeleine and what it had done to his memory. The girl was reluctant to say much about what had happened to her because of the plant. At that point, to cheer her up, he added to the berries some sweetwort from his bag, making the ink edible, and both of them dipped their fingers into it frequently as the diary progressed.

When they had finished, Syeira said, "You can make this your life story and add things every day."

"An excellent suggestion," said Sir Gemynd. "A dam against the onrushing years; that's what a diary is." He read again the first line and grew somber. "Can *you* remember what you did yesterday?" he said, glancing up at Syeira.

"Yes," said Syeira. "But I forget things, too." She thought for a moment. "Sometimes, just before I'm going to fall asleep, I forget what I was thinking about."

Sir Gemynd gazed sadly at the bark before him. "I wish I could remember just one thing from yesterday. What I had for breakfast, say. That's not much, is it? Then I would know I was *living* yesterday at breakfast time, that I was . . . here in the world." He gazed at Syeira anxiously. "Do you think I'll ever be able to do that? Remember just one thing?"

"I'm sure you will," said Syeira. "You'll have to keep this diary where you won't lose it. You know what you should do? Bind the pieces and attach them to your belt, right where your bottle used to be." She had noticed that he still plucked at that spot now and then, even though the bottle was gone.

Together they made a crude booklet of the bark sheets, putting holes in each sheet and binding them all together with twine, and Sir Gemynd attached it to his belt. Then they collected more bark, which Sir Gemynd placed (together with the ink) in the stable. He had decided he would live there for the time being. "It's very peaceful and civilized," he said.

He had actually forgotten what his house was like, but Syeira got him to look at his diary again. After doing so, he wrote, "You'd forgotten all this an hour after it was written. Don't get upset about it; just make sure you write in this diary at least twice a day. And don't lose it." He skimmed Syeira's story. "You are going to the end of the forest," he said, looking at her. "I can take you there if you wish."

"I think you should stay here," she replied. "On your way back you will probably forget everything, and maybe just wander around forever in the forest. We're past the worst part now, aren't we? Arwin can get me out."

"And have you recovered from the Pale Madeleine?" he asked, after glancing again at the account of her episode.

"I think so," said Syeira.

"Good. But be careful. Sometimes it stays in your system longer than you think."

Syeira couldn't help noticing how frail the man looked. "Sir Gemynd, listen to me," she urged. "You are back home, but you don't remember things, apart from long-ago things. And your manor house is a mess. It's filled with vines and moss and things. Do you want to come with us? Do you want to leave the forest? You *can*, you know."

But Sir Gemynd shook his head.

"No," he said. "I am content to live here." He looked around. "If my house is filled with vines and moss, then perhaps it is more suited to me now. The early stages of colonization are always fascinating." He turned back to Syeira. "You say I don't remember things, and it's true. But there is one thing I do remember, one very important thing, and it has no connection with long ago."

"What's that?" said Syeira.

Sir Gemynd's hand trembled slightly on his walking stick. There was more gray and less green about him now. His thin body seemed set at an angle, as if he were fighting a wind. But he brought his hand close against his side so the trembling wouldn't show, and when he spoke, his voice was steady.

"Pale Madeleine is gone," he said. "I sent her away."

Syeira put her arms around him for a long moment, and then she was up on Arwin's back and they were away among the giant trees.

Syeira never saw Sir Gemynd again. Often, years later, she would wonder how he was doing in the forest. She imagined him sitting alone in the stable, beneath the little mobile of the horses, reading about her and Arwin; and that made her happy. By then the events of her life had changed her perceptions of the past, and she had come to think differently about the stable charm. Perhaps it hadn't been meant so much for the stable. Perhaps it had been meant for Sir Gemynd himself.

⁕

That night they camped a good ten miles from Sir Gemynd's house, and it was then that Syeira had a dream. She never told anybody about it, for it was so terrifying that it made her sick to her stomach just to think about. But it proved one thing — that Sir Gemynd had been perfectly right about the power of the forest plants.

In her dream, Syeira was standing in Sir Gemynd's stable in the dead of night. A full moon hung in the sky, and by its light she could see the little mobile of horses, glittering beside her. Arwin and Sir Gemynd, she knew, were far away, but she felt that as long as she stayed beside the charm she would be safe. She moved closer to it. The three tiny horses danced delicately in the current of air she brought with her. She wondered about their beauty, about their colors, about their power to keep the forest away, and just then she caught a movement outside the stable.

She stepped away from the charm to see through the window. In a pool of moonlight stood a woman. For one wild moment Syeira thought it was her mother, and she darted to the door; but stepping out into the cool night, she realized her mistake. Vine thin was the woman and white as the moonlight. Her hair was the color of milkweed, her robe like the shed skin of a snake. She would have looked severely ill except that her body had a strange, wiry strength, like that of the thin creepers that wrap themselves around a big tree and strangle it. The only thing dark on her was her mouth, and when it spoke, Syeira could not take her eyes off it.

"Leaving so soon, child!" it said loudly. "Oh, you'll take away a part of me. Come here, just for a minute."

Syeira was badly frightened and knew she should go back inside the stable and shut the door tight. But she also knew this apparition had something infinitely precious, something of *hers*. The next moment she was standing before the woman. Now she could see the eyes, dead as marble in the dead face. The black mouth smiled again, like the edges of an old wound being forced open.

Syeira's mouth was so dry she could barely speak, but with a great effort she asked in a tiny whisper, "Why was my mother crying?"

The wound closed again and opened. The dead eyes blinked.

"I so rarely keep company with children," said the mouth, "that I'm becoming an old fuddy-duddy. I didn't hear what you said! What was that again, sweetheart?"

"Why . . . ," began Syeira, but that was all she could get out.

"Ah," said the woman helpfully. "I know what you're asking. Yes, dear, that's a sad story about your mother. I'm pretty sure it all had to do with a man. Somebody left her with a broken heart and a babe in arms, and generally that's a man's doing. But I don't really know the details; few people did. I think one or two of the old stable women knew — they generally know everything. And your mother's favorite mare, she knew in the way that horses do. The problem is, they're dead now. All dead and rotted."

She stepped close to Syeira, so that her mouth was only inches away. "But not in this forest. In this forest they're alive."

Syeira could not move. She felt as if her blood had grown clotted and hard. Suddenly the woman raised her own hand, and digging deep with her long white fingernails, she peeled off a thick strip of skin from her inner forearm. Taking Syeira's hand, she pressed into it the piece of flesh, moist and clammy as cheese.

"All you have to do," said the woman, "is eat this. Or make tea of it, whatever you like. You can have a tea party with the old man. Soon you will be seeing all your old friends again. Your mother, too." The woman's breath smelled like toadstools. "You don't know how much you look like her, dear. And think of seeing her again! Remember how they wouldn't let you look at her after she fell from the loft? Well, you can see her now. You can hold her and talk to her. And she'll tell you *everything*."

Syeira could not even drop the piece of flesh; she had melted in terror inside her frozen body.

"Stay in this forest," breathed the woman. "Every day I'll give you something good to eat, something of me. Soon you'll be able to see with my eyes. We'll be the same person. And then you'll know the beginning of your story — and when you know the beginning of a story, you can sometimes guess the ending. . . ."

Syeira felt the woman's vine-strong hand on her hair, forcing her head back. Just then she heard, very far away, the stable charm tinkling faintly. The sound seemed to thaw her blood for a moment, and she gasped, "Help me!" Then the tinkling became a cascade, as if the little horses had grown to full size and filled the forest around her. . . .

At that moment Syeira woke up. With one bound she was at Arwin's feet, wrapped around the horse's forelegs, coughing and retching. Arwin was startled, but saw at once that something terrible had happened to the girl, and breathed on her.

They remained that way until dawn came.

5

THURCKPORT

After sunset the ancient city of Thurckport grew quiet behind its walls, and the sea returned to fill the silence. Slow waves washed the night. The stars streamed overhead like the glittering wake of a ship. You noticed the salt in the air more, for the people and their livestock were gone. No merchants or beggars worked their trade outside the walls. With the closing of the city gates, everybody had retreated to the small *faubourg* towns that lay at least two miles south. The locals knew better than to linger after lockout. Bargemen were allowed to moor their boats just outside the walls, in preparation for a dawn entry into the city, but even they never strayed more than twenty paces from the canal. The shabby heath that surrounded Thurckport became, after sunset, a no-man's-land. Only the mad dared wander there.

Of these, there were a fair number near Thurckport. The men were all called Bill Mauditt, the women Betty Mauditt. Every night they flitted like bats through the darkness, chuckling and pulling at the air, or standing still to let the cool moonlight wash through their inflamed heads. Nobody knew why they came out at night, risking arrest and even death. Maybe the voice of the sea calmed them. Maybe the starry wake overhead made them think the earth was journeying away from conquest and empire, away from spikes and siege engines, away from their nightmares. At any rate, they were always there, regular as the nighthawks.

Syeira and Arwin saw the Mauditts each night as they rode the heath. The mare generally kept well away from them. She knew somehow that she had come to the last stage of her quest and was intent only on sniffing and listening, standing still to feel the distant vibrations of the city, endlessly searching for a way inside. They had been there a week and the task had begun to look hopeless. Very few outsiders were let into Thurckport. Tradesmen were admitted only if they had essential skills. Bargemen and farmers had to present a signed contract. Vagrants, jobbers, petty merchants, horse dealers, bards, actors — all were considered undesirables. Each morning Arwin and Syeira mingled with the crowds, watching and scheming; and each afternoon they withdrew, frustrated. Syeira knew the gatekeepers would never admit a dirty stable kid, even if she did have a horse of value.

And so the two of them would retreat to just outside the *faubourgs*, sleep for a few hours, and then return to the heath.

As dangerous as it was, Syeira came to prefer the nightly reconnaissance. She didn't like Stormsythe by day, didn't like the hard, orderly, *kept* look of the landscape. Everything had a purpose in Ran's country. Riding out of the Forest of Deire, she and Arwin had passed reservoir ponds, but no holy wells; orchards, but no wild apple trees; woodlots, but no forests. There wasn't much common pasture, either. Whenever she had lain down to sleep, she had always wondered whose property they were on, and whether dogs would come to chase them away. And the *people* . . . She remembered what Will Shanks had said: A lot of them looked the same. At first she had been astonished at the variety — in hosiery and hats and weapons. But the people were like the shrubs and hedges: many different species, but somehow all with the same *cut*. Long before reaching Thurckport, Syeira had begun to understand the nature of the empire. Ran had been twenty years building it and now lived to consolidate his domains; the people lived to consolidate their wealth. Even the vagrants here wanted more out of life than just life itself.

Once, trotting on the heath just after midnight, the mare checked herself and approached a hump on the ground, catching up sideways while still a good distance away. Syeira saw that the hump was a man, a Mauditt. He seemed to have dug himself a shallow hole and now crouched inside it. The girl could make out almost nothing of him, but his wheezy breathing sounded loud in the night.

Arwin stood quiet, ears forward, as if she wanted Syeira to talk to the man.

The girl slipped off and took a few nervous steps toward him. She wasn't sure *how* to talk to a Mauditt, and this one was just a dark lump on the ground.

"Only a shepherd," called the man in a cracked voice, as if he had been asked to identify himself.

Syeira stopped. "I — I just want to ask you about the city," she said. She added, "Shepherd," to put him more at ease.

The man was silent. After a moment Syeira asked, "Have you ever been inside?"

The man gave a sharp bark of a laugh. "Oh, yes. That's where I left my ears."

Syeira glanced back at the mare. What could a Mauditt tell them? They only spoke to the sea — or the moon, when it was out — and they made no sense to anyone but themselves.

"Are you a spy?" the man called out.

"No, no," replied Syeira.

"Then I'll tell you," he said. He scrabbled a bit in the earth and was quiet.

"Yes?" prompted Syeira.

Suddenly the man stood up and pointed to the sky, tracing an arc with his arm, as if he were following the path of a comet. "Watch out, Betty!" he wheezed. "Watch out, Bill!"

"What is it?"

"I'll tell you," he said, hunching down again. "Once, at twilight, I saw something fall out of the sky. Like a clot of brown honey, but alive. Spinning and twisting like a broken Catherine wheel, like a Catherine wheel that *knows* it's going to be broken, fighting the air but falling like a rock. I didn't see it land — it was beyond the hill — but I felt it *thud*. Then my sheep got bleaty. I left them and went to see what it was. Are you a spy?"

"No," Syeira insisted. "I just want —"

"Then I better tell you," continued the man. "I walked up the hill, then down into shadows. It was almost dark. I knew I was there because the grass was shiny." He wheezed a bit. "And I stepped on something. I bent down to touch it. I thought it was hair, a b-big head of hair. But it wasn't hair; it was a *mane*." He squatted down into his hole, his hands on the sides of his head, as if trying to block out a loud noise. He said something else, but his voice was inaudible.

"What did you say?" said Syeira.

"A lion," gasped the man. "A lion fell out of the sky. It was a mistake. I told them it was a mistake, I told them I was only a shepherd, but they wouldn't believe me."

Syeira had no idea what to make of this. She decided to try one last time.

"Can you tell me," she said slowly, "where they keep the horses inside the city? Where is the stable?"

The man only wheezed. In desperation, Syeira said, "Please, I'm not a spy. Can't you help me?"

Unexpectedly, the man stood up again, turned toward the city, and pointed. "There."

"Where?" said Syeira.

"Just inside the walls," he said. "The small stable. Near the bell tower."

"The small stable," repeated Syeira. "Is there a big stable?"

But the man had evidently decided he'd said enough. He was inside his hole again, hands on the side of his head. "Watch out," he said. "Lions and horses. *Up there*. If you see them, you're a spy. Watch out."

Suddenly he jumped up and skittered off southward, away from the walls. Syeira got back up on Arwin.

"He didn't know what he was saying," said the girl in a tired voice. "Why did you want me to talk to him?"

Arwin must have thought her reasons were self-evident; she gave an irritated shake of her mane and began trotting westward. Soon they were close to the point where the walls met the ocean. Thurckport stood on the northernmost tip of Stormsythe, guarded on the south by its huge limestone walls and on the north by the Gray Sea. The walls circled the city in a U, extending well out into the ocean to enclose the harbor. The first day there, Arwin had followed the walls westward and, where the water met the limestone, stood looking out. One glance had destroyed her hopes of swimming around. The sea was a live thing, sliding and seething, foaming and spouting, gathering itself hugely in a thousand places and then smashing itself against the walls. Now they stood in the same place, hearing but not seeing the angry waters. The line of watchtowers outside the harbor looked like a string of yellow droplets. Rain was gathering somewhere in the darkness. Syeira was thinking what a whole series of invading generals had wondered before her: *How was it possible to get inside this city?*

"The canal," she said out loud. "It's the only way."

She had already thought about selling Arwin as a barge horse. It was risky. She'd have to sell her own skills, too, and get the buyer to take her on as a handler.

"We'll come back late in the day," she said. "The barges will be moored up, waiting." She added thankfully, "We can sleep for a while."

They were trotting back, angling southward away from the walls, when Arwin suddenly stopped and lowered her head.

"What is it?" whispered Syeira.

Arwin was acting very oddly, moving her head up and down and snorting uneasily. Syeira glanced at the walls a quarter mile away. She could tell by the arrangement of lights on the parapet that the canal was close by. Guards stood on the parapet, she knew, scanning the heath. The two of them couldn't stay there long. She looked down at Arwin's feet but could see nothing in the darkness.

Arwin was clearly not going to move, so Syeira got off the horse and crouched down. Here much of the grass was gone because of the traffic, and her hands moved across the cool, damp earth. She felt the narrow, rounded impressions left by horseshoes. Military horses, probably. She crept ahead, feeling a wide swath of ground. At least half a dozen of them. She couldn't recall seeing any horses here that day. Maybe they had come out the previous night — early in the morning, after she and Arwin had retreated.

But Arwin had smelled plenty of soldier's horses in the last week and hadn't reacted like this.

"What is it?" whispered Syeira. She knew that none of the prints had been left by the colts; those two had never been shod in their lives. She glanced behind her at the lighted walls.

"We have to go," she whispered, and got back up on the horse.

Arwin must have felt the girl's anxiety, for after a few more passes with her nose she started southward again. From the look of the heath around them, Syeira knew that dawn wasn't far off. They skirted an old well, a ruined cottage that consisted of nothing more than two crumbling end walls and a skin tent that had probably been put up by a Mauditt; and soon they were among the oak trees that marked the outskirts of the *faubourgs*. (Around the walls the trees had all been felled so that invaders would have no cover.) Syeira lay down at once under the largest oak.

She slept long and deeply, slept through the light rain, slept through her dreams about high walls and the thrashing sea and twisting, honey-colored things falling from the sky. As she slept, people came and went around her, and once or twice Arwin stamped to deter the curious. Syeira awoke, hungry, late in the afternoon. *If I have to sell Arwin,* she thought, *at least maybe I'll be able to buy some food.*

They set off across the heath and soon reached the canal, which flowed directly into the city from the south. Under the cloudy sky the water was opaque and dimpled by feeding carp. But it was probably cleaner than most city canals in Stormsythe: Thurckport had strict laws against dumping things into it. Syeira and Arwin followed the barge-horse path toward the city. The canal narrowed as it approached the walls and then ran through a large tunnel, forty feet wide and guarded by two iron port-cullises — one outside the walls and one inside. The water-way was always busy. As Syeira and Arwin trotted up, the girl saw several empty barges moving out of the tunnel, one following another behind the slow-stepping barge horses. At least five barges were lined up in the holding area, waiting to go in. The bargemen were out on the grass, lolling, smoking, or attending to their horses. Syeira got down off Arwin and studied them. They all seemed to be mainly beard and belly, with voices that bristled like the snouts of boars; and some seemed very friendly with the soldiers on the parapet. She chose one that was keeping apart from the group. His tunic was as creased and dirty as a potato skin, his hair like a root cluster. Altogether he looked like some stubby old vegetable that had just been dug up. He seemed to treat his horse decently, though.

"That's a nice horse," said Syeira as she walked up. "Would you be interested in another one, to make a pair?"

"Don' need another one, chuck," said the man, who was adjusting the feedbag on his dray. But he looked Arwin over anyway, as everybody did.

"Looks a bit wicked," he commented.

"Oh, no," insisted Syeira. "She's as mild as a bluebell."

As a matter of fact, Arwin looked about as savage as a horse could look. Her mane was a tangle of knots and burrs. Mud had dried and cracked on her legs so that it resembled tree bark. She coolly returned the bargeman's glance — something no domestic horse would ever do.

"Yar," said the man. "And Ben here is a thoroughbred swanker. Sorry, chuck. I don' need no raw, yeasty horses today."

"I'll sell her cheap," Syeira offered quickly. "I'll sell her for a bit of food. Whatever you have."

"I don' *want* your horse," said the man distinctly. "Ben and me is doin' fine." Then, lowering his voice, he said less gruffly: "I'll give you some a'vice, chuck, 'cause I see you're new here, like meself. That there's a fightin' horse. Any soldier would be glad to have it, but they mightn't be towardly about payin' you for it. So I'd be careful around the walls, if I was you."

Arwin gave a warning nicker. Syeira looked up to see that four soldiers had come out of the postern door and were moving among the bargemen and canal rats and other hangers-on. Neither of them wanted anything to do with the soldiers. Without a word Syeira got back up on Arwin and urged the horse away.

Just then the rain began to fall. Several people around Syeira stretched cloaks over their heads. A bugle sounded on the parapet: lockout time. To the east and west of the canal, where the two main roads led to the city, the great gates began to close. Syeira and Arwin were now well away and the girl judged it safe to look back. The soldiers had closed and bolted the cage doors that covered the barge-horse path. Somewhere inside, another soldier was working the winch that lowered the two iron portcullises. Syeira watched hopelessly as the iron grids descended. Along the bottom they each had a row of foot-long spikes; dropped quickly, they would puncture the boats of invaders. Now the spikes divided the water at forty points. Syeira knew from watching beforehand that the grids extended about eight feet into the canal. After a minute the winch stopped, and the spikes came to rest on the bottom. Thurckport was now closed to all but the water creatures. Only a rat could have wriggled through the gaps in the grating. An otter, diving down eight feet, could have slipped through the larger gaps between the spikes; but even there it would have been a dangerous squeeze for a man.

For a full-grown man, anyway. A girl might have got through.

Syeira knew she had to do something; Arwin was getting increasingly restless and frustrated. But *swim* in? A week ago she wouldn't even have considered the idea; now she thought it might be their only hope. She knew she could dive down eight feet. It would be hard on her ears, but she could do it. Then, once inside, she could find the stable that Bill Mauditt had talked about. Even if there wasn't a stable — he could have imagined it, being a Mauditt — she might find out something useful. And a night like this would be perfect, with its cloak of rain.

Later, when they took shelter under their tree, Syeira put her head close to the mare. "I'll swim in," she said. "Tonight."

Arwin was swinging her head moodily. Syeira continued: "I'm small enough to get through, and with the rain they won't see or hear me. I'll find the stable. I'll find the colts."

Now, hearing herself say it out loud, she had doubts. How would she know the colts in the dark? Well, she would know their eyes, know their slightly splay-legged stance. They, in turn, would probably smell their mother on her; the water wouldn't wash it off completely. Syeira just hoped they wouldn't make a ruckus.

She looked up at the sky through the branches. The rain might not last; if she was going to go, she should go soon. She was starting to feel shaky, now that she had made her decision, and opening her satchel she took out the devil's scratch. Carrying this would be risky around horses, she knew; but she was thinking about the soldiers, and the spikes on the portcullis, and she knew she couldn't go without her amulet. "I'll put it inside Zephyra's spice pouch," she whispered to Arwin. "So it won't get wet." She made sure the scratch was well wrapped up, and tucked it into the waterproof pouch, adding the bottle of *Medic Synonyma* as a weight. Then she hung the pouch around her neck, slipping it beneath her tunic. Through all this the mare watched her intently.

"All right," said Syeira. The only question now was what Arwin would do once she learned that the girl planned to leave her. They hadn't been separated since Haysele.

The water of the canal was patchy in the rain. Cautiously they moved up the side until Syeira found one of several rough staircases that led down from the bank. All around them was the gray-black miasma of a wet summer night. They were more than half a mile from the walls, but Syeira had decided it would be safer to swim up than ride. She held her breath for a moment and then let it out, for practice.

"I just hope there's no rats in there," she whispered, getting off the horse.

Arwin was tense, her large eyes not moving from the girl. "I'll be back before morning," said Syeira. "I *hope*." Standing there, feeling the tightness in her stomach, she suddenly wished the horse would breathe something into her mind. Something strong and mint clear, something to wrap herself in. She remembered the old Hayselean story about the man who put on spring and wore it like a cloak. He was an old man, but he became young as he walked. She imagined how fresh his cloak must have smelled — all blue sky and honeysuckle and budding shoots. She needed something like that now, something to carry her through the dangers.

But Arwin only breathed *herself*, her own smell. It was enough, maybe. Syeira reached up and touched the horse's cheek.

"Well," she said, swallowing. "Good luck."

The water smelled like a distillation of bad beer and rotten fish. Syeira slipped in and looked up at the mare, who steamed lightly in the wet night. Keeping her head turned, she swam a few tentative strokes, and the mare moved along the canal beside her. Syeira stopped, treading water. "No," she whispered. "Don't follow me. Stay here." She knew she would have to give up if the mare didn't let her go. She began swimming again, and this time Arwin stayed where she was, standing large and still as a megalith.

The night ahead was grainy with moisture; it swayed and glittered like a curtain of shot silk. Syeira swam a silent breaststroke, her mouth an inch above the water. She wished her heart would slow down. She was making more noise with her breathing than her swimming. In her mind she saw the minnows that would gather by the wharf at home, near the river stable; when she moved, they would dart away in a silent green cloud. *Be like that*, she told herself. *Quiet as sunlight.* The canal crooked slightly, the shadows changed. She paused to look back at Arwin but saw nothing in the darkness. *I'm on my own now*, she thought. Down the length of the canal she could see the parapet lamps; they had halos around them. Now the dark shapes of the moored barges loomed ahead. She paused, treading water, and felt along the slimy wall until she grasped the iron tie-up for the barges. Her tunic felt like a second, ill-fitting skin. *Quiet now. Just rest.*

The rain would have been so soothing if she had been at home in her loft.

She had to wait; the fear was starting to rise from her stomach to her chest. Faintly through the rain came the voices of soldiers or bargemen. *They can't see me. Nobody can see me on a night like this.* She caught her breath and then struck out, passing the first barge. In the stern cabin she could see a smudge of candlelight. The second barge went by, and the third. *Easy, easy. Be a minnow.* She wasn't so much swimming now as gliding. Ahead she saw the glinting iron of the portcullis, and the darkness beyond it. This was where the soldiers might see her, if they looked down. The lamplight lay around her like a greasy slick on the water. She sensed the echoing space of the tunnel above and heard the water lapping against the sides. *Almost there . . .*

She was past the overhang of the tunnel. Weakly she clung to the portcullis with hands and feet, trying to still her breathing. *Don't pant. Just breathe. Breathe.*

After a minute she felt a bit better. Nobody had seen her. Now for the portcullis. *What if I get stuck? Don't think about that. And don't think about what lives down there, either. Nothing lives down there. Just wait for a good breath.* (Whenever she dove for horse brasses in the Hawkey, she always waited for a good breath.) *Just wait . . .*

She gulped and then submerged.

The water closed around her like a dark dream. She turned upside down and began pulling herself down by the grating. The tightness built inside her ears. *Have to go back up . . .* Her hand closed around a spike, but she knew she didn't have enough air and pushed off from the bottom. She rose as quietly as she could but still heard her own gasp echo in the tunnel.

Shhhh. She clutched the portcullis, fighting panic. *Quiet, quiet. Just wait.*

That wasn't a good breath.

Outside the rain fell steadily. She listened, trying to calm herself. The drops were small, but the rain was mighty. Given enough time it could alter the world — swell rivers, crumble castles, sweep away whole towns. She looked down the canal to where she thought the mare must be standing. This was one place where even Arwin couldn't go. *It's up to me.*

Again she took a deep breath. This time she *swam* down rather than pull herself by the grating. She felt the spikes and then the weedy bottom of the canal. *Tightness in my ears . . .* But she turned herself horizontal and glided through, scraping her stomach against the bottom. Bubbles slipped from her mouth and brushed her hand, soft as a moth's wing. She shot to the surface, her exhalation echoing in the darkness.

Through!

She couldn't see anything ahead. Silently she swam through the darkness toward the sound of the rain. After about thirty seconds she touched the second portcullis. Beyond it she saw another slick of lamplight on the water, but there seemed to be more of it here. She latched on to the grating like a limpet. *I can get through this one, too.*

Down she went a third time, hands pulling, ears hurting, squeezing through and up . . .

She came up facing the canal. There was only one barge here, a good distance away. She listened, forcing herself to breathe quietly. *I can't swim out into that lamplit water.* She slipped along the portcullis to the edge of the canal and then, after listening again, swam out into the shadows. From far away a dog barked. She reached the barge and went around it, leaving no more of a wake than a muskrat.

The canal widened and began to curve slightly. It seemed as dark within the city walls as outside them. Feeling her way along the wall, she found stairs leading up to the canal walkway. Cautiously, she pulled herself out and listened. Only the rain made any sound. She moved up the stairs and peeped over the canal wall.

The city of Thurckport rose up through the darkness.

Syeira saw houses like watchtowers — narrow and steeply roofed, with small turrets and minarets and high dormer windows. Most of them were stone, but a few were wood framed, faced with dark tile that shone in the rain. The windows were glass rather than oilcloth, for Thurckport was a wealthy city. In its markets you could buy basil, shark fins, fresh tomatoes, fine grass ropes, and rushes for your floors. Its cobblestone streets were in good shape. It had superb glassblowers, silversmiths, perfumers, and mirror makers.

And yet Thurckport was ill. Sometimes the children there would catch mice and insects and put the creatures inside toy guillotines. This did not bother the parents as much as the slight corrosion of their houses because of the salt air. On the streets, soldiers carried three killing edges apiece; the citizens were satisfied. At night the people rarely dreamed — they didn't need dreams. The dreams were all outside the walls, wandering the heath at night. The only thing their lives lacked, they thought, was light entertainment. They wished the gate watch would let in a few bearbaiters.

But Syeira saw none of this in the darkness. What she saw was an invincible city that *she* had invaded, single-handedly. She felt plucky and light-headed, even though, sniffing herself, she found she smelled a bit like the canal. She looked up and down the stone thoroughfare that ran the length of the waterway. Nothing stirred. Within a second she had scampered across the space, her sandals squelching, and was crouching beside a cistern. *Now for the bell tower*, she thought. Bill Mauditt had said it was just inside the walls. From the way he had been pointing, she'd got the impression it was here on the east side of the canal. The only thing she could do was wander the streets, keeping her eyes open.

It actually took her several hours to find the bell tower. By that time the rain had stopped and the exhilaration had pretty well ebbed out of her. Getting out would be more dangerous now. She looked up at the tower and saw beyond it a faint stippling of stars. The streets were silent except for the sound of water flowing through the gutters. She wondered how long it was till dawn. *What was I thinking of*, she asked herself, *to just dodge in and out of the city?*

Just then she heard, very faintly, the nickering of horses.

She crept past a long row of houses and underneath the

swinging sign of a public house. Through the darkness shone a single light — the only one she'd seen in the whole town. A few steps later she could make out the rounded gable roof of a stable. So Bill Mauditt had been right. She went closer, feeling the old knotted tension in her stomach. The stable was higher than those in Haysele, and older, judging by its sag. It had a single stone tower at the far end, roofed like the main building with slate tiles. At the front, one soldier stood in the lamplight. Syeira watched a moment, then darted through the streets to get around to the back. A shallow ditch led from one of the streets to the stable; she wriggled along it until she was ten feet from the building. The tower sagged a bit, too, and even in the dim light she could see that the stone was worn and seamed. About eight feet up there were black narrow shapes, like castle loopholes. Windows. Not glass or oilcloth windows; just empty holes.

Lying in the darkness, Syeira considered. It didn't look like a military stable. Only one guard, too. Probably a stable for "lubbers" — palfreys and geldings and other easy-tempered horses. The colts were unlikely to be here: Wild horses were not usually stabled with lubbers. But then she couldn't go back without at least taking a look. *The question is,* she thought, *can I get up to those windows?*

She crept close to the tower and felt the wall. Either the stones had been set poorly or they had shifted with age, for the wall was bumpy with crevices. A few were big enough for toes and fingers. She stepped up on one, steadied herself, then moved up to another. The stone was damp and crumbly against her cheek. She clung like a salamander, spreading herself to the very tips of her fingers, feeling the pull of the earth on her back. One leg was going a bit wobbly. *If anybody looked at the tower now,* she thought, *they'd see me clear as day.* She moved a foot weakly, like an insect's feeler, and found a ledge. Once more. Again. Her fingers gripped the sill of the window.

She was pulling herself up when she heard the last thing she would have expected — a nightingale.

It was inside the tower. Perched on the window ledge, she peered into the darkness. A pale cloud shimmered there, and she smelled blossoms. *A tree*, she thought in bewilderment. Then she remembered the Bayard tree she had seen in Sir Gemynd's stable. So this stable had one, too. They'd planted it in the tower, where it would have space and light. Now she was sure this wasn't a military stable. Soldiers had their own good luck charms, but trees weren't among them.

She sat, panting a bit, on the narrow window ledge. The nightingale had grown quiet. Below her the tower was in complete darkness. A branch twisted at an angle a few feet away; she saw it only because of the blossoms. It looked thick enough to hold her. She listened. Farther inside, the darkness was faintly alive with the snuffle and twitch of horses.

She shifted on the sill and leaned toward the branch.

With a sudden whirring of wings the nightingale darted away. Syeira hung from the branch, holding her breath, but the stable remained quiet. Quickly she moved hand over hand to the trunk, the blossoms rustling rhythmically with each grasp, and then lowered herself down. Now she could see a dim light at the far end of the stable. Her feet touched straw. She felt her way through the darkness, alert for things like buckets and hayforks. The air had the familiar close, dry smell, as if it had been filtered through burlap. She smelled hay and old wood and manure; she felt the warm nearness of horses.

Some were asleep, she knew, and some were aware of her, wondering if she brought food. She just hoped they wouldn't make too much of a fuss. She crouched for a moment, getting her bearings. The layout seemed very much like that of King Hulvere's stables. The horses were arranged in a series of two rows, facing one another but separated by a hay lattice — a narrow barrier of mesh topped by a walkway. To get close to the horses, she would have to go down the walkways.

She took a few steps forward, and her hand closed around the mesh of a lattice. Stealthily she hoisted herself up on the walkway and moved along it, wary of squeaking boards. One or two of the horses nickered. She studied their eyes, watching for the green-tinted pupils of the colts. She was sure now that these were not chargers; they didn't smell right. She reached the end of the walkway, lowered herself down, and felt her way to the next one.

This might take a little while, she thought.

But she felt safer here than outside. An old stable is a good place to hide, with its lofts and stalls and pitch-black crannies. And anyway, she had always felt that horses were on *her* side. She whispered softly to these ones as she moved down the rows. From the front she could hear voices, but it was the languid drawling talk of men who were just filling in the hours.

At that moment she felt the breathing of the horses change. It was as if she had been standing in a field of wheat and heard the stalks rustle, stirred by an imperceptible wind. Someone was coming — someone the horses knew well.

She glided to the end of the hay lattice and crouched down. Near the front of the stable a lantern was moving waist-high through the darkness. She saw two figures and heard a deep, raspy voice. The lantern stopped at a stall, and one of the figures disappeared into the darkness. Suddenly a large bird flashed across the lantern's beam. *A hawk?* thought Syeira. *No, too big.* From behind a stall she strained her eyes. The bird, perched on a beam, stretched its wings just at the edge of the light, and Syeira realized it was an owl.

Owls, she knew, could see in the dark.

Unthinking panic seized her. Had they trained owls here to seek out intruders? She scuttled along the back of the stable toward the tower. The blossoms plumed whitely before her, and she saw the midnight blue sky through the tower window. In an instant her head was engulfed in leaves. She heard no more voices, but she could tell by the shifting patterns on the straw that the lamp was moving closer. Frantically she clawed her way around the trunk so that she would be hidden by the tree. Her hands had just closed on the escape branch when she heard footsteps behind her and saw the lamplight flickering below. She drew back and froze. The yellow light moved upward, illuminating the foliage around her. Someone was standing fifteen feet away and holding up the lantern.

Syeira held her breath. A breeze from the windows rustled the leaves above her. Then came a voice — slow, heavy, and sulfurous, like lava moving down a darkened hillside.

"What, no tunes this eve, nightingale?" it said. "With the night sweet as an apple and the stars waking up over your shoulder? Come, lay down a bit of the moon-fleckered charm. I'll lead you."

And the voice broke into a song:

Two brawm coursers came riding at a run
Riding like the moon and riding like the sun;
One was honey to the roots of her hair
The other was spiced like the midnight air. . . .

6

In the Compound

S yeira could not think; she just gripped the tree and hoped she was hidden by the trunk. She heard footsteps, then another voice — much lighter and smaller than the first — saying, "Everything looks fine at the back, Mr. Davy."

Davy. The name brushed Syeira's memory but did not take hold; she was too numb with panic.

A grunt answered the small voice, and then the lamplight shifted back and forth across the tree.

"Where's our nightingale, then, Pouty?" said the heavy voice.

"I don't know, sir," replied the other nervously. "He *was* here."

There followed the raspy breathing of the man called Davy.

"I'm hoping," he said with menacing calm, "that no tabbies got in here."

"Oh, no, sir," said the light voice quickly.

Syeira heard straw crunching softly underfoot and knew that the smaller voice — Pouty — was approaching the tree. She closed her eyes.

"He might have just gone out for some bugs," said Pouty.

"For your sake I hope so," said Davy, his voice becoming even softer and more menacing. "We don't need tabbies here, Pouty. Just howlets and nightingales. The first does for the mice, and the second pours out the charm pure as an old fiddle."

"Yes, sir."

Suddenly Davy gave an angry bark that almost scared Syeira out of the tree: "What constellation is that, Pouty?"

Pouty must have jumped, too, although Syeira couldn't see him.

"Constellation, sir?" he replied shakily. Syeira tried to keep still; she knew that both men were looking through the window just above her.

"I . . . I think that might be the Boar constellation, sir," said Pouty. "The . . . er . . . Major Boar."

Davy laughed scornfully. "Does that look like a *boar* to you?"

"Well . . . Now that you mention it, sir —"

"That's a *bird*, Pouty. That's the Zinga Ree. You don't know about the Zinga Ree?"

"No, sir."

"That's 'cause you're a callow and babberlupped little georgie. Listen now and I'll tell you what the gypsy knows about the Zinga Ree. Long ago, Zinga was like other birds, chipping out the symphonies all day but living no longer'n a bee. Well, he gets to thinking this a'n't fair, and one day he goes to the Mare Arwina, the Mother, and says, 'Lady, I die with the mayflies. I flare out like a moth. Why can't I live a good long life like the elephant, who does nobbut honk and lumber?' Arwina says, ''Cause he's a great big gen'man and you're a nabbity little cuss, that's why, Zinga.' Are you listening, Pouty?"

"Yes, sir. A nabbity little cuss."

"That's so. 'Well,' says Zinga, 'but I toss out the songs so sweet and trilly; a'n't that worth having for a long time?' And he keeps yammering away like this, and at last Arwina says, 'Enough, Zinga! I'll tip you a gift, then, but not the one you want. You'll live the same span as all birds, but you alone'll be able to fly 'cross the years, fly ahead to the world as 'twill be, and bring back beauty for the Zinga song. At the end of your weedy little life you'll have more years in you than a hun'red elephants. And all your bairns, and your grandbairns — they'll have the same gift.' So that's the father Zinga Ree up in the sky, Pouty. He's only there in the summer, 'cause in the winter he's back in the warm green early of the world. And if you ever find one of his bairns here on earth — you won't, 'cause they're as shy as the outer planets, but if you do, forget about trying to catch him. He'll only stay around if you got some good tunes yourself. And he'll only stay around till winter, just like his pater. When the leaves turn, he gets to hankering for summers past — and summers to come. But you might want to listen to him real careful while he's here. He's the man who's seen great joy afore its day, and great woe, too. That's why his song is such a cutting silvery thing. Cutting and silvery for sinners like you and me."

There was a silence. Davy hawked and spat.

"Know your constellations, Pouty," he said.

"Yes, sir."

"And remember that birds are needful creatures in my stable. Much more needful than 'prentices."

"Yes, sir."

The lamplight went up again. "Where's our man the howlet?" asked Davy.

"He's at the front," replied Pouty. "Eating a mouse."

Davy grunted, then said, "Let's hope the nightingale comes back, boy. Otherwise *you'll* be up in that tree, tipping us a few airs."

"Yes, sir."

The lamplight shifted, and Syeira heard the scrunch of foot-steps on the straw. The voices faded. Darkness closed around her again.

❧

Davy, breathed Syeira. She felt weak and dizzy. Now she knew who it was — Blacklock Davy, the same gypsy who had captured Arwin years ago. What was *he* doing here? She listened again, and faintly from the front she heard Davy's heavy voice. He seemed to be in charge. How could she and Arwin ever find the colts if Davy was here? How could they even get close to the sta-bles? Davy would recognize the mare for sure, and then —

The thought spurred her into action; she had to get back to Arwin. Grasping the escape branch, she swung along it like a monkey, her legs swinging in a jerky arc. Getting out was not as easy as getting in: She had to swing from the waist and hook her feet over the windowsill. But she did it, with only a bit of grunting. On the window ledge she took a quick look, lowered herself till she clung by her fingers, and dropped to the ground. Then she was away like a hare in the night.

In the east she could see a faint glow. *It can't be*, she thought. *Not already*. She dodged frantically through the streets, nearly turning her ankle several times on the cobblestones. A few people were out with lanterns — fishmongers on the way to early market, street cleaners with their heavy boots and long brooms, and one or two mounted soldiers in their black and silver armor. She kept out of their way, chafing every time she had to crouch down in the shadows. Even before she reached the canal she heard the bugle ending lockout. She was winded by then, fighting a pain in her chest, but she kept going. As she drew close to the waterway she heard the cranking of a winch.

And there, at the canal's edge, she slumped to the ground, holding her side. Too late. The portcullises had been raised and the first barges were now gliding through the tunnel and into the city. She raised her head, panting. What had possessed her to try this stunt? Now she was in for the day. She just hoped Arwin would be all right by herself. After a moment she had to get to her feet and move back; she was standing right in the path of the barge horses. The clop-clopping of their hooves echoed in the early morning silence.

"So you gave up your horse, did you?" somebody called out.

She turned. The barge before her was being guided by none other than the man in the potato skin, the bargeman she had talked to. As he came abreast of her he gave his reins a gentle tug, bringing his horse to a stop.

"She's . . . tied outside," said Syeira distractedly.

"No, she a'n't," countered the man.

Syeira stared at him. "What do you mean?"

"They took her inside last night."

"*Inside?*" said Syeira wildly.

"Inside," confirmed the man. He shook his head. "You don' leave your horse alone here, chuck. That's the way you lose it."

"But . . . where did they take her?" said Syeira.

The man shrugged. "Lord Ran's stable, I suppose. There was a bunch of other horses with her; I guess they was roundin' up loose ones. Saw 'em go in the door beside the canal."

"This is awful!" Syeira cried. She stood stricken, one hand on her head. "What should I do?" She stared at the bargeman, who was now standing with his foot on the gunwale, watching the barges ahead of him. "What should I do?"

"What you *don'* wanna do," said the man, "is get theeself into a froth. That won't help."

"Where is the stable?" asked Syeira desperately. "I mean the *big* stable?"

The man shook his head. "Dunno. I'm pretty much new here meself." At that moment the barge ahead of him started to move, and he snapped the reins to get his horse going again. Syeira followed the boat dazedly, unthinkingly.

"Here," said the man, glancing at her. "You'd best go down to the harbor and find Spicetrader Marlow. His ship's the *Reynard*. Got a fox painted on the hull. I know he's got some dealin's with the stable, so maybe he can help you. He'll probably want money, though. Man's a spicetrader. And *don'* get in a froth," he added. "That never helped no one."

"All right," said Syeira. She watched as the barge drifted down the canal, then blew her hair out of her eyes and looked around.

"I'm *not* in a froth," she said in a low voice.

Around her the blue morning was starting to fill with light.

The thin clouds on the horizon were underlit with a seashell pink, faint as the glow of a buttercup when it's held under somebody's chin. From the streets came an ever-growing clatter of iron cart-wheels, horseshoes, and hobnailed boots. Thurckport was wak-ing up. Syeira began moving warily along the thoroughfare, keeping well to the side. The only thing she could do was follow the canal; she hoped it would take her to the harbor eventually. People brushed past her — burghers jowled and dewlapped like old trees, young goodwives in silk, bent and gnarled tradesmen. Everybody seemed in a hurry. The goodwives had the eyes of sparrow hawks. Nobody paid any attention to Syeira.

After a while she didn't pay attention to them, either; she was too busy with her own thoughts. Why had Arwin let herself be captured? Well, because she wanted to get into the city, of course. But she didn't know about Blacklock Davy. Dall and danker that man. Arwin's worst enemy, apart from the wolves of Arva. Now Arwin would be taken to the main stable, the military stable, and Davy would surely recognize her. But maybe Davy had no con-nection with the military stable. Maybe he only worked with the lubbers. And even if he did work in the big stable, he might not notice Arwin when she was brought in. They must have hun-dreds of horses there. If they put her in some small, out-of-the-way stall, and if she didn't suddenly decide to take on Lord Ran's entire army . . .

Syeira noticed a salty edge to the air. There were no houses around her now; just old sheds and warehouses. The canal widened and the flagstones gave way to planks. She felt the cool air of open water. Turning a corner she saw a spindly forest of masts and yardarms and furled sails. Flags snapped in the wind and hulls — tall and narrow, low and squat — rocked in the waves. Syeira had never seen so many boats. Ancient bulk carriers sat at their berths like huge floating cradles, their decks a mass of rope and tackle. Schooners, bleached by sun and wind but still grace-

ful as cranes, pulled and slacked on their lines. Small vessels —
dories and rowboats and skiffs — clustered around the big ones
like ducklings. All the boats bore the ensign of the empire — a
black and silver falcon. Everybody here worked for Lord Ran.

The water — what she could see of it — was a milky, flecked
green, but out toward the center of the harbor it was a cold blue.
She stopped and looked out. The harbor was perhaps half a mile
across, enclosed by the wall jetties. The eastern end was reserved
for Ran's fleet — mainly *taride* and his compact, high-prowed
warships. The entrance to the harbor was a line of quicksilver
etched by the sun. Two watchtowers stood on either side, flying
Ran's ensign. (Syeira couldn't see this, but at the base of each
tower, pointing seaward, was a row of four catapults. Any unau-
thorized vessel that tried to enter would be caught in the cross-
fire.) Beyond the harbor entrance she could barely see more
watchtowers and then the sea, showing white where it hit the
rocks. To get in, a ship would not only have to have authorization; it would have to know the waters well.

Syeira made her way along the main wharf, looking for a
ship with a painted fox on the hull. Carts loaded with grain and
fabric and clay bricks rumbled past her. Soldiers directed the
loading of goods while sun-darkened stevedores hoisted and
strained. The smell of pitch and kelp filled the air. She had covered the length of the wharf twice when she finally spotted the
Reynard, on a side dock. It was as weathered as an old barn, about
thirty-five feet long and "beamy," as the sailors say. Two ragged
sails the color of tobacco were furled to the boom, and a section
of webbed rope was stretched out around the prow to act as a
safety net. The ship was too small for a fighting ship and too deep
for a galley. It was one of many mongrels in the Thurckport harbor, pluggy as a bulldog and given to rolling when it moved.
Unusually for an oceangoing boat, it had a loading door in the
front hull. (Probably, like a lot of the large-bellied boats there, it

had once carried livestock.) This door was now open, and a gangplank led to the dock. Tacked beside the door was a parchment sign that bore a short message in the script of Stormsythe. Syeira couldn't read it, but it said, CREWMEN WANTED.

Inside the hold she could see somebody moving. She stepped down to the edge of the gangplank and coughed. Nothing happened.

"Are you Spicetrader Marlow?" she called.

A black-haired man was passing the doorway, carrying a sack on his shoulders. He paused just long enough to say, "Sometimes," and then disappeared again.

Syeira took a few steps along the plank. The large square doorway was edged with strips of oakum that fluttered in the breeze. Inside, dust motes whirled languidly in the sunlight.

"The bargeman said I could find you here," she said uncertainly.

Again the man appeared at the door — a man sun-darkened like all the sailors, yet somehow sallow about the eyes, as if he had once fought off a severe fever. He didn't have the build of a Thurckport seaman. Most of the sailors were as muscular and illproportioned as orangutans, but this one might have been a judge or a scribe. Only his eyes — slitted from staring into the sun — spoke of a life on the ocean. His shirt and breeches were the same color as his sails, but cleaner. His rope sandals were white with age. He looked both monkish and world-weary: He might have been a prince who had long ago run away to sea and was now just about ready to go back to being a prince again.

"You're too short for a crewman," he said.

"I . . . I didn't come here to be a crewman," said Syeira. She hesitated, wondering if he was trustworthy. "The bargeman — I don't know his name — said you deal with the stable."

The man's cool gray eyes never flickered. "Sometimes."

"I need to get into the stable," said Syeira.

"Why?" he countered.

Is he a spy of Lord Ran's? thought Syeira. *Is he a smooth-looking pirate?*

"I just need to," she said.

Without a word the man went back inside the hold. Syeira, nervous but determined, moved along the broad gangplank and into the ship. There her step slowed; her eyes closed; she stood still.

She might have just opened a window on a flowered, pinnacled city. The air around her was warm and clover soft and filled with echoes. She kept her eyes closed; she didn't need to see. She was in a garden of almond and jasmine, a garden that quivered with the incantations of a hidden bird. She was lounging in a green-scented, white-tiled room, and the harps and hautboys had just finished playing. She was drinking thick coffee in a bazaar, among peddlers who hawked hemp and ginger and ink that smelled of patchouli. In the palm dusk she listened as turbaned old men, their beards suffused with frankincense, talked of countries that could only be visited when the comets blazed. She was in a land where the very angels were made of musk. For this was the hold of the *Reynard*: Anyone who entered it breathed in a different world. Myrrh, sandalwood, star anise, lemon grass, aloe, cassia, eucalyptus, balsam apple — Syeira didn't know the names, but they transformed the air as the sun does over desert sands, creating islands and continents out of nothing. She opened her eyes and looked around. A lot of the casks were empty, despite the lingering scent shadows: The spicetrader must have been at the end of his run. Now she turned to the man. She noticed that he wore a single shark's tooth around his neck.

"Once again," he said curtly, "why?"

She had to take a risk; she had to get to the stable quickly. "Because," she replied in a low voice, "my horse was taken from me and is being held there. Against her *will*."

The man named Marlow looked bored. "Are we talking about a rescue mission?"

Syeira was silent; she dared not say more.

The man didn't need any more. "I don't carry out rescue missions," he declared. "I'm a spicetrader. Good-bye."

"Wait," said Syeira. "Just wait till I —"

"Parting gift," said Marlow, reaching up to a spice net and tossing something chalky to Syeira. "For the complexion. Rub it on and you'll be beautiful in two days. You won't be bothered by bugs, either. Good-bye."

"*Listen!*" Syeira cried, ignoring the tossed spice. She took a few steps forward and suddenly felt the weight of Zephyra's pouch around her neck. That gave her an idea. She fished inside her tunic and drew out the bottle of *Medic Synonyma*. "I'll pay you," she said, and held up the bottle. "I'll pay you with this."

"What, your cough medicine?" said Marlow.

"It's not cough medicine," said Syeira. "It's a word potion." She didn't use the technical name because she had a problem saying *Synonyma*. "It creates words. You think of a word, and it creates others in your head. Words that mean the same. A *tree* of them."

Marlow raised his eyebrows. "A tree of words," he echoed.

"Yes."

"In your *head*."

"*Yes.*"

He held out his hand for the *Medic Synonyma*. Syeira didn't really want to part with it until he agreed to help, but she was in no position to bargain. Marlow took the bottle and looked at the label.

"The very thing to keep a sea dog eloquent," he said dryly. "I suppose this is for those far-off days when I'm old and fat and can do nothing but sit around telling stories?"

"Yes," Syeira replied earnestly. And, because Zephyra had always stressed this, she added, "It's herbal."

Marlow uncorked the bottle and gave it a sniff. He was

amused by all this, in his sour way. From a kid, too. On the whole
he had a low opinion of kids and their ability to spin a yarn.
Twice in his life he had almost got married — to a pirate queen
and a female witch doctor — but at the last minute he had
backed off, knowing that marriage was bound to end in children.
And probably (he had told himself) his wife would ask him to tell
stories to the children. He only told his stories to those who could
appreciate their subtlety and sophistication. In practice this
meant that he told them to nobody in the Thurckport harbor.
Now he glanced at Syeira with distaste. She had come as close as
she dared, afraid he was going to steal her *Medic Synonyma*. For
some reason Marlow suddenly felt depressed.

"Herbal, is it?" he said irritably. "Probably some gut-flaying
poison."

"No, it's *not*," insisted Syeira. "I'll take some of it, if you want."

Marlow didn't look at her. He recognized the black feeling
now. It was the feeling he sometimes had late at night, when he
woke up, got up on the dock, and looked out over the dark profile of Thurckport.

"I'll take some of it," Syeira repeated. "You'll see."

If any of his friends had seen Marlow's face just then, they
would have thought he was in for a return of his old fever. The
pallor around his eyes seemed to have deepened. Syeira, watching him uneasily, said, "But we have to hurry. My horse was just
taken last night, and —"

"Enough about your horse!" snapped Marlow.

Syeira fell silent. Marlow tossed the *Medic Synonyma* into his
basket of knickknacks, where it joined a bit of dried ambergris, a
harpoon head made of bone, a parchment map of the trade winds,
a roll of sail twine, an old seaman's almanac bound in wood, the
birdlike skull of a small dolphin, and a mermaid's purse (actually
the egg case of a skate). Then he lifted up a spice bag and thrust
it into Syeira's hands.

"What's this?" she asked.

"Just take it outside," said Marlow, scowling.

Syeira, puzzled, hoisted the bag with an effort and moved out onto the gangplank. Marlow fitted the hold door into place, and Syeira could hear him barring it from inside. Then he appeared at the hatch on the deck, carrying another spice bag. He locked the hatch door, lowered the bag onto the gangplank, and finally lowered himself.

"Let's go," he said shortly.

Syeira understood, with relief and gratitude, that he was taking her to the stable. She didn't ask him why he had changed his mind; she just followed him up the dock. "You didn't try the word potion," she said.

"Later," said Marlow. "When I need a pick-me-up."

The main stable was apparently farther east, in the direction of Ran's fleet. The street Marlow chose was wide and flat-flagged to make it easier on the horses' hooves. As they walked, Syeira avoided the eyes of passersby, but now and then she would glance up at the houses. Their upper stories leaned slightly over the street; they looked as if they were watching everything — including one another. A lot of them had balcony gardens or wall trellises, and here and there she could see clusters of tomatoes and cucumbers.

"What are we carrying?" Syeira asked.

"Zembala," Marlow answered.

"What's that?"

"The resin from the zembala tree," said Marlow shortly. "You heat it and mix it with oil. Makes a good dressing for horse's hooves."

"Oh," said Syeira. They walked on a moment, and then she remarked, "In Haysele we use pine tar."

Marlow said nothing. Syeira's bag was getting heavy, but she didn't want to complain. They went up a hill, and on the way down, when Syeira wasn't straining so much, she said, "Tell me, do you know a man named Blacklock Davy?"

"Everybody knows Blacklock Davy," said Marlow.

"Is he . . . one of Lord Ran's men?"

"Of course. Head farrier and master of the stables."

Syeira was silent; she had been afraid of this. After a moment she asked, "How did a *gypsy* get to be head farrier?"

"Talent rises to the top here," said Marlow acidly. He was about to say more, but just then they passed two mounted soldiers who were policing a junction. In the sunlight their armor looked chillingly beautiful: The chest plate was fire-blackened and the rest of it a bright burnished silver. Both the men carried glaves — the very long bladed pikes that were so dangerous to horses. In the melee of battle, a foot soldier with a glave could slit the throat of any charger that wasn't well protected. Marlow nodded slightly to them, but they remained impassive. Syeira looked up only when she was well past them. As she did, her eyes fell on a tall tower of black stone.

"Lord Ran's donjon," said Marlow, before she could ask.

"He lives there?"

"All alone with his black and silver dreams. He's not there just now; he's in Broak, dealing with rebels."

Rebels. Will Shanks had also spoken of a rebellion, Syeira remembered. She wanted to get more details from Marlow, but right then he looked forbiddingly tight-lipped and grim. They walked in silence until the road ended at a wall and a gate — the military compound.

"Now," said Marlow in a low voice. "You're here helping me with the zembala. Don't say a word about anything else, and don't even *think* about your horse. We'll have to see what we can do once we're inside."

On either side of the gate were towers that held three soldiers each. Syeira was steeling herself for a challenge from the guards, but they waved Marlow through with barely a glance.

"I sell them exotics," whispered Marlow, by way of explanation.

"Exotics?"

Marlow gave a sardonic smile. "Love potions. Hair restorers. Infallible specifics against fainting on the battlefield. They all work if you *believe* they work."

Before them were several grassy fields, pitted and furrowed by hooves, and across the fields moved clouds of men and horses. Soldiers rode chargers and stable boys led chargers-in-training. Wheelwrights carried wheels, bowyers carried bows, and beefy men carried bundles of glaves over their shoulders. Syeira saw a man pushing a wheelbarrow that held nothing but rallying bugles. She and Marlow walked down a dirt path in the center of the fields. To their left, running at right angles to the stable and about a hundred feet from it, was a high limestone wall. Smoke billowed above it, and Syeira could see something else in the corner, something that looked like the rounded dome of a tent. She gazed in awe at the stable, which stretched out before them at the end of the dirt path. How many horses were kept there? They passed through the immense doors and found themselves in the farrier's alcove. Two men were shoeing horses, another was clipping and filing their hooves, and a boy was sweeping up the clippings. Syeira and Marlow put down the zembala in the corner.

"Zembala's here," Marlow announced.

A man wearing several hoof rasps on his belt paused long enough to say, "Other end. We'll mix it later." Then he hurried outside. It seemed a busy place.

"Where's Blacklock Davy?" whispered Syeira nervously.

"Could be anywhere," said Marlow. "Could be asleep. He keeps late hours."

They both looked down the rows of horses that stretched to the end of the building. Marlow's face was expressionless.

"All right," he said, speaking as if he were just making conversation. "We'll take the roundabout way to the other end. You're going to have to carry that zembala a bit longer. *Don't* look as if you're looking."

They moved down between the hay lattices. Many of the soldiers were there grooming their own mounts, since, as any good horseman knows, this is the way to create a firm bond with a horse. They all seemed to know Marlow and nodded to him. Most of them were dressed in the leather jerkins, streaked here and there with rust, that they wore under their armor.

Syeira kept a good lookout for Arwin and the colts but saw no horse that faintly resembled them. When she and Marlow got to the end of the row, they switched over and went down the other one. They did this for all seven rows; it took them half an hour. Neither Arwin nor the colts were there. The two of them set their zembala down at the far end of the stable.

"She's not here," whispered Syeira, perplexed. "There must be another stable."

"No other stable," said Marlow.

"A holding paddock somewhere?"

Marlow shook his head. "If your horse isn't here, we're leaving."

Syeira was looking off to the west, through a small window, at the limestone wall she had seen coming in. "What's over there?" she asked.

"Weapons yard," answered Marlow. "Never been there. Don't want to go." He was getting restless. "Come on. We're done here."

Syeira looked around hopelessly. Where could Arwin be? Where could the colts be? The stable hands must have them holed up somewhere, in a special stall. She sensed there were large sections of the compound she hadn't seen yet. "I want to stay here," she whispered to Marlow.

"No, you don't," said Marlow. "Believe me, you don't."

"I can't go until I've searched everywhere."

"Listen," said Marlow, lowering his head. "*Listen* to me. They'll cut off your ears if you're caught trespassing here. No horse is worth your ears."

"This one is," whispered Syeira, her eyes darting around her. "I didn't tell you before, but . . . she's a *magic* horse."

Marlow was looking ill again. Syeira picked up a nearby bucket; she knew she would stand out more if she were empty-handed.

"They won't notice me," she said. "I'm just another stable kid. There's dozens of them here."

"And what am I supposed to tell the boils at the gate?" Marlow hissed. "That I left you to snoop?"

Syeira had forgotten about that. "You can fix it, Marlow," she whispered urgently. "Please. Arwin's here somewhere, I know it, and the colts, too. I must find them before Davy does."

"The colts," repeated Marlow in a voice of wonder. "I'm hearing about some colts now, to go along with the marvelous magic horse." He took a breath. "All right, dammit. I'll tell them at the front that I left you here to mix the zembala, as a favor to the stable hands. Another example of Marlow's largesse."

"I don't want to get you into trouble," said Syeira.

"You won't get *me* into trouble," said Marlow. "I'm the man with the love potions and the oriental hair restorers. But *you* — you're nothing to them. If you end up having to carry around your ears on a string, don't come crying to Marlow."

He said this as one last attempt to scare the girl into leaving with him, but Syeira only bit her lip and said nothing. Marlow exhaled in exasperation. "Fine," he said. "The bell in the compound sounds at twilight; that's when all outside workers have to leave. I strongly advise you to get out when they do."

"All right," said Syeira.

"As for me," he concluded tightly, looking around, "I need a holiday. As soon as I get a couple of crewmen, I'm gone from this city. Bloody capital of the empire."

"Thank you, Marlow," said Syeira.

"I'm leaving now," he replied. "Good-bye, squit. You're lucky you tried to flim-flam *me* with your word potion; I do that all the time with my own exotics. But here you won't find such a sympathetic audience for your yarns. In particular they are *not* moved by animal stories. So make sure you leave the compound with everybody else."

Syeira watched him go, feeling subdued. She just hoped the word potion *wasn't* poison.

But she had other things to worry about now. Bucket in hand, she went down the aisle and stepped out the main door. On the quads around her, training was going on. Young chargers were learning battle moves: At their handler's signal, they would go back on their hind legs and kick with their forelimbs. Elsewhere a small phalanx of horses was learning to wheel and retreat. This was actually one of the most important — and difficult — moves in the cavalry repertoire. It involved training all the horses to change their lead foot at the same time. When it was done well, it was beautiful to watch: The horses seemed to surge through a single corridor in the air, as a flock of birds does when it changes direction. These horses had almost got it, but not quite. Syeira turned to the southwest field. There, riders with lances were charging a quintain — a dummy soldier holding its own lance, set up on a swivel mount. A soldier had to hit the dummy just right; otherwise it would spin around and give him a whack with its lance. These soldiers went at intervals of twenty seconds, riding fast and hitting sure; none of them were cuffed by the swinging quintain. All along the sidelines, watching the exercises, were grooms and standard-bearers and stable hands.

Casting her eye over them, Syeira was suddenly aware of

something she should have noticed long ago. They were all men or boys. She was the only girl there.

She began edging away. She looked toward the weapons yard on her right; there seemed to be less activity there. The wall was almost as high as the city wall, with a wide arched gateway in the center. Through the gateway she could see a fire-blackened lawn. She knew she should just go back to the main stable and hide until the bell tolled, but she was curious about the smoke and the dark tentlike thing, which still showed just above the wall. Now she could see on the lawn a catapult and several large wicker baskets. Setting her bucket down, she took a step inside, in order to peer around the corner.

And she stood rooted to the spot, staring upward.

Ten feet from the ground floated a huge shape, twice as big as a haystack. It was made of coal black fabric and resembled nothing so much as a giant tapered pillow, broad at the top and narrower at the bottom. It seemed to be filled with smoke. Black wreaths trickled out from the open mouth, and the air below it shimmered with heat. Two ropes held it to the ground. It had the taut, weighted look of a skin bottle heavy with water, but Syeira could see that it was pulling *up* on its ropes, straining like a sail to leave the earth. She was marveling at the thing, wondering how it managed to stay up, when a harsh voice yelled, "Hey, you!"

Syeira turned swiftly. A man with a shaved head and soot-blackened face glared at her from the center of the weapons yard. Beside him was a long, deep pit in which the remains of a fire still smoldered.

"You here to gawk?" he said. "Get back to the sewin' room!"

Fortunately for Syeira the man jerked his thumb over his shoulder. She scurried off in that direction, going well around the man. The yard was as busy as a village fair. In small lean-tos along the wall, fletchers were putting feathers on arrows and leather workers were cutting out bracers, the gauntlets worn by bowmen. Here a man was making mantelets, the iron-reinforced body shields that stuck in the ground and protected archers; there a man stood fifteen feet up on a siege tower, hammering in a brace. For all the smoke and banging the lawn might have been a blacksmith's shop.

At the far end of the compound was a long thatched building — the sewing room, Syeira guessed. She looked over her shoulder. The smoke-blackened man wasn't looking her way, but he had moved close to the gateway. She couldn't sneak out now. To her right was a large cage door that led into some kind of keep, but two men were working around it. To her left was a postern door — leading out of the whole compound, she guessed — but it was padlocked. She had no choice but to take her chances inside the sewing room. Drawing a deep breath, she stepped through the doorway.

Three women looked up as she entered.

They were sitting on three-legged stools, and between them on a very large, low table was a huge swath of the same dark fabric that Syeira had seen floating near the wall. Each woman had a section of it and was darning away. They were all middle-aged, grayed and hunched by toil. Behind them on the walls hung shears, measuring tapes, and some of the litters used for carrying horses aboard a ship. Even as the women looked Syeira over, the steady stitch and draw of their hands did not stop.

"And who might you be?" asked one of the women.

Syeira returned their gaze anxiously. They did not look hostile, but neither did they look particularly friendly.

"I'm Syeira," she said. "I was sent here."

The woman eyed her doubtfully. "You a seamer?"

Syeira swallowed. She had no idea what she had got herself into.

"Sometimes," she said earnestly, remembering Marlow's reply.

The woman sighed. "All right. Get a stool. There's needle and thread on the table there."

Syeira did as she was told. The tabletop was strewn with sewing tools: pincushions, large-eyed embroidering needles, and wafers of beeswax (to wax the thread so it wouldn't knot). Syeira chose a needle and a spool of thread and took a place beside the woman, who gathered up some material and spread it before the girl. "I'll get you started backing up this seam here," she said. "You know what you're supposed to do?"

"Um — no," said Syeira.

One of the other women gave a snort of irritation. "There! Two days to finish this gallin' warboy and they hand us a squab!"

"Well, we'll have to make the best of it, won't we, Hanna?" replied the first woman. "Here, girl. You see this seam's already been done with a main stitch; you put in a backup. Like this."

She began putting in the stitch, easily and fluidly. Syeira caught on without much difficulty (she had sewn plenty of bridles in her day) and was soon sitting quietly, moving slowly down her seam. The fabric, she noticed, was held to the table with clamps in the shape of birds. She knew they were sewing the same kind of floating thing she had seen outside. She had no sense of the shape, but the women seemed to know exactly where they were amidst the huge piles of material. The one called Hanna finished a section and held it up.

"There," she said. "Now all it needs is a line of lace. Nothin' too tarty, but somethin' to draw a bright eye."

The other women chuckled.

"Why stop there?" chimed in the third woman, one with a tiny, delicate face and boxy figure. "Let's sew a big train onto the bottom. A weddin' dress in the sky!" She sighed. "I swear I'm losin' the know, doin' nothin' but warboys day in and day out. To think I was once the best dressmaker in the city."

"You mean the *second* best, dearie," said Hanna sweetly.

"We was *all* the best," said the first woman, the one who had spoken to Syeira. "And we'll be the best again, when we're back in civvies."

"Not much chance of that, Jayce," said Hanna sourly. "With all the hoo-ha in Broak, we'll be sewin' warboys for years." She smoothed out the fabric with an impatient gesture. "You'd think the blimey mechanicals could learn to sew."

"They *can* sew," said Jayce. "They just think it's lowering theirselves to do it. They want to make things with points and spikes, and flying things as you can drop boiling oil out of."

"*Some* mechanicals do," said the woman with the small delicate face, lowering her voice. "But there's others who'd rather die than make them things. What do you think is behind the hoo-ha in Broak?"

Hanna glanced furtively at the open doorway, but Jayce kept her eyes on her sewing.

"You seem well up on the fortunes of the empire, Triese," she said mildly.

"Well, a flung stone sends out ripples," returned Triese, "and there's more than one stone bein' flung in Broak, let me tell you. A lot of mechanicals there never liked bein' part of Lord Ran's war machine; we all know that. Now things have broke wide open." She leaned closer to Jayce. "And Lord Ran a'n't takin' it lightly, that's plain. I was down at the harbor last week, and I saw 'em loadin' catapults by the dozen. Catapults and warboys! That's a lot of weaponry for just a ragtag bunch of mechanicals. I'm wonderin' if —"

"You might want to save your military speculations for after work, girl," said Jayce, in the same equable tone as before. "More healthy that way, know what I mean?"

They all worked on, for the most part in silence. The women said very little to Syeira, and she didn't want to ask too many questions. But she felt relatively safe there, even though she had to work hard to keep up with the others. In midafternoon they stopped for bread and salted fish, which Syeira wolfed down gratefully; and then, after a cup of tea, they were back at work. Now she wanted desperately to sleep — she'd been awake for almost twenty-four hours. She opened her eyes wide, put her head back, and returned to her sewing. The women never looked up. Slowly the light changed outside the window. Syeira's fingers were cramped and sore by the time she heard the bell ringing out in the compound. The women stood up stiffly and began to gather up their sewing bags. Syeira sat with eyes closed; fatigue held her to the stool like a great soft hand.

"Where's your home, then, girl?" said Jayce.

"Um — in the stable here," said Syeira, opening her eyes. She didn't know what else to say, and she wanted a chance to investigate the place at night.

All the women began clucking and shaking their heads. Jayce eyed her skeptically. "Don't you got no home in Thurckport?" she asked.

Syeira was getting uncomfortable; soon they would be asking who she was and where she had come from. "I'm a stable kid," she replied, as casually as she could, "and the stable is fine for me."

"You a'n't no stable kid here," said Jayce. "They don't take girls here."

Syeira began to squirm. She was racking her brain for a credible story when Hanna said, "Take her to Grulla's place. She'll be safe there."

"Aye, that'll do," said Jayce, slinging her satchel over her shoulder. "Let's go, all."

They left the hut, Jayce closing and locking the door, and began walking toward the entrance. Torches had been lit on the wall above the weapons yard. Most of the yard workers had disappeared, but the fire pit glowed faintly. The great pillowlike thing was hanging in the sky. There seemed to be a fire directly under it, in a large kind of pan. A wicker basket hung below the pan, and inside the basket, looking out at the main compound, stood a soldier. He had climbed up there by rope ladder; Syeira could see it swaying gently in the torchlight. The whole contraption was tethered to the parapet by two thick ropes. Syeira stared at it openmouthed.

Noticing her awestruck expression, Jayce said, "Yep, that's the top of the line, that one. That's the sentinel warboy."

Syeira wanted to ask more questions about it, but she grew silent when she saw ahead of her the man with the fire-blackened face. She kept her head down, but the man ignored her and said, "On schedule, Jayce?"

"We are, sir," replied Jayce shortly.

"Good, 'cause we'll need another one by the end of next week."

They passed out through the gateway. Syeira shot a glance over her shoulder. The man in the basket was about fifty feet above the wall.

"Does it stay up all night?" she asked.

Jayce nodded. "They keep the fire going, so it has heat to stay up. You see, from the top of the wall they can just look out over the compound; but from the warboy they can look right *outside* the compound, and into all the dark corners."

Within two minutes they had reached the main gate. The soldiers in the gate towers watched them without expression as they passed out of the compound. Once they were outside, the two other women turned east while Jayce and Syeira began walking southwest, following the same street taken by Marlow and the girl earlier that day.

"Grulla lives in the old town," said Jayce. "It's a bit of a walk."

"Who is Grulla?"

"Grulla the fighting crone," replied Jayce. "Now retired and full of spleen toward all. *Especially* the military."

They were silent for a time. Once again Syeira felt fatigue wash through her veins; she felt she could almost fall asleep while walking. To keep awake she said, "I don't know any crones."

"Sure you do," Jayce corrected. "You met three of 'em today. Grulla's like us, 'cept even more of a brawling old bag of bones."

"But she *is* a friend of yours," pursued Syeira; she was getting nervous about meeting this fighting crone.

Jayce shook her head. "Grulla has no friends. 'Cept maybe the Weerlings."

"The Weerlings?"

"You'll meet 'em soon enough," said Jayce shortly. "Be decent to 'em and Grulla will be decent to you. They're all she's got." They crossed a bridge over the canal, and Jayce said, "I'll tell you right now, Old Grulla's house is no palace. I think it used to be an old dovecote, and the yard was for bees. But it's close to the Wall, and there's a nice broad walk along the canal — just what she needs for the Weerlings."

The city around them did indeed begin to look old. There were more leaning houses and fewer bright colors, and on the walls hung the skeletons of ancient vines. At length Jayce stopped before a small rounded house and tapped on the door.

"Are you here, Grulla?" she called.

There was no answer. Jayce pushed the door gently and it swung open. "Grulla!" she hollered.

They heard fumbling, and a lamp was lit. In the dim light they could just make out a small bent figure shuffling toward them. "What is it?" a harsh voice asked.

"A guest," said Jayce.

"I don't want any guests," replied the voice.

"She's a seamer," Jayce continued patiently. "No home to go to. Wanted to stay inside the compound, but we wouldn't let her."

There was a silence. The tiny woman limped to the doorway, bearing a lantern. "In the *compound*?" she echoed. "What would you be thinking of?"

Syeira took a step back.

"Thought she could stay with you," said Jayce. She turned to Syeira. "You're part of the group now. Be at the gates tomorrow at dawn. You'll get two good meals a day, which I reckon you can use."

She walked away without another word. Syeira was not at all anxious to be left alone with Grulla. The little woman had the face of a monkey and only patches of hair on her head. She stood lopsidedly and held a small walking stick in her hand, yet she had an ocelot's glare and a pointed, aggressive chin. She looked as if she would know how to use any weapon you put in her hand.

"I suppose you want some food," she said.

"No, I'm fine," Syeira replied nervously.

"Good," said Grulla. "Because I don't have any. Unless you eat hay."

The woman turned and disappeared into the darkness, Syeira at her heels. There was the sound of a door being scraped open, and a rectangle of night sky appeared in the darkness. Syeira was looking out on to an overgrown yard, a good hundred feet long and about half as wide. She smelled alfalfa and horse-hair and then, over the woman's crooked shoulder, she saw horses — maybe ten of them. She moved forward, excited, but suddenly stopped.

There was something wrong with these horses. Healthy horses wear the dusk easily; these ones were rubbing and scratching at it. One, a shaggy-maned dray, was making a soft buzzing noise as if it had a fly trapped inside its forehead. Another one had strange white eyes, white as a squid in a dark sea. Directly in front of Syeira, a small mare was swinging its head back and forth. As the girl watched, it put its head back, scratched at its ear with a hind hoof, and then went back to swinging. Most of the horses had the bulk of war steeds, but they stood and moved like skittish colts. They were old children: Something, some gall or plague, had clouded their souls.

"The sons and daughters of Ran's empire," said Grulla.

Just then Syeira gave a half-stifled gasp of joy. In the far corner of the yard, half-hidden behind a tree, was a profile she knew well. Arwin's eyes flashed in the darkness. Syeira started forward, but the mare moved even further into the shadows. Syeira stopped; Arwin stayed where she was. It was as if the horse wanted to remain unnoticed.

"What is it?" Grulla demanded sharply.

Syeira hesitated. "What's the matter with your horses?"

"A falcon et their livers," said the old woman grimly. "Just like it et mine." She gestured to the yard. "You can make your bed here; there's only room for one in the house. Take some of the fresh straw and sleep next to the well, under the tree."

"All right. Thank you."

"And don't affright the horses. They go Mauditt easily."

She hobbled back into her small round house, and at once Syeira moved across the yard toward Arwin. The other horses shied away from her nervously. As she got closer to the far end, she broke into a run. For perhaps the hundredth time in her life she wished she was a horse. She didn't want hands; she knew Arwin disliked being touched. All she could do was go right to Arwin's breast bone, under her neck, and smell her.

"How did you get here?" she whispered furiously.

But Arwin was impatient to get the girl's news. She put her nose down close, sniffing, and Syeira knew that she was looking for the scent of the colts.

"No," whispered Syeira. "I didn't find them. But I will, don't worry." She added urgently: "Arwin, Blacklock Davy is here. He was in the small stable, and it looks like —" She stopped. *Well,* she thought, *maybe it's just as well that you don't understand me. You're tense enough as it is.* The girl sighed and slumped down beside the well. One thing was certain now: Arwin couldn't go near the stables. Blacklock Davy was bound to recognize her — after all, Zephyra had. It would be up to Syeira to do the low work, as Will Shanks called it.

"The colts must be around *somewhere*," she said. "There must be another paddock."

Her whispering was starting to bother the other horses. She looked around at them; never had she seen such waifs, orphans, damaged ones. She remembered the hoofprints that had bothered Arwin: These must have been the horses that had made them. The small mare, the one with the ear problem, was very curious about Syeira. The horse had come within ten feet and stood there, still swinging her head and scratching at her ears. Syeira guessed her to be well over twenty years old, but there was a certain brittle quickness to her movements. The girl slipped over to her, approaching at an angle so that the mare could see her clearly. "Shh," she whispered coaxingly. Very gently she put her hands on either side of the horse's nose, but still the head swung back and forth, back and forth.

7

THE FIGHTING CRONE

At work the next morning, Syeira asked Jayce about the horses in Grulla's yard.

"Aye, the Weerlings," said Jayce, without looking up from her sewing. "They was all military horses, once. But the fighting got into their heads and left nightmares inside like slivers. They're broken up now, bad as the Mauditts."

"But if they're in pain," said Syeira, "wouldn't it be better to put them down?"

"They a'n't in pain," interjected Hanna. "They're just crazy. That's no worry to Grulla: She's got a like disposition."

"She said a falcon ate her liver," remarked Syeira.

The women laughed sourly.

"One way of putting it," said Jayce. "She'll probably tell you the whole story, sometime. Then again, she might chase you out tomorrow with her crossbow. She's a tetchy old scrub."

That day was just like the one before. Syeira was getting used to the heavy lake of fabric around her and the ache in her fingers. She saw that they were sewing the warboy in three large panels, reinforcing each one at the top and bottom. As they progressed, the warboy got more and more unwieldy, and several times they stopped to roll and clip the section they had finished. Once again Jayce was doing the main stitch and the girl the backup. Hanna and Triese did "extras," such as the reinforcing and the sleeves to hold the guide ropes in place.

In midafternoon, after tea, Jayce and Syeira went outside to bring in two new rolls of fabric that had been left by the compound workers. Syeira was glad to be able to stretch.

"What's in there?" she said, nodding to the cage door on the east side of the weapons yard.

"Lord Ran's menagerie," said Jayce, as the two of them hoisted a roll of fabric. "Bears, big cats, rhinos, and so on."

"What are *they* used for?"

"For fighting, naturally. And for entertainment. The rhinos are chargers, and the cats and bears are executioners. Ran keeps 'em all half-starved when they're on duty, so they do a good job." She backed into the hut with one end of the fabric roll. "Most of 'em are in Broak now. I'm sure they're putting on a show with the rebels."

"Don't the horses smell them here?" asked Syeira.

Jayce shook her head. "There are several walls and a field between here and the stables. I've never heard of any problems."

They toiled away until the light faded, and Syeira thought she had never worked at a more tedious or mind-numbing job. *Soon I'll be a crone myself,* she thought. She was looking out the window yet again, wondering when the bell was going to ring, when she saw a wheelbarrow coming toward them across the lawn. Behind it was a young man, stooped and portly. Stacked on his wheelbarrow was something that looked like mats.

"More work," sighed Jayce, looking out the window. "Rot and rile all stablemen!" She got up just as the young man nudged open the door, his arms full of the matlike things. "Did you hear that, Pouty?"

Syeira looked up furtively. Pouty — the man who had been with Davy. He was very young, no more than a boy, flabby and seal-like. His protruding underlip made him look like a young camel. He put down his load and wiped his brow.

"Sorry, ladies," he said. "To be done for tonight."

"Tonight!" the women chorused in dismay.

"Mr. Davy's orders," said Pouty. Syeira, looking at the stack in the corner, saw that they were shabracks — the soft, tailored mats that went under war saddles. They all had the black-and-silver falcon embroidered on them.

Jayce grimaced. "How many?"

"Six," said Pouty. "Davy got you a dispensation. You can stay another three hours."

"A'n't he a gen'leman, that Blacklock Davy!" said Triese. "Why didn't you get the bleedin' things to us earlier?"

"You know what it's like," said Pouty. "Saddler's run off his feet, and they need 'em tonight for the maneuvers."

Just then the bell in the compound tolled. Jayce put a toe against the mats and moved the top one. The underlying mat bore several circles in chalk, which marked the frays and tears. "Well, they don't look too bad," she observed. "Shouldn't take us three hours."

"That's the spirit," said Pouty weakly.

Jayce glanced at Syeira. "You might as well go; your fingers a'n't no use to us anymore." She turned to Pouty. "Escort this lady out."

Pouty sighed; he seemed the sort who was always being told what to do. Outside he went around the wheelbarrow and began striding across the weapons yard, ignoring Syeira. She didn't feel shy about speaking to him.

"What are the maneuvers you were talking about, Pouty?" asked Syeira.

"That is not a seamer's concern," said Pouty tightly. "And I'll thank you to address me by my real name."

"What *is* your real name?"

"None of your business!" snapped Pouty. "Stop talking. And stop *looking* at me."

Syeira did as she was told. The sentinel warboy was up, she saw; she heard the fabric ripple above her as she walked through the gateway. Ahead she saw a dozen stable hands out on the quad, shovels and rakes in hand. Beside them were a few wheelbarrows full of earth. Syeira knew what they were doing, for she had done it many times herself: They were combing the field for holes.

Pouty veered off to the left, toward the stable. "You've got two minutes," he said over his shoulder. "Escort *yourself* out."

Syeira took a few steps toward the gate, then hesitated. All around her, moving toward the gates in knots of two and three, were the artisans and laborers who had been here for the day. Stable hands were coming and going among them. To the north she could just see Pouty's back disappearing into the twilight. Beyond him was the dark hulk of the stable, now lit up inside by isolated coronas of lamplight. Elsewhere the compound was settling into darkness. *This may be my only chance*, she thought. Quickly she started toward the stable, keeping her eyes straight ahead. Pouty disappeared through the front doors, but she kept going, skirting the immense wall of the stable.

At the back of the building, she crouched in the shadows and took stock. This part of the compound looked deserted. On her left, purple in the fading light, was a small field. Ahead of her was a squat building — the feed house, she guessed, judging from the smell of hay and oats. She glanced across the field on her left, to the high wall of the weapons block. It did not extend right to the end of the compound but stopped about twenty feet short. Behind that was a grassy, sloped alley. From her vantage point she could see timbers and what looked like an old cart wheel. *Better have a look*, she thought, and darted across the field. Yes, a storage alley — and a drainage area, it looked like. She could see several sluice ditches running down the slope to the compound wall. She recalled what Jayce had said about the war menagerie: The ditches were probably for draining the cages. The ditch nearest her went through a low grating and out of the compound. She felt the grating to see if it was solid. It was. No escape route there.

She looked back at the stable, pondering. *There might be some cell stalls tucked right at the back*, she thought, *that Marlow and I missed.* It was just a question of getting in. She crossed the field again and, feeling along the back wall, found what she was looking for — a feed chute. She'd figured there'd be one, with the feed house so close. The trapdoor was closed but not locked. She hoisted herself up, keeping the door open with her head. No light showed inside. She worked her way through and then, turning awkwardly on the edge of the rollers, lowered the trapdoor without a sound. The rollers were tricky, but she went down them on all fours, keeping to the edges. Though the air had the stable feel, she had a sense of space around her. The rollers ended among bags of oats and bales of hay. She crouched and listened. There were no horses here, but she guessed from the smell and shape of the darkness that there were plenty ahead.

And then, directly in front of her through the gloom, she saw four blue-green lights, moving in a small circle.

What witchery is this, *now?* she thought. She crept forward, her heart pounding, and peered out from behind a pillar. In an open, straw-covered space a man was standing in a semicircle of horses. He was *juggling* the lights. She could hear him now faintly, saying things like "Hup!" and "Hola!" and once, as he stepped close to a horse, "Not bad, eh, courser?" She couldn't really see his face, but he was wearing the sleeveless leather jerkin of a blacksmith, and his large arms gleamed sweatily in the blue-green light. As he turned, Syeira caught a flash around his head. He was wearing an earring.

It was Blacklock Davy.

Very quietly she began to back up. The gypsy had stopped his juggling and had mashed all the balls into one. Now he cupped the blue-green light in his hands, and it shone through his fingers as if he were holding a candle. Syeira stopped her stealthy creep and listened.

"All right, lads," he said, in his raspy voice. "Enough foolery. Back to work."

He moved ahead to the first horse and, holding up a handful of light, dabbed a bit on the horse's back, near its croup. She could see now that he wasn't very tall but very broad and stone-solid. He seemed to have a lot of hair at the back, but not much on top — at least, his head gleamed there when the torchlight caught it. Syeira watched, tense and curious. Why was he rubbing that glowing stuff on the horses? It was like a hackler's vision, something out of an old book of horse magic: a man rubbing *light* onto horses, and the horses enjoying it. For they were enjoying it, she could see. She wondered if it was true what people said — that certain gypsies had been horses in another life, and so could witch and charm the ones in this life. These horses were making a soft sound, almost a humming, deep in their throats. Syeira knew it well. It was the same sound *her* horses made when she came to see them in the river stable.

Suddenly she felt deeply uneasy. Something darker than the night around her had begun to seep into her bloodstream. She began to back away again, keeping her eyes on Davy, until she was able to scuttle back to the rollers. She turned for a last look: The streaked horses moved in the darkness like phosphorescent currents in the ocean. It was then that she remembered: *moonscatter*. Davy was marking the horses with his moonscatter. She had no idea why and didn't want to know. She just wanted to get away.

She turned, and her hand slipped into the gap between two rollers.

Down her head went, hard, her chin banging on the roller. But in a flash she had wrenched her arm out and pulled the trapdoor open. She couldn't tell whether Davy had heard the noise, but she wasn't going to wait to find out. She wriggled out of the opening and jumped down, the trapdoor banging shut after her.

She was looking around wildly when she heard a scraping

noise — a door being opened. It came from just around the corner, on the east side of the stable. There was a door there, one she hadn't even known about.

She ran without thinking, blindly, stupidly. The jumbled shadows of the alley seemed the safest place. She stumbled as she reached the first drainage ditch but kept going. The last ditch was almost right against the wall of the compound; that was as far as she could go. She crouched down inside it, gasping. Blood was trickling down her chin. Voices sounded across the field, but she dared not look. She snaked her way along the ditch — it was deeper than the others — to the wall of the animal keep. There her scrabbling hands felt a low opening. The hole had probably been no more than a few inches high at one time, but that part of the ditch had lost many of its flagstones, and over time the drainage water had deepened the channel and enlarged the hole. She had just enough space to wriggle through.

The recent rain must have sluiced the ditches thoroughly, for this one didn't smell any worse than the canal. Inside, the darkness was absolutely impenetrable. As she stood up, she felt she was in some open area — a pit of some kind. She felt only stone on the ground.

But she knew by the air, by the *feel* of the darkness, that there was something alive in the space with her.

A pair of large eyes flashed at her, and then, from farther away, another pair.

Then she heard a shallow blowing sound, a sound she had heard countless times in her life, and she slumped against the wall in relief.

She had found the colts.

◈

It was strange, to smell the sea in a cage. It was strange to smell Arwin so intensely, again and again, large as a cinnamon forest.

Bears, too, rank as wet goats, and a leopard hot and clear as the liquid wax on top of a candle. For hours Syeira lay on the cold floor while the smells moved through her head. When she crept out at dawn, the world seemed glazed and airless, as if everything were under glass. The danger and tedium of the day passed vaguely, for she was thinking of the strange fragments that the colts had breathed into her mind. When evening came again, she was telling Arwin all about it.

"Davy probably thought that the cage would settle them down," said Syeira. "Just stone and bars, and no other horses. I don't think there are any animals left there, but the *smells* still are. The colts told me."

They were standing at the far end of Grulla's yard, away from the Weerlings. Syeira had come home at twilight to find Grulla gone and the door locked; she had got into the yard by climbing over the wall. Arwin had been restless all day and was now even more restless, having smelled the colts on Syeira. The Weerlings watched them nervously from the front of the yard.

"They're *fine*," said Syeira, who was getting tired of being nosed by the anxious Arwin. "They hate the stone, but it's better than being in a ship's hold."

The colts had, in fact, been almost savage in their bewilderment when Syeira had surprised them. She had actually thought they were going to attack her. They had circled the girl, sniffing and snorting, not knowing what to make of this human who had the smell of their mother on her. All Syeira could do was crouch in the darkness, whispering, "It's all right, it's all right. She's here." After a while they calmed down, but then began to breathe a storm of living pictures into Syeira's head. It took a while before the girl understood that the colts were telling her what had happened to them. She smelled horse nausea, and wet oak, and old straw, and saliva-dampened rope, and the harbor smell, and torches, and the prowling animal shades that still lingered in the keep. She had stayed in the cage all night, after deciding it was too risky to go out. At dawn she had sneaked out to join the seamers in the sewing hut, telling them that she had arrived late at the main gates and come in on her own.

"But Jayce was suspicious," she said out loud. "She said if I'm late again, I'm through. I think she knows I'm up to something in the compound."

She slumped down gloomily. Arwin had no idea of how bad the situation was. The colts were in a kind of pit cage — stone on three sides and bars on one — which was sunk about six feet below the main aisle of the animal keep. Syeira had found, by feeling around, a gate that led up to the main aisle; but of course it had been locked. To get the colts out, she would somehow have to steal the key to the door and get them into the weapons yard. Then she would have to smuggle them out of the whole compound. And *then* she and all three horses would have to get out of the city. "And it's *me* who has to do it," she said, rolling over and putting her head in her arms.

Beside her she felt Arwin touch a foot to the ground.

She sat up. Grulla had just come out of the house carrying a cloth bag. She set it down beside an old stone brazier which stood in the corner, under the awning.

Syeira got up and approached the woman. She expected questions about her absence the previous night, but Grulla just said, "There's a bucket there. I'll need some water."

Syeira picked up the bucket and went to the well. The old woman was kindling a fire in the brazier when the girl returned. "So it's *your* mare I found," said Grulla.

"I — I was hoping to sell her in Thurckport," said Syeira.

"No ordinary horse, is she?" said Grulla, keeping her eyes on the growing fire. "When I saw her outside the other night, I knew she was something rare. My mare Perlina went right up to her and wouldn't leave. I didn't want the soldiers to find her so I took her inside. She went along nice and gentle, like she was *waiting* to come in."

Syeira glanced down at the end of the yard; Arwin was watching them closely.

"Why did you leave her outside?" Grulla asked.

The girl looked away. Grulla eyed her for a moment and gave a faint, dry chuckle.

"I take you both for outlaws," she said, removing some carrots from the bag. "Otherwise you would not be staying here." She passed the cloth bag to Syeira, along with a knife. "You do the potatoes."

Syeira sat down beside the table and began peeling. A long silence followed. Arwin approached the awning, and the Weerlings moved aside to let her through. Glancing up, Syeira saw the mare Perlina standing in a corner, swinging her head as usual.

"What happened to Perlina, Grulla?" said the girl.

Grulla was chopping the carrots. "Same thing that happened to me," she replied curtly. "We sailed a mighty ocean, you might say."

"An ocean?" said Syeira. "Which one?"

Grulla stood still and looked up. Smoke from the brazier swirled toward the stars that, in the twilight, were faint as milkweed seeds.

"That one," said Grulla.

Puzzled, Syeira followed her glance skyward. "I don't understand."

Grulla stopped cutting. "Didn't Jayce and her gossips tell you about me?"

"No. They said that you would tell me yourself."

Grulla gave a crooked smile. "Well, perhaps you *should* hear the story plain, not dressed up in the seamers' fashion. And then perhaps you can tell me why you're *really* here, and what you whisper about to your horse."

Syeira said nothing. Grulla glanced at her briefly and said, "Good. You don't trust me. That's wise." She put a pot of water on the brazier and then sat down beside it. "Well, you shall hear my story, anyway. Then you can judge whether I am on your side." She looked at Arwin. "Come closer, lady; I want you to hear my voice, know me, know my travails. Closer still. Now.

"Look at me: an old sparrow now, but once a swallow that could strike like a falcon. I was taught to fight by my father, a great baron. He was small, too, and so I learned all the feather-weight tricks — shooting a crossbow at full gallop, leaping from one moving horse to another, that kind of thing. Lord Ran saw me ride years ago, just after he came to power, and offered me a position. I became the only female soldier in his army. After many campaigns I was given an official title — marshal of the bowmen — and an unofficial one: the fighting crone." Her voice was as dead as last year's leaves. "Crone — and I was only thirty-seven years old. But deep down I knew the name was right. Fighting makes you hard, makes you old. I was old when I was young. It is the greatest sin.

"But it was my life; I knew nothing else. I watched Ran's army grow, watched his weaponry become ever more savage and powerful. He needed the men to make these weapons, and most of them he got from Swebban, the city of mechanicals in Broak. They built catapults and firethrowers and all manner of killing engines. Then about ten years ago they built a flimsy little thing — just air and animal skins — that would become the greatest weapon of all. They built a warboy."

She gave a grim smile. "It was a beautiful idea. So beautiful that I don't believe the mechanicals were thinking about war when they invented it. They were remembering their childhood — kites and sky sails and so on. But of course Ran looked at this little thing floating over the trees and saw only an army in the air. Soon he had a whole corps of mechanicals working on the warboys. They switched from animal skins to cotton and built special looms to weave the fabric. They got the pit fires down to an art so that sparks wouldn't fly up and burn the envelope. Within a year they were making warboys big enough to carry animals aloft. By this time Ran had a lot of fighting animals to experiment with. Big cats especially. One of his schemes was to send up at night a fleet of warboys carrying starved cats and let them come down over enemy lines. He had his mechanicals working on cages that would open on impact, but the early ones were faulty. Sometimes they would open in midair. The cats didn't have a hope."

Syeira saw in her mind's eye the crazy man on the heath, hunched down inside his hole. "Bill Mauditt," she said. "He told me he saw a lion fall. I thought he was —" She stopped, remembering what the man had said about his ears, and how he had held the sides of his head. "I think they cut off his ears for it," she added.

"The usual remedy," said Grulla. "To keep him from talking. Didn't work, obviously."

"But" — Syeira was still bewildered by the whole idea — "how do the warboys stay *up*?"

Grulla leaned down painfully, picked up a bit of straw, and let it go over the brazier. It was wafted up the flue briefly before settling down into the fire.

"That's how," she said. "Hot air carries them up. A warboy is just a bladder filled with hot air. You fill it by staking it — carefully — over a fire. The smoke particles from the fire will coat the inside and trap the hot air. Eventually the bladder will rise. If a vessel is tied underneath, the bladder will lift whatever is in the vessel. A small bladder cannot hold a lot of hot air, and so will not lift much. A big one — say, the size of an oak tree — will lift a man." She paused. "Soon they were making warboys that could lift *two* men. But Lord Ran wanted more than that. As he said, a spy set down by warboy wouldn't be much use without his steed. He always believed that a horse could be trained to do *any-thing* — fight with its hooves, walk a suspended bridge, catch spears in its teeth. Horses were just another kind of engine to him. More valuable than the cats, but engines just the same.

"Well, one day my regiment captain comes to me and says I have a chance to be a hero of the empire. I had a fair idea of what he had in mind. My mare Perlina and I were by far the lightest members of the army; evidently we had been chosen for Ran's great experiment. You do not say no if you are chosen by Lord Ran.

"Of course, we had to be trained. I went up in warboys, but I also spent time on ships — the best place to learn about winds and knots. As for Perlina, she had to get used to smoke and swinging platforms and heights. They made us a special wicker vessel, turned up at both ends like a sleigh and reinforced with pine in the floor. It could be lined inside with straw balks, so that Perlina wouldn't shift around. Many times we went up in that together, hoisted fifty feet by a pulley system. Meanwhile the seamers were stitching together the immense warboy that would take us into the heavens.

"Finally the great day arrived. We had chosen a field far inland. Early in the morning they strung a rope an inch thick between two trees and fastened to it the crown of the warboy. The mouth was staked open above the pit and the fire lit. They had endless problems with wind and sparks, and it wasn't until noon that the big black warboy began to belly out. The thing was *gigantic* — three times as high as the city walls. I remember think-ing that if anybody saw us, he would have thought we were sim-ply trying to raise an oversized circus tent. Well, we wrestled with it for hours, and the day grew hot. We went through several wagonloads of firewood. It wasn't until midafternoon that the warboy had filled out completely. We both felt skittish looking up at it, Perlina and I. Even with all her training, it took some tricky work to get her into the wicker vessel without spooking her.

Finally we were inside, and the balks were secured around us. The last tether ropes were cut. We were tilted and swung, as if in a cradle, and then carried straight up."

She paused. The yard had become absolutely silent, as if the horses were also listening to the tale. Perlina had come to stand beside Arwin.

"I tell you," resumed Grulla in her quiet, gray voice, "my heart was beating as it had never done in battle. I looked over the side of the vessel, and the whole group — all the mechanicals and soldiers and Ran himself — were watching me in silence. I had to smile. Their faces were so serious — and so black from the smoke. The fields expanded below; after a minute I was looking down on a green-and-tawny checkerboard. And then I saw three birds fly beneath me, in a perfect whirring line. *Beneath* me. I thought, 'This is what it is like to be a god.'

"Up and up we went. I was surprised at how quiet it was. Sounds from the earth seemed very close. I could hear cows lowing, children calling, and a miller's wheel grinding. Big trees looked like tiny puffs of lichen, a cottage was like a seed case, and people — well, I laughed when I saw them. I actually laughed. Yes, I was a god. But then I heard Perlina snorting, and I turned and put my hand on her. 'Easy, Perlina,' I said. 'We'll be down in five minutes.' *Five minutes.*" She passed a hand over her eyes.

"You see, I thought — everybody thought — that the warboy would come down very soon. They always did. The hot air inside them would cool quickly, and they'd sink back to earth. That was why the mechanicals started making them black: They knew the dark fabric would trap heat from the sun and keep the envelope aloft a bit longer. But they'd miscalculated with this one. It was far bigger than any of the other warboys. It trapped a *huge* amount of heat — and it had already been sitting in the sun for almost eight hours. Rising, it lost the fire's heat, but not the sun's. And that kept it up.

"But I didn't know, I didn't know. I saw that Perlina was having a problem with her ears, as I was, and I got her to raise her head and open her mouth. The next minute we were plunged inside a thick mist — a cloud. A soft, sizzling sound came from far inside the warboy. I could feel that Perlina was foaming slightly at the mouth, and that's when I began to get uneasy. But then we were out of the mist, and when I looked down at the huge cloud below, I forgot everything."

Grulla's eyes were suddenly hot and alive.

"A land of clotted cream, that's what it was like. Piled hills and ladled-out valleys and white spires rising up two hundred feet below the warboy — all *pudding*. I felt as if I could scoop off the crags and eat them. I wanted to get on Perlina's back, open the wicker door of the vessel, and leap — jump — capriole down onto the whiteness. How could we hurt ourselves on a *cloud*? And then we would ride across the shifting fields, all the way to the mountains at the edge — wispy around their peaks like real mountains. Oh, the cloud mountains, I remember the cloud mountains. Light and yet solid they were, like molten rock billowing up underwater . . ."

She sat back, and the grayness returned to her voice. "But then I looked out at the blue beyond and felt in the pit of my stomach the huge emptiness below us, the shoreless ocean of air. And it was only *air* that was keeping us up. I glanced up through the guide ropes at the warboy: Across the black mouth was a shimmering film. It was still hot inside. I could see our shadow on the cloud below, getting smaller and smaller. We were rising, ever rising.

"Suddenly Perlina jerked her head, and I looked down to see drops of blood on my arm. She was bleeding from the ears. I put my arms around her neck and soothed her, but I felt the cold hand of panic close around my heart. *Why weren't we going down?* The clouds were gone now: Around us was a bubble-clear eternity of blue. It was much colder, and I felt as if I were breathing against a pillow. Perlina began to sag in my arms, and I tried to lower her carefully so as not to tilt the vessel. Her body was racked by an awful pumping wheeze, and every minute she would snort a mist of blood onto my fingers. I cursed, I cried, I called out —"

Grulla suddenly stopped and half-raised her hand, and Perlina came close to nuzzle it. Syeira noticed that the horse did not stop swinging its head even then.

"Yes," said Grulla. "We will relive that journey for the rest of our lives, Perlina and I." She stroked the horse's nose briefly and then continued. "Still we rose. I grew tired, so tired. A great cold thickness filled my chest. I remember looking up and wondering if I could climb up the guide ropes and cut a tiny hole in the fabric with my knife — then the hot air could escape, and we would descend. But even in my stupor I knew that the time to do that was long past. With such a hole the warboy would go down slowly at first, but after a thousand feet it would be plummeting.

"I don't know how long I slumped there. Perhaps I swooned. Most of the time I was just looking at the sky. No human artist could have ever manufactured such a holy color. Imagine if the whole world — everything, the earth and all the heavens around it — were filled with the purest mountain water. Then imagine that it had all been tinted with the blue of gentian or cornflower. It was as if the world had been immersed in a single blue *thought*. I looked at the sky for a long time and it seemed to be changing. It was getting *bluer*. I raised myself a bit on the floor and looked out between the wicker mesh. Far beyond the curved rim of the earth, the sun was sinking. This took a long time to impress itself in my brain. Finally I struggled to my feet. Yes, we were descending; the air inside the warboy was cooling. Clouds floated below us, and as I watched they came a tiny bit nearer. I turned to Perlina, who was unconscious, and began massaging her forequarters and blowing into her nostrils. After a while I found I could breathe with less difficulty. With my knife I ripped off some of the straw balks and slipped them under Perlina. Wisps of straw floated off into the sky. We seemed to be going down at a feather-slow rate, but I knew it would be fast enough to break our bones when the earth stepped up to meet us."

She shook her head. "We were lucky. We landed in a copse of big spruce trees, ripping a swath from their crowns to their trunks. Branches broke like fireworks going off. Perlina came off the best of it; the straw balks must have cushioned her fall. I broke my leg in two places. One of the pine planks on the floor splintered, and an edge went into my side. For about a minute we hung ten feet above the ground, and then something snapped, and we fell with another huge jolt. I think that's when I broke my leg the second time.

"Well, it had been a success. For Ran and his mechanicals, that is. They wanted to hear everything. For months afterward, sick and sore as I was, I had to tell the story again and again." She shrugged. "And I did tell them everything. Everything except . . ." Here she leaned close to Syeira. "Except the white shape."

"The white shape?" said Syeira.

Grulla nodded. "It happened when we were very high up. By then we were lying beside each other and breathing in tiny sips, like beached trout. My cheek was against the floor, and I could see the blue between the slats. And I heard something, a soft rustling. Something like the sound of far-off rain. Between the wicker and the pine, a good distance below us, I saw something flash by. It was whitish gray, but I thought it *shimmered* a bit at the edges. A bird? It couldn't have been a bird, so high." She shrugged. "But I was so fevered then that I may well have invented it."

For some reason this caught Syeira's imagination more than anything the woman had said so far. She looked at Arwin. Perlina had brought her nose close to the big mare, but Arwin was paying no attention.

Grulla's face became hard again. "I've kept it to myself all these years. I certainly had no wish to tell my superiors. Because of my shattered leg they judged me unfit for Ran's army. I was given this house, this *hovel*, as a pension. And that was it, after a lifetime of service. They couldn't resist adding one final indignity: I was never to leave Thurckport, since I knew too much about the warboys." Her eyes shone with a savage light. "So I took Perlina with me — she, too, was considered unfit — and came to live here. But I would still visit the stables, and I found that there were other horses like her, horses that Ran had destroyed. And thus I became the keeper of the Weerlings." She gazed at her charges around her. "Soldiers are superstitious, you see. They will not destroy the horses that become mad from war. They believe that the horses shoulder the burden of madness for *them*. The beasts of war swallow war's nightmares, and the men are left to dream only of military glory. So the fantasy goes." She shook her head wearily. "I am permitted to take my Weerlings outside the city walls twice a week, for exercise. But it has to be late at night, and only outside. They don't want the Weerlings around the good horses."

There was silence in the yard. Grulla stood up and tested the soup she had been making. "Now," she said brusquely, "who's in charge: you or your horse?"

"She's in charge of me," replied Syeira, "and I'm in charge of her."

Grulla smiled. "I see. And what crimes are you planning in my yard, the two of you? Treason, insurrection, murder? For mark me, girl: If you are merely conspiring to get the best price for your horse, then you must leave."

Syeira was silent. She knew that Grulla could help them; the woman probably knew the military compound thoroughly. She glanced at Arwin, who stood quiet, her ears forward, studying Grulla. Syeira decided to risk it.

"We're here to free Arwin's colts," she said in a low voice. "They were taken from her in Haysele. She's an Arva horse, and —"

She realized then that she would have to tell Grulla everything, including the part about Blacklock Davy. "It's a long story," she concluded.

"Can't be any longer than mine," said Grulla. "Here, take some soup."

They each went through two bowls of soup during Syeira's account. At the end Grulla was silent for a long time, and then she got up and stoked the fire, which had almost gone out.

"Yes, I know Marlow," she said. "So you have two allies inside Thurckport. A limping crone and a spicetrader who hates kids."

"Maybe he hates kids," said Syeira, "but he helped *me*."

Grulla nodded. "That's the odd thing about the man. Every once in a while he will do something to prove to himself he hasn't completely sold his soul to the devil. When I'm down at the harbor, he sometimes gives me leftover zembala for the Weerlings — always with a bad grace, of course." She blew on the fire. "You'd never know it to hear him talk, but Marlow's a storyteller. He likes tales of unlikely heroes who take on the all-powerful authorities and win. Got his start telling them in Broak. They appreciate that kind of thing there."

"Broak," said Syeira. "That's where the rebellion is."

Grulla gave the fire one last stir, then hobbled back to her seat. "Where the rebellion has finally *ignited*, yes. It's simmered for a long time. Years ago, Broak became part of the empire — voluntarily, people pretended. Most folk in Swebban got rich making things for war, but not everybody liked it. The place still belongs to Ran, but a lot of mechanicals have turned against him.

We can only live in hope. In the meantime, our own worries are right here in Thurckport, which isn't exactly a fermenting vat of dissent." She took hold of her cane and dug in the dirt, thinking. "But back to your colts. The first order of business, as I see it, is to get them up from that dungeon."

"But how?" asked Syeira. "I'm sure Davy keeps them there because they're so savage. He probably can't even move them."

"Probably not. And that must have him chafing. I'll wager he nearly broke into song when he saw what Ran had brought him — two prize Arva horses, just like the one that got away from him years ago. It'll be a feather in his cap if he can train those two. But now he finds he can't do a thing with them." She gave the dirt a good poke. "So I say, why not help him out a bit? Show him a trick or two that not even the gypsies know. Keep him from losing face with the soldiers."

From beneath her jerkin she brought out a long knife and glanced at Arwin. "Yes," she said, fingering the blade. "We need a bit of practical magic. We need a *charm*."

She stood up, knife in hand, and moved toward the mare.

Arwin laid her ears flat back and turned to face the woman head on. Grulla only smiled.

"Your mane is in a frightful state, lady," she said politely. "I hope you will consent to a little grooming. I shall stand right in front of you; if I do anything you don't like, you may break my *other* leg."

Late that night, Syeira came awake to see Arwin and Perlina standing together at the edge of the yard. The darkness was absolute. She could only see the two horses when they raised their heads against the backdrop of stars. Arwin, perhaps sensing that the girl was awake, took a few slow steps toward Syeira. Perlina followed. Syeira, sleepy and comfortable, turned on her side to watch them. With the stars overhead she was feeling a lot more hopeful now. She had heard Grulla's plan, or at least most of it, and had been mulling it over when she'd fallen asleep. *At least*, she thought, *I'm not* alone *anymore. . . .*

The two horses came close. Arwin seemed very awake and alert; she breathed as easily, and as hugely, as the sea. Perlina was unusually calm. The girl couldn't help thinking that the two horses had told each other their thoughts, just as she and Grulla had done.

Arwin, apparently, had something to say to the girl.

Syeira lay there, sleepy but curious. The big horse put her nose down and breathed something into the girl's head. Syeira barely smelled it, so fast did it move. It was a wild smell, but soft, too — like a chamois jerkin that had been washed in spring water and spread to dry on a holly bush. Sun and wind coursed inside it like blood. It moved through her head like lightning through a tree, leaving a faint musky stillness. She sat up quickly.

"What was *that*?" she whispered.

The stars looked down on her, grave and noncommittal, as they always are — even in tumultuous times.

The scent was long gone, but it seemed to have left a faint, far-off sound in her mind, like the bells they attach to the feet of hunting hawks. Her eyes moved from Arwin to the sky. The smell was a bit like the colts, but not earthy like them. It was the smell of something that lived high up, like those big seabirds that ride the winds all day. . . .

Gazing into the white-berried night, she suddenly remembered what Grulla had seen from the warboy.

"The white shape," she murmured. "The white shape that Grulla saw."

She stood up, wide awake. She understood now. Perlina had breathed a *memory* into Arwin's mind. She must have been conscious in the warboy; she must have caught the scent then.

Syeira stared at the sky for a long time. Though the scent had disappeared, it had stirred up so much — bits of tales and songs — that when she finally lay down she had a clear picture in her mind. She saw them racing across the cloud fields, eddying the mists as they went. At night they would alight to feed in the alpine meadows, their wings folded along their backs. They would breathe as a waterfall breathes. And if she were to stand among them with her eyes closed, she might think — for a moment — that they were ordinary horses.

8

Stratagems of
an Old Soldier

Grulla's fighting days may have been over, but her time as a strategist was just beginning. She seemed to make it her personal mission to free the colts — and make Ran's men look silly while doing it. But first she would have to get around Blacklock Davy, and (as she told Syeira the next night) the man was no fool.

"Some of the officers grumbled when he got his position," she said. "A *gypsy* for head farrier? But I guess the Broak contingent had great things to say about him. He'd worked for them for years, apparently — ever since he gave up horse trading after losing his entire stock. But I guess you and your mare know all about that."

"Did you talk to him today?" asked Syeira.

Grulla shook her head. "Not him. I thought it safer to go for the weak link."

"The weak link?"

"Pouty." She took a sip of tea. "The boy wants badly to impress Davy. He's been a 'prentice for two years now and hasn't done a lot in that regard. But I left him pretty excited today." She chuckled. "I made sure I caught him early, when I knew Davy would be asleep. Said I'd heard he had two wicked Arva colts locked up. Said I knew more about savage horses than anybody, being the keeper of the Weerlings. After some grumbling, he took me to the colts' cage (he's a bit afraid of me, you know). And you're right — they're spruce ones. They looked like they could almost jump over the compound wall if they had a run at it. Well, I looked at them, and they looked at me, and then they came a bit closer; and that's when they smelled the hank of their mother's mane inside my sleeve. They tensed right up, and I could see their nostrils flaring.

"So I say to Pouty, 'Having a bit of trouble moving 'em, are you?' He starts telling me about how wild Arva horses are, how they thrash and buck and trample; and in the meantime the colts have come right up to the cage and are standing as still as the grass. I move to the other end of the cage, going around Pouty, and the colts follow me as if they're on a lead. Pouty just stares. 'What have you got there, Grulla?' he says. I say, 'I've got aching bones and a corroded heart, Pouty, and memories of a time before the empire, and more smarts than your average stable hand; and I've got a bit of horse magic, too.'"

She smiled her monkey's smile.

"Of course, he doesn't want to seem too eager. 'Oh, well,' he says, 'Mr. Davy's got plenty of tricks in that line.' And I say, 'Yes, I know all about his sweet-smelling fakery. But it's not helping him much with these two, is it?' So then he starts talking about the code of the stable, how we're all supposed to share our knowledge. I just laugh. 'I live by my own code, boy,' I say, 'and these Arva horses are *your* problem, not mine.' But before leaving I gave him my usual harangue about the Weerlings. Said it's a shame that we can't go out for exercise *every* night. Said that if the stablemen were a bit kinder to me, I might be a bit kinder to them. That's when I left him. I'm sure he had a hard time keeping his mind on work today."

She reached down into a pocket and withdrew the piece of mane. "I'll hang this over my doorway, as my own charm. We can take a fresh hank from your mare when we need it."

Syeira leaned forward to smell the mane. "It doesn't have much of a scent, to me."

"It does to the colts," said Grulla. "A bit of undermane can't help but absorb some odor, especially if the horse has been anxious or fretful — as yours has been."

"So what do we do now?" asked Syeira.

"We wait," said Grulla. "But if I know Pouty, it won't be long before we can start thinking about the next stage."

⤞◈⤝

"You're early tonight, Grulla," said the soldier on the parapet.

Here at the walls, the night crouched in twitching vigilance. The wind made a lonely sound over the parapets, stirring the pennants into a martial snapping. Lanterns flickered watchfully. Beside the canal, stamping and blowing, stood a restless line of Weerlings, with Grulla at their fore. The soldier squinted down at the woman and shook his head. A bent little thing like her, he thought, and in charge of the Weerlings. Most of them were too broken to be dangerous, but once in a while you got a skittish one. Like that big mare in the front there. He'd never seen it before. Must have been a fine bruiser before it went Mauditt. Well, some conscripts could take it and some couldn't. He'd been on the battlefield; he knew all about *that*.

He was about to descend to open the canal door when he noticed a small figure at the back of the group.

"Who's that?" asked the soldier.

"War orphan," said Grulla. "She's helping me."

"War orphan," repeated the man suspiciously. "She got authorization?"

"She's with me," said Grulla shortly. "That's authorization enough."

The man sighed. "You know that a'n't enough, Grulla."

Grulla took a few hobbling steps ahead and glared up at the man. "Scrabber Jones, how do you expect me to look after these horses by myself? I've got a new Weerling coming in every month now. And barely enough money to keep them all in hay, let alone mash —"

The horses, hearing the agitation in her voice, began to grow even more restless. Suddenly the big mare half-shied, turning its head away as if it were fighting a bridle. Scrabber Jones started forward nervously; he never liked dealing with the Weerlings. But the girl, moving ahead quickly, put her hand on the horse's flank, and it lowered its head and stood quiet.

Grulla eyed them for a moment, then turned to face the soldier again. "I need that girl," she said. "I'm going to have to pass the torch pretty soon."

Scrabber Jones knew that the longer the Weerlings stood there, the more restless they would get. "All right, all right," he said. "Stay out on the east heath tonight."

He descended the interior staircase, appeared at the door just inside the tunnel, and opened the inner and outer barge-horse gates. The horses filed through in the darkness. Once they were outside the walls, they seemed more at ease. They moved about on the heath in a gradually expanding circle, with Grulla in the center, leaning on her cane. Syeira came up to her.

"That was close," she whispered.

Grulla shrugged. "They know you now. Next time they won't hold us up with a lot of questions." She glanced back at the wall. Another soldier had joined Scrabber and they both looked down on the heath. "As long as it's Scrabber here, we'll be all right. He'll do whatever he can to avoid incidents. He's afraid of being sent back to the battlefield."

Like her charges, Grulla seemed to enjoy the heath. There were no Mauditts around, so close to the walls; only the sea-flavored wind rustled through the grass. The old woman leaned on her cane, eyes upward.

"A Mauditt's dream," she murmured.

"What?" said Syeira.

"A winged horse is just a Mauditt's dream. Something invented to console and comfort. That's what I would have said, anyway. But I was wrong, you tell me. The horses know better. They often do."

They were all silent for a moment, looking out at the night. Then Grulla turned to Arwin.

"You make a good Weerling, lady," she said. "Let's hope your sons are equally convincing."

⋘⊱⊰⋙

Yes, she's here, I told you. You'll see her soon. Now listen: They might take you outside, on the grass. Just go along with them. Don't fight them at all, because you want *to be taken outside. Understand?*

Syeira sat back in the darkness, feeling worn out. The colts had been quiet while she whispered to them; they hadn't breathed any pictures into her head — except Arwin's. The girl stroked their noses. Getting inside the cage had been a bit less difficult than before. This time she had stayed behind to do extra work, repairing a few horse litters, and afterward had slipped into the animal keep by the back way. Once again she'd have to stay there for the night. But she wanted to make sure the colts were all right and then carry their scent back to Arwin. The mare was getting dangerously restless; any moment she might decide to go after the colts herself. She might hold off a bit longer if she knew the colts were still nearby and in good shape.

The colts' eyes were the only thing Syeira could see in the cage. *I wish you understood just a few words,* she thought.

She wondered what Grulla was doing. Working with Arwin, probably. The old woman had discovered that the mare liked quince and had spent some of her precious pennies on a supply of the fruit. With the quince, and a lot of patience, she'd already made good progress. She had even managed to teach Arwin how to catch a thrown rope — an essential skill for the next stage of the plan. As for Arwin, she seemed to go along grudgingly with Grulla's efforts. Maybe it was because she was going crazy from inaction, and maybe it was because Grulla's touch with horses was just as good as Syeira's.

Just then the girl heard voices. A torch was coming down the main aisle of the animal keep. She didn't have time to get out; she was only able to dart behind some hay bales. She was scrunching herself down as far as she could go when Pouty and Davy came up to the colts' cage. Davy was speaking; his voice was harsh and belligerent.

"Grulla's come over wise, of a sudden," he said. "Knows all about Arva horses and Arva charms."

"Well, she says they're a bit like her Weerlings," replied Pouty. "And I think she's right because they were pretty interested in her the first time they saw her. I laughed right to her face when she finally told me her secret. 'All right, then,' she said, '*you* try it.' And it *worked*, Mr. Davy. I tied the mane to my belt and went up to the cage, and they came close and watched me real quiet. Just like they're doing now."

The colts were standing rigid and quivering, like thrown knives, in the middle of the cage. Syeira couldn't see Pouty and Davy, but she could see the torchlight flickering on the horses.

"Let me see this 'charm,'" said Davy.

The light shifted as Pouty put the torch in a holder on the wall. Davy must have taken the hank of mane then, for the colts moved a bit closer to him.

"Pouty," said the gypsy.

"Yes, sir?"

"If you waved a bit of your toenail in Skandall's Inn, would all the ale maids come and sit on your lap?"

"No, sir."

"No. Well, a bit of mane is like a bit of toenail, Pouty. It a'n't got a lot of magic in it. And if some old cheat says it *is* magic, a brisk head would start to wonder what the old cheat is —"

Suddenly he stopped. Syeira, eager to see what was happening, peered around a hay bale. Just above the colts, on the main aisle of the keep, the two figures stood in the torchlight. Davy was holding the mane to his nose.

"What is it, Mr. Davy?" asked Pouty.

Still Davy said nothing. Syeira watched, spellbound. She couldn't see Davy's face, but she could hear him very faintly sniffing the mane. When he spoke again, his voice had changed completely.

"Where'd Grulla get this?" he asked.

Pouty hesitated. "She . . . Well, I actually didn't believe *that* part, Mr. Davy. I may be just a 'prentice, but —"

"Where did she *get* it?" barked Davy.

Pouty swallowed. "She said . . . the Stablecharm Man gave it to her."

"The Stablecharm Man."

"Yes, sir. Came from a wild horse, Grulla said. The Man had fixed a horse's leg, and the horse let him take a bit of mane. As a charm." He hesitated; his doubts were deepening. "It sounded a bit too much like the old thorn-out-of-the-lion's-paw story to me. Um . . . I don't know how you feel about it, sir."

There was a long silence. The torchlight flickered; Pouty blinked apprehensively; one of the colts stamped. Then Davy was tying the hank of mane on to his belt.

"Get ready to open that door," he ordered.

"Are you going to try it, sir?" Pouty asked excitedly.

"Put your key in the lock," said Davy shortly, taking the torch from the holder. "You won't be able to see it in a minute."

There was a nervous clinking of keys; Pouty was having a hard time finding the keyhole. Davy, torch in hand, moved down the aisle and disappeared; the colts followed him until they were up against the wall. The cage was now in near darkness.

From down the aisle Syeira heard the clanking of the large

keep door. The dim light wavered slightly as the torch flame flickered in the draft. Then came Davy's voice, echoing faintly in the gloom: "If they come after you, hie yourself up the cage. Even these lads can't follow you there." There was a pause, and the torchlight shifted. "*Now*, boy."

The key squeaked as it turned. Immediately the colts went up the ramp, snorting and blowing. Pouty, snorting and blowing as well, wrenched open the door and quickly got behind it; but the horses ignored him and thudded off toward the torchlight.

"You see, Mr. Davy?" called Pouty hoarsely. "It *does* work."

The dim light remained steady; Davy must have put the torch in a holder before darting out. "I *told* him," came Pouty's voice. He slid out from behind the door and vanished down the corridor. The cage was suddenly plunged into darkness; Pouty had taken the torch and closed the door.

Syeira let her breath out. *Well, it's working,* she thought.

She weighed the risks of staying where she was. All in all she thought she was safer there than anywhere. She would have liked to watch the colts in the weapons yard, but the chances of being spotted were too great. She just hoped they wouldn't go wild and hurt themselves. Davy wanted to see them move, learn their responses, figure out how he could get a lead on them. He'd let them spend some of their energy, then he'd draw them right back into the keep.

She waited for just over half an hour, and then she heard the clanging of the keep door. The torch wove through the darkness again. Davy tossed something into the cage and backed away, the smoking torch held up as a weapon before him. A clattering of hooves followed. The colts streamed into the cage, their flanks shiny with sweat, and made immediately for the tossed bit of mane. Davy slammed the door on them.

"You lose this one, lads," he said.

The colts raised their heads, their eyes flashing with hatred. They had chased the smell right back into their prison — and no doubt Davy had kept most of the mane for next time.

Syeira heard panting from down the corridor and Pouty appeared. "We did it!" he exalted. "That's the first step!" He laughed, then coughed, then laughed again. "I bet Lord Ran never thought these horses could be gentled. But when he comes back, they'll be ready for pre-rider training."

"We're a good ways from that," growled Davy, who was still holding the torch. "They'll soon cotton to what we're doing, and we'll have to come up with a new dodge. But for now the smell is lighting a fire in their heads. I wonder . . ." He came close to the cage and looked in.

"I'd like to know what Grulla wants out of all this," he said finally. His voice was thick with suspicion.

"Well, she wants to take the Weerlings out every night," replied Pouty. "That's what she said."

Davy glanced sharply at him. "Did she, now?"

"Yes, but she's always asking for that, sir. Twice a week outside has never been enough for her precious Weerlings."

Davy turned back to the colts, studying, thinking.

"We'll take these colts out every night, in the weapons yard," he said. "Keep the gate closed; I don't want them near the other horses."

Pouty hesitated. "Yes, sir. But, sir, night maneuvers will be going on for another few days, and —"

"Never mind the night maneuvers. We'll be in the yard and they'll be out in the quad. Make sure you light the pit fire; that'll keep the colts away from the wall." Davy held up the torch, took one last look at the colts, and turned to go. "As for Grulla and her Weerlings . . ."

Syeira strained to catch what he said, but the words were swallowed up by the echoes as the two stablemen moved down the corridor. The torchlight faded. One of the colts snorted heavily and shook his mane, as if in relief.

In the darkness the hoofbeats were like a roll of surf, crashing against the night. Again and again the breakers of sound spilled over the wall and on to the narrow street below; and then they ceased, and the snorts and blows of the horses could be heard. Above them came a sudden shouted command, and once more hoofbeats filled the air.

Grulla and Syeira crouched in the darkness of the street, just outside the western wall of the compound. From their hiding place behind an old cart, which stood at the front of a derelict supply house, they could hear the horses training on the other side of the wall. Syeira's heartbeat had finally slowed to the point where she could take stock. The warboy was there inside the compound, hanging about forty feet up. The black envelope was almost invisible in the night, but she could see the glowing line of the firepan below it. Inside the basket was a dark form. From the slant of the man's body it was clear his attention was fixed on the southwest quad before him. He was there to watch the horses.

Syeira glanced down the wall in the other direction. About a hundred feet away was the locked postern door — the only way out of the weapons yard. And, according to Grulla, only Davy had the key.

Now the warboy began shimmying in the light of the firepan.

"All right," whispered Grulla. "The captain's coming down."

They could just barely make out the soldier descending the rope ladder. They lost sight of him after a moment, but Syeira knew he had stepped onto the walkway that topped the wall.

"He'll talk to the men for a while," said Grulla. "Out by the quintain. Tell them what they're doing wrong. Then he'll go up the ladder and watch them again."

"But how can he *see* them from the warboy?" whispered Syeira.

"Davy's got this glowing stuff to mark the horses," replied Grulla. "Makes it out of mushrooms or something —"

"Oh, yes, the moonscatter," said Syeira. "So *that's* why he was putting it on the horses."

Grulla nodded. "He dabs their croups and their legs so that the captain can see if they're changing leads right." She shifted uncomfortably; a crouch was much harder for her than the girl. "Yes, night maneuvers are a serious business. Ran would never have got to where he is if his troops hadn't been able to fight in the darkness. I've heard it's quite something to watch them from the warboy. It's as if you're looking at a thick cluster of blue stars that suddenly start turning in whorls — the way cranberries do in a bog, when you stir them with a stick. After a while they stop swirling and line up in one direction, to wait for the captain. But you can still see them moving ever so slightly because the horses are breathing hard."

The compound had grown silent; the soldiers were waiting for their captain. Just then, from the other end of the weapons yard, Syeira heard a different sort of neighing. She half-rose, craning her neck, but Grulla put a warning hand on her arm.

"Aye, they're out there," whispered Grulla, speaking even more quietly than before. "I guess our charm is still working."

Syeira, listening intently for more sounds from the colts, suddenly remembered what she had seen in the animal keep. "I saw Davy *smelling* the mane," she said. "Do you think he can tell it came from an Arva horse? You don't think — does he actually *remember* the smell?"

Grulla made a careless movement of her head. "Who knows? He's got the senses of a horse, they say." She shifted again. "I couldn't resist tweaking his nose with that bit of fluff about getting the mane from the Stablecharm Man. He told me once that he used to have one or two charms that were even more power-ful than the Man's. But he gave them away to a deserving woman, so he said. Looked all sorry about it, too, the old fraud."

"I bet he wasn't as sorry as *she* was," said Syeira.

They were silent again. Just in front of Syeira was a black puddle of rainwater that held the cool, observant moon — the only calming presence in the whole scene.

"Have you ever seen the Stablecharm Man, Grulla?" she said. "I mean, really?"

"No. Not many have. But I know he often takes ordinary things, like a hank of mane, and makes charms out of them." Her eyes were on the warboy. "You know what the gypsies say: 'Dreams and memories make the best charms.' Well, Davy's got one of those charms right now, and it's got him interested. He's a gypsy, after all — even though the other gypsies won't have any-thing to do with him, now that he works for Ran." She was sud-denly alert. "Right, this is the crucial time. Listen."

The flow of night seemed to suspend itself, in order to catch the captain's monologue. They got the strong impression that on the other side of the wall, the whole compound was occupied, intent.

"The warboy is empty now," continued Grulla. "The sentinel is in the barracks. The captain is out on the field with his regi-ment. And this is where *you'll* come in."

Syeira hadn't yet heard the details of the final stage; Grulla had been saving them until they could see the layout together.

"What do I have to do?" asked the girl nervously.

Grulla was still watching the glowing line in the sky. "Set loose the sentinel warboy."

Syeira let out her breath in dismay, then hastily clapped her hand over her mouth.

"It'll be the perfect diversion," said Grulla calmly. "That warboy is the most valuable thing in the weapons yard. If it's set loose, believe me, everybody will drop what they're doing and go after it."

Syeira was overwhelmed. On the whole she would have pre-ferred just to jump on the colts and try to ride them out of the compound.

"But we don't want to set it *completely* loose," continued Grulla, in the same even-tempered voice. "We want to snag it in just the right place. And as long as your mare does what —"

Suddenly, from some distance behind them, came the sound of men's laughter. They both crouched down further behind the cart.

"Soldiers," whispered Grulla. "That's Skandall's Inn over there. I don't think we should prolong this little sight-seeing tour."

She led the way back, moving carefully and sticking to the shadows. The streets were empty as always; only bats and night-hawks took their usual skittery inventory of the night. Above the darting shapes, the stars were vivid nicks and gouges of light. Grulla thought aloud as she hobbled along. "I'm hoping that Pouty has already talked to Scrabber Jones, as he promised, so we'll be able to get out the main gate," she said. "We'll be taking all the Weerlings, of course. I'm not leaving a single one."

They got back to Grulla's house without incident. "You'd better get some sleep," Grulla advised. "We can talk about it tomorrow."

She spoke casually, but she knew that they couldn't put the escape off much longer. The colts might balk anytime and refuse to be lured out into the weapons yard. Night maneuvers would only last a few more days. She silently berated herself for taking so much time already.

"No," said Syeira.

The girl was standing beside Arwin, threading her fingers through the mare's mane. "Tell me exactly what I have to do. About the warboy and everything." She let her hands fall. The mare gave a restless shake of her head; the cascade of her mane was like two large waves meeting. "Arwin won't wait any longer."

Grulla studied the girl for a moment, then nodded slowly. "I know you can do it," she said. "You're smart and quick, and you know the weapons yard thoroughly now. You can do it." She looked around. "Very well. I'll need props if I'm going to explain this. . . ."

Tomorrow night, thought Syeira, looking into Arwin's eyes. *Please hold on till then.* She fell silent for another long moment, arranging things in her mind, preparing herself. Then she reached inside her jerkin and withdrew the small bag that was in her spice pouch. "Here," she said to Grulla. "You'd better take our secret weapon."

Grulla gave a tight smile. "Ah, yes. The gift of Will Shanks." She reached for their secret weapon — the devil's scratch, the aromatic that could make horses bolt in terror.

The night was breezy, luckily. From where Syeira crouched, behind the wheel of a half-constructed siege tower, she could see the sentinel warboy rippling in the wind. Now and then the firepan would clank; she could hear it even above the hoofbeats from the southwest quad. She was thankful: The noise and movement would provide a bit of cover. She'd had a difficult time of it — and the dangerous part hadn't even begun. First she'd had to stay behind in the sewing room and wait until the weapons yard was almost empty. (Jayce had turned a blind eye to this; the woman was hard-pressed to meet the quota demands and couldn't afford to lose a seamer.) Then she'd had to creep out across the weapons yard, keeping to the shadows. Now she was close to the wall that divided the yard from the southwest quad. Before her was a flight of steps leading up to the wall walkway. She rested, trying to gather her courage.

Well, she thought, *it's over tonight. Either we make it, or I won't have to worry about meeting a quota.*

She looked up at the warboy. She could just make out the two thick tether ropes that held it to the parapet railing. In her mind she went over the setup, as Grulla had explained it. The tethers were hooked onto the railing by means of ringbolts, which had been woven into the ropes at twenty-foot intervals. With this rig the men could let the warboy float at whatever height they wished. (It could go as high as one hundred and fifty feet.) For the night maneuvers, it would only be about forty feet above the wall, which meant there would be plenty of slack rope on the walkway. The rope was what she was after. She had to unhook one tether from the parapet railing and get its whole length over the western wall.

Just then she felt the hoofbeats grow silent in the southwest quad. Maneuvers had ceased; the regiment was waiting. The glowing line of the firepan moved, and in its faint light Syeira saw the dark form of the captain, climbing down the swaying ladder.

Be quiet, she told herself. *He'll hear you breathing.*

The captain descended the steps and paused at the gateway that led into the southwest quad. Looking down the weapons yard, he gave somebody a nod, then opened the gate just enough to get out. A yard worker arrived to close it behind him. The worker paused to give the pit fire a rake — Syeira could hear the hissing of coals — and returned to the other end of the yard.

Then came the clang of the keep door. *Finally.* The colts were coming out.

She crouched down even farther. She could only hope the colts wouldn't smell her and betray her presence. The fire in the pit was burning well; like all wild things, they hated fire, and would stay away from this end of the yard. That was the idea, anyway. Now she could sense their unruly presence, hear their neighs, feel the vibrations of their hooves under her feet. She knew that Davy would have torches and lassos ready, in case they turned on him. . . .

The thought of torches spurred her on.

This is it.

She put a hand to the spice pouch under her jerkin. The devil's scratch was with Grulla, but in its place she had put the hank of Arwin's mane, the original one that Grulla had cut off. She couldn't have taken on a job like this without a charm. She took a deep breath.

Now.

She darted up the stairs and, crouching low behind the parapet, scampered along the walkway to the warboy. Yes, it was just as Grulla had said. Tether ropes, ladder, slack neatly bundled on the floor. First she had to unhook the tether rope nearest the western wall. She unscrewed the bolt in a second — that was the easy part — then looked up, her hands on the rope. *Don't rush, don't rush.* She held her breath, watching the wind knead and ripple the warboy, waiting for . . . *yes, there.* The wind lifted the warboy on the other side, and the tether rope slackened perceptibly. At once, she hung on to the rope using all her weight. The ringbolt slipped off the railing. *Got it.*

She let go of the rope. The other tether went ominously taut; the warboy jumped up and settled at a different angle; something slid with a metallic sound overhead. She winced at the noise. She hoped that if anybody heard it, they'd think it was the wind. Now she really had to move. Scooping up the slack of the tether, she sped along the walkway. At the western wall she peeped over. *Please, please be there.* Yes: Arwin's eyes flashed in the darkness and Grulla stood right beside her. Syeira fed the rope over the wall as quickly as she could. *Take a good hold, Arwin. . . .*

From the weapons yard came the sound of Davy's voice, chivvying the colts. "Hey! Hup! Away there, lads!"

Syeira paused for just a second. From the sound of the hoof-beats, she knew that the colts were no longer ranging all over the yard, but running back and forth close to the western wall. She barely heard Pouty's voice: "What's got into them, sir?"

She knew perfectly well what had got into them. They had caught Arwin's scent on the other side of the wall.

Don't panic. Grulla had said this might happen. The girl scurried back to the other tether, still keeping low. She didn't have to worry about unscrewing this bolt; she could just cut the rope. Once the men saw the warboy hanging over the west wall, with the tether rope *outside* the compound, they would be after it in a flash. Davy would have to open the postern door — and the colts, frantic for their mother, would be through it faster than a shot arrow.

With her knife, Syeira began carving into the tether rope. Strands gave way with the speed of darting silverfish. The warboy dipped and rippled above her.

Suddenly she heard a call from inside the weapons yard: "Hey! What's with the 'boy?"

Syeira's heart turned over. She gave a desperate slice at the rope, and several things happened at once. With a snap, the last strands broke. The warboy rose into the air, tipping the firepan and sending a cascade of bright embers onto the parapet. The coil of rope ladder disappeared as the warboy shot upward. And the man below — no doubt the yard worker — began pounding toward the wall where Syeira was.

"It's snagged outside!" he yelled. "Open the postern door!"

Everything was a blur to Syeira. The warboy had swung over on a tangent and was now above the western wall. She sprinted along the walkway and hoisted herself up. She had planned to let herself down by the tether, but she saw now that it was hopelessly out of reach. The rope ladder was there, though. The end dangled three feet away, at the level of her chest. She jumped and barely caught the last wooden rung. She heard faint shouts, followed by the banging of the postern door as it was wrenched open.

Then the shouts were joined by a savage neighing.

"Look out, sir!" came Pouty's voice.

"Lassos!" roared Davy.

The colts were breaking free.

But now the yard worker had reached the top of the wall steps. He dashed down the length of the walkway while Syeira, wild with panic, clambered up the rope ladder. Below, the rope in her teeth, Arwin took a few stumbling steps. The man reached out as high as he could go, but the end of the rope ladder was just out of reach. He swore and stepped back two paces, fumbling at his belt for his knife.

"Arwin!" yelled Syeira. "Away from the wall! Go!"

She knew she could only get down if the mare pulled the warboy closer to the ground. But at that moment something happened to throw everything else out of Arwin's mind. One of the colts gave a neigh that was almost a scream. Arwin wheeled toward the sound, and in doing so she let go of the tether rope.

"Grulla!" Syeira shrieked.

But it was too late. Without the mare's weight the warboy shot upward. The yard worker stood up on the parapet, trying vainly to grab the dangling ladder. Into Syeira's numbed mind flashed the thought that she had to jump, but already she was thirty feet off the ground. As the warboy rose, she swung wildly with the rope ladder, so that at one point she was almost upside down. Below her was a chaos of neighing and yelling.

And then, above it all, came the bellow of Blacklock Davy: "I know you, Arva jade!"

Syeira dared not look down; she was already dizzy with fear. She clung dazedly to the rope ladder as the warboy rose. The last thing she saw was Grulla who, turning away from the action, flung something over the wall and into the southwest quad.

Two things managed to shake Syeira out of her terrified trance as she swung through the darkness. One was a sudden din from the southwest quad. Horses — dozens and dozens of them — were neighing and stamping in terror. She could feel the thunder of their hooves even from where she was. The second thing was a large, burning ember that alighted on her arm. She shook it off with a yelp and looked up. The warboy's basket was on fire.

The warboy had received a good jolt when the last rope had been cut, and the firepan had been thrown off its moorings. Now the firepan hung by one hinge; below it on the wicker floor of the basket was its load of burning pitch. From Syeira's vantage point there seemed to be only a few flames, but the movement through the air was fanning them.

It was then, drifting above the rooftops of Thurckport, that Syeira knew complete despair. She cried out in the darkness. How long would it be before the flames reached the rope ladder and burned through it? She would fall like that lion, fall scrabbling at the sky, and in the morning someone would find her broken body on the cobblestones. For the first time, she looked down. She could see the glittering line of the canal, and Ran's tower, but everything else was shrouded in darkness. In vain she looked for any sign of Arwin and Grulla and the colts.

She had to get hold of herself. Another ember floated off behind her, and she realized that the only thing she could do was try to put out the fire. Without the heat source, the warboy would cool and descend on its own. *Gently,* she hoped. She looked up and, gritting her teeth, began to climb the ladder. The smell of burning pitch and wicker came to her. Through the ladder hole she went, coughing from the smoke. The wicker was smoldering badly, but the flames were not high. Feeling around, she found the woven covering that fitted over the trapdoor. With this she managed to scrape the smoldering pitch out through the ladder hole. The coals glowed briefly as they fell and then became a part of the blackness. Once they were gone, she put the cover on the flames, to smother them.

She didn't like to stand, so she crawled cautiously around to the far side of the basket, avoiding the hot spots. The guide ropes creaked around her like the rigging of a ship. With the burning pitch gone she could smell the clear night air. She peered down through the ladder hole. The warboy had drifted over the harbor: Far below she could see the lights of the watchtowers. She was heading out to sea.

She slumped in the corner of the basket. *If the others did escape,* she thought tearfully, *they will have to leave me. What else can they do?*

She lay there for a while, looking at nothing, and then checked the fire. Part of the basket had been burned away, and there was still some smoldering around the edges, but the fire was essentially out. She got to her feet carefully, holding on tightly to the edge of the basket. Below her she could faintly hear the sound of waves. She could tell there was a good stiff wind out here. Slowly the sound of the waves got louder. The warboy was descending.

She looked out again; she could now see whitecaps in the darkness. She guessed she was about two hundred feet above the water. The warboy was coming down on an angle — and at a good clip, too. She dreaded the thought of landing in the ocean. She crouched down, her arms around her legs. A hundred feet from the water now. She heard the wind; heard the sound of the sea beneath her. Then, after about a minute, she heard the ladder end bump and skip on the waves.

The basket hit with a jolt. The ladder-hole cover flew up in the air as if it had been kicked, and water spouted up through the hole. Syeira was flung hard against the side. Overhead the warboy snapped and fluttered, yanking the basket over, and Syeira scrambled up on the side, gasping. There she hung on, clinging to the damp wicker, while the waves splashed around her. She could see the warboy still flapping and billowing on the waves, as if some sea creature were floundering beneath it.

"Help!" she screamed. "Help!"

She screamed herself hoarse, clinging to the basket, and then fell silent, panting and sobbing. For a while the basket rose and fell in the wet darkness. At length, very cautiously, she turned around on the basket. Some distance away — she could not tell how far — she could see the lights of the watchtowers. She watched them for a while, and it seemed that one was moving. It bobbed up and down on the water.

"Help!" she called faintly.

The light was definitely coming closer. Syeira held on with cramped, ice-cold fingers. Now she could see it was a longboat — one of the sturdy oared vessels that were used for rescue along the coasts. On its prow she could see the silver-and-black falcon. It actually had two lamps, one on the prow and one on the stern. These heaved up and down as the longboat crested the large waves. Through the darkness Syeira could hear the squeak of oarlocks.

The boat sculled close. Syeira saw that it was manned by seven men — six oarsmen and one pilot, who stood in the prow near the lamp. This man steadied himself in the boat and, as it bumped against the basket, reached out and roughly lifted Syeira into the bow. She didn't struggle.

"I am the captain of the harbor watch," said the man harshly. "Who are you?"

"Syeira," said the girl faintly. "A . . . seamer."

The captain was looking at the water, where the warboy slid

and rolled with the waves. "I'll be damned," he said. He brought his face close to Syeira. "You *stole* a warboy?"

The girl said nothing. Nothing mattered now. She hunched in the boat, shivering.

"The basket's damaged, cap'n," said the first oarsman.

"We'll need to take it back, anyway," said the captain. "Can we tow the warboy?"

"Hell of a weight, sir, but I guess so."

"All right. Take the basket aboard, and tie the warboy to the stern." He picked up Syeira by the scruff of the neck and sat her down on a bench, directly opposite him. "Sit there and don't move," he ordered.

With some difficulty, the men wrestled the basket into the boat, laying it across the back seat. The two oarsmen who had been sitting there moved to the very stern, where they fished out the tether ropes of the warboy. When it had been secured to the transom, the boat started back toward the watchtowers. It was going slower than it had been. This was partly because of the weight behind it, and partly because the two oarsmen, their places gone, now concerned themselves with monitoring the warboy.

"Stole a warboy," said the captain grimly. "Can you believe it?"

Syeira was facing inland while the captain faced the same direction as the oarsmen. Looking toward the mouth of the harbor, she saw a black shape rise up through the darkness. A sail showed faint as a ghost against the night sky. Syeira watched it numbly. The captain turned and, seeing it, swore.

"What the hell is *this*, now?" he said.

He watched for a moment, then detached the lantern from the prow and, bracing himself in the bow, swung it in a shallow arc. The sailing vessel was moving well with the wind. It altered its direction slightly without coming about; now it headed straight for the longboat. The first oarsman, who had turned around to watch, said, "He's not paying attention, cap'n."

"Bloody hell," replied the captain. "I'll bleed him a cup at a time, whoever he is. Hard a-port."

The men changed their stroke, to swing the bow around, and then began rowing eastward. But they were slowed by the extra weight, and the sail came about and started bearing down on them once again. Now they could see the ship itself: It seemed to have a foresail as well as a mainsail, which, in the strong wind, made it much faster than the longboat. It was about two hundred feet away and closing fast.

"He's chasing us," said the captain, in a tone of mingled rage and disbelief. "Cut loose the warboy, and all hands to the oars."

The men in the stern moved quickly: One slashed the ropes of the warboy while the other tossed the basket overboard and took his place at an oar. By then, however, the sail was less than a hundred feet away. Now Syeira could hear the rippling sails of the oncoming ship and the waves crashing against its bow. "Hard a-port!" roared the captain, and at the same time he stood up and bellowed, "In the name of Ran, *come about!*"

It was too late. A high dark prow took the longboat broadside. There was a tremendous splintering, the boat was spun around, and the captain was pitched headfirst into the water. Two of the men had already dived in. Syeira herself felt as if she had been thrown by a horse; she found herself in water, winded, hanging on to an oar. The hull of the ship sliced past within five feet of her. Then she heard sails flapping in the wind; the ship, after ramming them, was coming about.

After a moment the men stopped yelling and concentrated on getting close to the broken sections of their boat. They sputtered and swore as they pulled themselves up. Oars and tackle bobbed around them. The ship was twenty yards away; it was now rocking sideways on the waves. Then, over the wash of the sea, came a man's voice. He sounded as if he were talking to himself, but he spoke loudly enough for the men to hear.

"Whoops," he said.

The captain had pulled himself up on the overturned hull of his boat. "You *fool!*" he bellowed, spitting out water. "I'm going to have your guts for rigging!"

There was a sudden *thwack*, and a crossbow arrow stuck in the wood, not a foot from the captain's arm.

"Keep quiet and stay with your boat, captain," said a different voice — a thin, scratchy voice. With a stab of joy, Syeira recognized it.

"Grulla!" screamed Syeira. "Here!" She began swimming furiously toward the ship.

"Don't shoot anybody, Grulla," said the first voice, the man's voice. "I'm already looking at a hefty increase in my dockage fees."

Marlow, thought Syeira in a daze, still thrashing away. The captain recognized the voice, too. "Marlow," he called slowly and savagely, "you are a dead man." But before he'd finished speaking he had let himself slide into the water so he wouldn't be a target for Grulla.

The girl was now by the side of the *Reynard*. A rope snaked down beside her, and she was pulled up, her feet scrabbling at the hull. She collapsed into Grulla's arms.

"Mainsail, Grulla," shouted Marlow from his place at the tiller. "We have to get out of here."

There was a flurry of movement. Grulla let Syeira slump to the deck, then hobbled to tighten the mainsail. It billowed, caught wind, and the ship began to bump eastward over the waves, away from the watchtowers, away from the harbor. Syeira, exhausted, got to her knees.

"No," she gasped. "We have to get Arwin."

Marlow laughed from the tiller; he seemed to be enjoying

himself. "Rest easy," he said, then glanced over the ship's balustrade at the waves. "You don't think this is fast, do you? You don't think this is fleet or swift? I've been full to the brim with spices and I haven't been wallowing like this. Waddling like this. *Wambling* like this."

"*What?*" replied Syeira, still dazed.

"Below!" shouted Grulla from the other side of the deck. Syeira crawled to the hatch and stuck her head down into the hold. Over the spice smells came the scent of horses. She could tell from their wheezing that they were already sick as dogs.

9

Flight

In his mind, Marlow put out a hand and plucked a word from the tree there. He found that he couldn't just pluck *one* word; a small bunch came with it. Standing at the tiller of the *Reynard*, eyes closed, he looked like a wine taster who had just sampled a superb vintage. The words in his mind all had a slightly different flavor. He laughed aloud, opened his eyes, and gripped the tiller. He'd taken a bit too much of that potion, he knew. Great nets and webs of words had sprung up in his mind, and they were *catching* things. All right, he told himself, just *sail*. Get away from Thurckport. But he couldn't help looking up at the night sky, which was the color of a deep tropical lagoon and faintly phosphorescent. There must be a name for that color, he thought. In his mind he stuck out a hand again. Well, it was a mixture of Barbary black and parrot green, with a touch of . . . pirate blue. Pirate blue! He wished he'd had his notebook with him; he had a place in one of his stories for just that color. . . .

So the kid *had* spoken the truth about that potion, he thought. Strange, to get something like this from a kid.

The lamp hung from a slanted peg in the hold. By its light Syeira could see the horses lying crossways over the keel, as Marlow had wanted them. They had their heads low, and before them on the boards was a small pool of saliva. Horses get seasick very easily, and the pitching floor can cause them to stumble and injure themselves. This was why these ones were all lying down. And yet even in her nausea, with the sweat coming out in patches on her coat, Arwin looked calm. She had her colts back; that was all that mattered.

The girl turned to Grulla. The old woman had just finished applying a last layer of oakum and resin to the cracks of the loading door.

"Maybe you'll be able to go back someday, Grulla," said Syeira tentatively.

"I can never go back," said Grulla. "They know I was behind the escape. They know I lobbed that devil's scratch into the compound. They know I shot at the captain of the harbor watch. I am marked for death ten times over."

She crossed the hold, moistened a rag in the water barrel, and moved close to the colts. Syeira saw now that one had a raw patch at the base of his neck. From a lasso, she guessed. He must have neighed loudly when he got it around his neck. Maybe that was when Arwin had let go of the warboy. Somehow, though, he'd thrashed it off.

"Well, you did everything right, you two," said Grulla, as she washed the colt's neck with the damp cloth. "Except trample Davy. I heard him bellowing the whole time — right up to the moment when the regiment horses got a whiff of that devil's scratch. Then he might as well have been a squeaking mouse."

"I heard them even in the warboy," said Syeira, smiling.

Grulla nodded. "Aye, whoever your man Shanks is, he's got the wise. Probably took Davy and the others a good fifteen minutes to get those chargers under control. And that gave your horses and me a head start. I actually managed to stay on your mare's back." She refolded the damp rag. "I wish I'd been there to see Davy's face when he got to the city gates. He'd thought we'd all be there, helpless, surrounded by the gate watch. He didn't know about Scrabber Jones."

That was a bit of luck, thought Syeira. Scrabber had come alone to Grulla early in the evening and told her Davy's orders: No

Weerlings were to be let outside until further notice. She remembered Davy saying something to Pouty just before the two left the animal keep; that must have been when he gave the word. Fortunately Scrabber went beyond his orders. He thought he was saving himself trouble by privately warning Grulla, but actually he had saved their lives. Grulla knew she'd have to find another way out, and so had gone to the harbor with the horses. Syeira looked at the woman in admiration. *You could have been a general,* she thought.

"They won't let the Weerlings perish, Grulla," she said gently. "You said yourself that —"

Suddenly the old woman turned on Syeira, her eyes blazing.

"Of course they won't let them perish," she snapped. She passed her hand over her brow. "But I had no choice; I had to leave them. We all would have been caught and executed. Ran would have won."

Grulla had no tears in her; they'd been drained out by war and death and disappointment. But standing there in the lamplight, she suddenly seemed to curl and wither, like a flower that's been dipped in alcohol.

"I just hope Perlina's ears don't bother her too much," she said in a small voice.

Syeira took a step toward her, but the old woman said harshly, "Well, you're free now, you and the horses. Where will you go?"

Syeira had never really thought about that. "Well, to Arva, I guess," she said.

"You, too?"

Syeira glanced down uneasily at the mare. What *would* happen when they got to Arva? Arwin wasn't looking at the girl; like the colts, she was dully watching the rolling floor in front of them. Syeira conjured up in her mind what she knew of Arva — vast empty grasslands and rolling hills stretching off to nobody knew where. A home for horses, yes. But a home for *her*?

"Well, I can't go back to Haysele," she said, with just a tinge of sadness. "I stole a horse." To ward off further questions, she added, "And you, Grulla? Where will you go?"

"It doesn't matter where I go," said Grulla. She turned and put her hands on the ladder to the deck, but Syeira moved forward.

"Here," she said. From her spice pouch she drew out the hank of Arwin's mane. She took Grulla's hand off the ladder and pressed the mane into it.

"Ah, a charm," said Grulla, in the voice of one about to lie down inside her own tomb. "This will make me happy."

"It will make *me* happy," said Syeira, "if you always keep it with you. Then you will remember what we did together, you and I." Her eyes were obscurely alight. "You said yourself that memories and dreams make the best charms."

Grulla's face was a mask. "The *gypsies* said that, not I."

"But it's true," Syeira protested. She did not let go of the woman's hand. "I know where you can go, Grulla. Where you *must* go."

The woman did not respond. "You must go back to the heath around Thurckport," Syeira urged. "But not as Grulla. As Betty Mauditt."

"Something to look forward to," said Grulla.

"Someday they will bring the Weerlings out again," continued Syeira earnestly. "They'll have to; even broken horses need to run. And Perlina and the others only have to smell you once."

Grulla raised her eyes to the girl's face.

"You're the only one who really knows how to look after them, Grulla," said Syeira intently. "Maybe it's time they left the city along with you. And then . . ." She paused, thinking about the empty spaces of Arwin's homeland. "Then you can all come to Arva."

"Arva!" snorted the woman, and for a moment she was again

the Grulla that Syeira knew. "So you think it's time I was put out to pasture, eh?"

"Yes," said Syeira. "Along with me."

Without looking at the girl, Grulla put the charm inside her cloak and turned to climb the ladder. Syeira stepped back with a sigh and watched her go. The woman moved very slowly, since she couldn't bend her bad leg. With her head just above the deck, she paused, and Syeira heard: "Arva! Not much of a place to retire to, is it?"

The girl gave a hopeful smile. She'd just have to keep after Grulla; the woman would come around eventually.

After a moment Syeira lay down beside the horses. *It's over*, she thought. *They're free*. Marlow had said they wouldn't be able to land for a good while, because of the reefs, but that didn't matter. She smiled then, thinking of how Marlow must have looked when the horses had shown up on the dock. But he'd come through. He'd been a bit tipsy, Grulla had said. Good old Marlow. It was a lucky thing the warboy *had* caught fire: Otherwise the spicetrader would never have been able to track it outside the harbor.

She ran her fingers through her hair. That dip in the ocean had washed out a fair amount of dirt. Good: Now that she was free of Thurckport, she wanted to be free of its grime.

She wasn't seasick, not yet. Above her the lamp clanked gently with the rolling ship. The smells around her were mainly woody — sassafras, sandalwood, and the oak of the floor — but there was something else in the shadows, something tart and smoky sweet. Cloves. She remembered Davy's song about the horse of cloves and the horse of honey. She felt sure it was a nice song, even though Davy had sung it. The horse of honey would be a light sorrel mare, the color of buttered toast. And the horse of cloves? Was it *made* of cloves? She must ask Grulla about it. Or Marlow . . .

Later, asleep in the rolling darkness of the hold, she dreamed that these two horses were standing in the shadows of the river stable, nibbling on each other's necks, as horses do. She couldn't see them very well, but she could smell the cloves. She found herself inside her dream, walking silently over the straw toward the horses. The dark one, the horse of cloves, gave her a brief glance from the shadows and then went back to its nibbling. *He knows me*, thought Syeira. She was suddenly glad the ocean had washed her clean, glad she was recognizable again.

⤜⤛⤝

It was Syeira who first spotted the sail. The sun had been up for an hour, and they were running through choppy water about a mile from shore. Around them, the sea was one color — aquamarine — but elsewhere it was many. At a distance, the sunlight strained out the blue green, leaving only a glittering silver. Over rock and seaweed it flowed a purple blue, the color of a bruise. Above a shallow beach it could be almost lime green. Grulla and Marlow both had their eyes forward, watching the changing waters. Syeira, looking back from her perch beside the tiller, saw a dark smudge on the horizon.

"Is that a fishing boat?" she asked.

Marlow turned around and was on his feet instantly. "Take the tiller!" he barked. Syeira took it while he fumbled for his pocket spyglass. He gave a quick look and then cursed loud and long.

"What is it?" asked Syeira.

Marlow just turned and yelled, "Grulla! Foresail!"

"What is it, Marlow?" Syeira repeated, feeling the first twinges of panic.

"It's a warship, that's what it is," he said tightly. "They're after us."

Syeira looked back in dismay. It wasn't fair; they had just *escaped*. "We have to land," she said urgently.

"We *can't* land," snapped Marlow. "It's all reefs. I'd tear the bottom out of her. Here, hold it steady." He gave her the tiller and sprinted across the deck.

Syeira didn't like to steer; under her hand the ship felt like a huge restless ox, ready to tear off in the wrong direction. But she held it steady enough that Marlow, who was now shinnying up the mast, wasn't thrown onto the deck. Grulla had already raised the foresail at the bowsprit. Marlow, legs wrapped around the mast, got out his spyglass again. "They're making good time," he said. "Dammit! Probably took the fastest ship in the fleet."

"We have to go out farther, Marlow!" called Grulla.

"Not on your life," answered Marlow, clambering back down the mast. "With that rig they'll move even faster out there." He stood still, feeling the ship under his feet. "We're too heavy, that's our problem," he said in a low voice. A second later he was at the tiller again.

"What are we going to do?" asked Syeira.

Marlow kept his eyes straight ahead. "I'll tell you what we're going to do," he said. "You got your knife? Get below and start digging the caulking out of the door."

"Why?"

"Because you and your horses are going to swim, that's why."

"*Swim!*" Syeira was aghast.

"It's the only way." Marlow saw the look on the girl's face and kept his voice calm. "Once you're ashore you'll be safe. They probably won't even see you in the waves. And without the weight I *might* be able to get away."

"But . . . the horses are *sick*, Marlow!"

"I know, I know. But in half an hour that man-o'-war will be alongside to grapple us, and then we'll all wish we had been killed quickly last night." He raised a hand against the sun. "The first bay I find, I'll put in. We'll be out of their sight for a while."

Syeira looked down at the waves below her and wondered

how on earth they could possibly get the horses out without swamping. But Marlow said, "Go!" and she had to move. As she scrambled down the ladder to the hold, she felt the ship change tack and move in toward the shore.

"Arwin!" called Syeira. "There's a warship behind us!"

Arwin raised her head, and the colts put their noses close to hers.

"We have to *swim*," said Syeira. She unsheathed her knife and began furiously to dig out the caulking.

The colts, unnerved by Syeira's feverish activity, struggled to stand. Above them came a yell from Marlow.

"No, stay down!" instructed Syeira, gesturing. "You're rocking the ship."

Arwin could feel the rocking of the ship, too; she nickered and the colts settled back down. Syeira knew that, sick as the colts were, they would rather stay in the hold than swim through a churning sea.

For several minutes she dug away at the door. The oakum, sticky with pitch, stuck to her fingers. There was a small pile of caulking at her feet, as well as a few pools of seawater, when Syeira felt the ship come around and heard the sails flapping. Against the hull, the wash of the waves grew louder. A few seconds later Marlow appeared, swinging down the ladder.

"This is as close as I could get," he said, moving toward the door. He yanked out the two wooden support bars, took hold of the handle, and gave the door an expert kick at the bottom. It came out in his hands, and he thrust it to one side. Sunlight flooded into the hold. They felt the cool breath of the ocean, less than six inches below the doorway. A wave broke over the oak planks, and fingers of seawater began creeping toward the horses.

The shore was about a quarter mile away.

"Any sign of them, Grulla?" yelled Marlow up the ladder hole.

"Not yet!" shouted Grulla.

"All right," said Marlow. He was sweating freely. "We'll have to do this carefully. The big one goes first. We'll have to get the other two to back up as she moves ahead."

Syeira wasn't sure whether Arwin actually understood that they had to swim; she thought *she'd* have to jump in first. But Arwin had realized the plan as soon as she'd seen the door come off. She rose to her feet — forequarters first, as horses do — and the colts followed. The unlit lamp clanked with their movements. With the horses standing, the hold seemed small and wobbly.

"All right," said Marlow to Arwin. "Easy does it."

Arwin took one step forward, then another. The tilt of the floor changed as she moved. Syeira, moving between the colts, got them to back up a step. The mare had to keep her head well down since, standing, her withers were barely a foot from the ceiling. She lifted a foot, tested the floor, shifted her weight. More waves crested into the hold, but the weight of the colts (plus that of Marlow) was enough to keep the doorway above the water-line.

A foot from the opening, Arwin paused. Even with her lowered head she was too tall for the doorway and had to go down slightly on her knees. Water sloshed in around her. Syeira felt the ship begin to heel dangerously. Marlow had just opened his mouth to yell, "Go!" when Arwin, with a thrust of her back legs, half-slipped and half-fell into the water. From the splash they might have just unloaded a medium-sized catapult. The whole vessel bobbled violently. All of them — horses and humans — took one stumbling step forward and then one back. Behind them the lamp fell with a smash. The colts flung their noses away in fright, but Syeira kept her hands on their shoulders, and a second later they were standing, ears back and eyes wide, exactly across the keel. The floor steadied.

Just then Grulla yelled down through the ladder hole, "Marlow! Warship's in sight!"

Marlow kept his cool. "All right," he said, grabbing a bailing bucket. "Next one. No, just *one*. And *you* move back as *he* goes."

Syeira touched one of the colts on the shoulder and he started forward, trembling. He tried to go out as his mother had done, but his front feet slipped and he fell with his forequarters overboard and his back legs scrabbling on the floor. Water streamed ankle-deep through the hold. Syeira pushed with all her might against the colt's haunches, and he went in like an elephant seal. At once he rose, blowing hoarsely, and began swimming off in the wrong direction. Arwin was churning the water to get close to him.

"Last one!" said Marlow, stooping to bail furiously. Seawater swirled and foamed around him like tattered, angry spirits.

The remaining colt seemed to have learned from the other horses. He stepped forward at a slight angle, skidded, lowered his head, and rolled into the water. His head went right under for just a second, but when he came up, he was swimming in the right direction.

"Good-bye, Marlow!" said Syeira, standing at the doorway.

Marlow stopped bailing just long enough to put out his hand. Syeira grasped it tightly with both of hers.

"Good-bye, horse girl," he said. His face was taut with anxiety. "I'll remember you."

And he would. Under that lagoon sky he'd felt something new and exhilarating. For the rest of his life he would be buffeted by the hot windblown spicery of words, and though he would find himself in some pretty tight spots later on, he'd never be at a loss for a synonym. For this he had the girl to thank.

"Remember me!" cried Syeira urgently, as if only that would save her. "Good-bye, Grulla!" she called through the ceiling. "We'll meet again in Arva." And from the deck above came Grulla's answering cry: "Arva!"

Syeira turned, slipped, found her footing, and then pitched herself into the sea.

∼⊙∼

The waves caught her in their cold, heavy smother. She rose, spitting out saltwater, and began swimming frantically. In the rolling sea she could hardly make headway. She slowed down then, trying not to fight the waves, and suddenly Arwin was there. Syeira grasped her mane thankfully. On either side of the mare, the colts were swimming hard — too hard. "Easy!" called Syeira over the waves. At that rate they'd never make it to shore. Alongside the mare's back she flutter-kicked steadily. The sea would take them all in, eventually. They just had to *ride* it.

Still hanging on to Arwin's mane with one hand, she half-turned in the water to look back. The loading door of the *Reynard* was in place. She saw the tiller move, the mainsail belly out with the wind. Marlow was going to make it.

Then she saw, moving in from the mouth of the bay, the warship.

She turned back and began kicking again. *They won't see us. The waves will hide us.* Looking ahead, she caught glimpses of the hilly shoreline and the spouts of white that marked the reefs. They were still a good two hundred yards away. The colts were wheezing badly now. The one on her right could barely keep his nostrils out of the water; his eyes were wide with terror. Syeira let go of Arwin's mane and swam over to him.

"Just float!" she urged. "Float!"

She put one hand under the horse's chin and kicked and sculled frantically to keep herself up. The colt's eyes were almost underwater. Syeira knew the only hope was to get the other horses close, to support him. She opened her mouth to call Arwin but swallowed seawater. At that moment the colt stopped swimming and tilted his nose up. *"No!"* cried Syeira, grabbing at him frantically. Beneath her she felt the colt's hooves scrape against something. Now he seemed to be *standing*.

"A reef!" she gasped. "Arwin, a reef!"

At once Arwin and the other colt were beside them. Syeira felt a hoof strike her shin. Heavy bodies moved around her like tree trunks in a mudslide. Now all the horses stood precariously on the reef, blowing and hacking, their hindquarters swaying with the pull of the sea. Sliding sheets of water met and drew apart over their backs. Syeira floated in a pool created by their bodies; the water was violet because of the shadows. She put out a hand to one of the colts and felt his flank pulsing in spasms. The other colt was shivering, his mane rising and falling on the swell.

"Not far now," she told them. "Not far now."

She looked seaward, treading water. The *Reynard* was moving away, all sails up. "Go, Marlow!" she breathed. She watched for a moment, feeling the cold seep even deeper inside her. The *Reynard* seemed to be outdistancing the warship easily, and now she could see why. The latter had come to a stop, sails flapping, its deck a mass of activity. Shouts came across the water, ropes swung in arcs. Then Syeira saw a longboat being lowered from the side.

"They've launched a boat!" Syeira cried. "We have to go!"

She pushed out between the horses and began swimming again. Arwin nosed at the colts. They neighed weakly and moved their heads away; they didn't want to leave the reef. But then the mare struck out herself, and in a second they were after her. Syeira shot a glance back. The boat was powering through the choppy water; there must have been at least eight oarsmen. She recognized a hefty, pink-faced figure near the gunwales — Pouty. She couldn't see Blacklock Davy, but she could hear him yelling, "Stroke! Stroke!" A burly man stood in the prow, bracing himself against the swell. He raised something in his hands, something that glittered. Syeira saw that it was a crossbow.

In a second she was swimming like a demon. She didn't look

for a mane; the horses had formed a wedge around her and, shielded from the waves, she could just keep up to them. From the shouts behind her she knew the boat was moving up on their left. Dimly she heard Davy's "Stroke! Stroke!" On land, the horses would have been in range of a good crossbowman, but not in a choppy sea. Everything was slow and heavy around her: the waves, the horses, her terror. One of the colts, its breath almost gone, was making an awful coughing sound.

She couldn't see how far she was from shore; she just kept swimming. The colt on her left was crowding her, trying to get away from the boat. She expected at any moment to hear the sickening *whick* of a crossbow arrow and feel the colt stop swimming beside her. Then, very dimly, she heard Arwin's hooves scrape against the bottom. The colts, now surging through chest-deep water, were moving ahead of her. The shouts behind her grew louder. She stumbled through the shallows and went down.

"Help me!" she gasped.

Less than fifty feet behind her, the crossbowman raised his weapon. Who knows if he intended to shoot the girl? He'd been trained to see only a target; perhaps it didn't matter that the target, helpless with terror, now held up a hand before her — as if it was a bee and not an arrow that sought her out. The man steadied himself, one foot on a gunwale, and squinted down the crossbow. But he never got his shot. Davy had clambered forward and now stood at the marksman's elbow. For an instant he stared at Syeira with wild eyes, like a man jolted out of sleep by a thunderclap. Then, with a yell, he brought his hand down hard on the crossbow. The crossbowman staggered, and his arrow disappeared into the shallows like a whiplash.

At Syeira's cries, Arwin had wheeled about in hock-deep water. The girl, splashing forward, now pulled herself up on the mare's back. Davy had jumped overboard and was wading through the shallows, bellowing. The horses paid no attention. Laboriously they scrambled up the hilly shoreline and in a second had disappeared into Broak.

And the crossbowman stood ominously quiet in the midst of the shouting men, watching Davy with narrowed eyes.

10

The Dream Hunter

Northern Broak was heathland. It was swells of heather and moor grass rolling away from the sea. It was tufts of bracken, and tiny spruce like mange on the hills, and ancient standing stones showing through the grass. It was deer and fox and hawk and rabbit. The forests had long ago been cut down to serve the empire, and few people lived there except shepherds and, on the coast, the odd fisherman. But it was a good place for horses — grassy, open, and not too many flies.

Through this land stumbled the fugitives. They had no strength to gallop; they kept up a dragging trot, panting and wheezing. Syeira, on Arwin, could feel her changing her stride slightly every hundred yards or so, as horses do when they're very tired. Soon they slowed to a walk, and Syeira slipped off. All the horses had twitching chests or flanks. They seemed bewildered at how tired they were.

After a while they came to a stop at the foot of a hill, behind a small thicket of larch. Syeira guessed they were a good five miles from the coast. Unless their pursuers had landed and got mounts, they were safe. The horses stood with their heads down, still breathing hard. The salt had crystallized in their manes and tails so that it glittered in the morning sunlight.

"What happened back there?" said Syeira, more to herself than the horses. She had sensed that something had taken place in the boat, but in her terrified state she had barely been aware of it.

Later, as she rubbed the horses down with a handful of grass, she said, "He missed. He shot and missed."

They drifted further inland. Slowly the horses began to take mouthfuls of grass. They listened for sounds of pursuit — the horses could feel the vibrations of hoofbeats from a long way off — but heard none.

"He *didn't* shoot," murmured Syeira, who was standing by herself, away from the horses. "Why didn't he shoot?"

When night fell, the colts slept standing up; Arwin lay down. Syeira, stretched out beside the mare, listened to the breathing of the horses. Even in their sleep they were aware of the world around them. At one point Syeira held her breath noiselessly, to see what would happen; instantly Arwin was awake beside her. The girl smiled. For most of the night she slept a secure and dreamless sleep, but sometime just before dawn she came awake. One of the colts had lain down and, judging by a slight movement of his hoof, was dreaming. Syeira inched closer to him. He woke just enough to determine that it was her, and then was back in his dream. A few smells, very faint, wafted into Syeira's mind. The colt was dreaming of Arva. She smelled grass and myrtle bush and endless clear air, atmospheres piled on atmospheres, the air of a wild place.

Home, she thought. She tried very hard to think of it as *her* home, but she couldn't help imagining the vast empty spaces and the wind blowing lonely through them.

Syeira rode Arwin, who kept up an easy pace south and east. The colts did not keep up an easy pace. They had been cooped up for a month, in ship and cage, and they wanted to run. Whenever Arwin stopped to feed, they would stand around her, alert and quivering, like fencers. Very soon one would take a small jump. His forefeet would clear the ground by only a few inches, and he would land with a shallow pounce, like a butting ram. His brother would eye him gravely and do the same. Then they would stand still for a moment, serious and still. The wind would lift their manes haphazardly, the way it lifts the sedge fringes along bogs. Their tails would move once or twice with the sound of a grain flail being swung through the air. They would lower their heads, study their back feet, and look up again. Suddenly, as if on a signal, they would tear off across the grassland, and wheel and tear again, churning up identical fountain jets of divots.

They took to jumping, too. They were born jumpers. Whenever they came to a stream or a shrub, they would stop and eye it suspiciously, as if it had insulted them. Then one colt would give a swing to his neck, as if feinting, and take off sideways. He might have been tethered to a powerful crosswind, so quickly did he move. He'd race storm-driven toward the obstacle — *thupetty-thup, thupetty-thup* — scattering dirt and echoes. Six feet away from it he'd leave the ground, and there would be silence: He had become wind. For an instant he would be sculpted and weightless, high above the earth. His back would be straight, his nose forward, his forelegs curled like those of a begging dog. He would be lodged in the air like an axe head. Then time would split along its sunlit grain and let him through, and his forefeet would come down with a thud, and he would be off balance for a fraction of a moment until his back feet hit; and he would turn in a wide loping circle, blowing and tossing his mane. After a moment his brother would try to outdo him.

"Again!" Syeira would call. They always did it again.

The good weather held; their spirits rose. They hurried no more than the butterflies that moved over the fields in a kind of confetti meander. Syeira rode Arwin; the colts were really too young to be ridden — except in emergencies. But she was fascinated by them and would often try to coax out scent pictures by breathing on *them*. They found this behavior very odd, for a human. She would come close to a colt, blowing softly, and he would turn his nose away, as if bothered by a fly. "Do I smell *that* bad?" she would ask. She wanted to share their scent stories from Arva — stories of wolves hunting, stallions fighting, night flowers blooming, the wind carousing through the long Arva grass. But the colts didn't seem that interested in talking to her. Whenever they weren't running or jumping, they liked to stand by themselves, pondering stilled time or their own shadows. After a while, Syeira gave up on them and contented herself with catching bits and pieces of Arva as they slept.

They rode on toward the horses' homeland, sleeping on high ground (to better catch distant smells) and often rolling in the grass. The girl's only problem was food. The moors had berry bushes and mushroom patches, and the horses stood up on their hind legs to help her get nuts from the trees; but altogether it wasn't much. She had seen no signs of habitation since they arrived in Broak — no cottages, no farms, no places to beg food. Now they had even less chance of finding a house, for the land was becoming flat and wet. The colts didn't do as much racing around. Syeira saw a lot of glittering dragonflies, and herons with their kinked necks, and once a weasel darting away with an egg in its mouth.

One sunny morning they were skirting a large swamp, the horses squelching warily over the spongy ground. Syeira, riding low over Arwin's neck, was watching for bird's nests in the reeds. At the edge of the marsh, plants like tiny green parasols stood limply in the quiet air. The swamp was a hot green meadow of scum, dotted by stumps and logs and clumps of reeds. Looking out into the middle of it, Syeira was surprised to see a small island. They went into some trees and then out again, and glancing across the swamp again she saw a crumbling chimney through the island greenery.

"Look," she said, turning in her seat.

Arwin and the colts stopped.

"There's a house on that island," said Syeira.

The horses lowered their heads, found nothing worth eating, and raised them again.

"It's a ruin," said Syeira. The island was probably a hundred yards away, and she could see better at that distance than the horses. "There may be something there," she added. She meant twine for making snares, or wire for making fishhooks, or a flint for making fires, or anything that might help her get *food*. She was getting hungrier with every passing day.

The horses clearly had no desire to wade through deep, sticky mud. But Syeira felt sure she could get out to the ruin: There were enough logs and boulders and reed patches to allow her passage. Besides, the swamp didn't look that deep.

"I won't be long," she said, slipping off Arwin.

The mare sniffed the air in the direction of the house but picked up nothing except swamp smells. The colts were lowering and raising their heads, as horses do when they're trying to focus on a distant object. One of them touched a forefoot to the edge of the swamp but drew back in distaste. The scum had the consistency of soup.

Syeira was already twenty feet out into the swamp, walking along an archipelago of small rocks. Two pale yellow butterflies wobbled past her, darting and weaving in perfect concert as if they were joined by an invisible wire. She crouched to look at the thick pond scum. It was alive with tiny insects, darting over the surface like blown dust particles. She jumped from the rocks to a patch of reeds, and from that to a half-submerged log, and from that to another boulder. The lichen on the rock looked like dried smoke rings. It felt crumbly under her feet. She had been right about the depth of the swamp: When she put her foot in by accident, she went up just to her knee. "It's shallow," she called to the horses.

But she didn't like the grasping feel of the warm mud on her calf. She drew out her leg — it wasn't easy — and continued on. Now she could see part of a wall on the island and a big branch crooking up through a window. Close to the island there was nothing to step on. She had to follow a narrow islet of reeds around to the side, where she found a log that gave her access. Then she stood, muddy and hot, on the island.

It was about fifty feet in diameter and heavily overgrown. She slipped through brambles and branches, and after a moment was standing at the house. One look at it and she knew there wouldn't be anything worth taking there. The house was probably hundreds of years old. It had one wall left, with part of the chimney and fireplace, and around it was nothing but greenery. Near the fireplace was a relatively clear patch; she moved into its dappled green light. The trees were large and still around her. A small bird flew through the undergrowth, but it moved too quickly for her to see what it was.

Before she went back to the horses she wanted to have a look at the far side of the island. Again she worked her way through the greenery. The bird, still keeping to the undergrowth, darted ahead of her. When she got to the edge of the island, she found a section of log, flattened on top. She sat down and looked out. Here, too, the swamp was littered with reed patches and stumps. Because of the reeds, she couldn't tell where the shore actually began.

She was just about to get up when, looking down beside the stump, she saw something dirty white showing through the bed of moss. She peered close. *A bone or a shell*, she thought, and began to clear away the moss and dirt. She didn't think it could be anything valuable, but she was curious, anyway. After a moment she had scraped away enough soil to see that it had a rounded shape. Then, with a shudder, she stood up quickly.

It was a human skull.

She stood there uneasily, shaking the dirt from her hands,

when she became aware that the bird was perched not far away. It was robin-sized, black and gray, with a slight hook to its beak. For a moment it scrutinized her, and then said in a small, scratchy voice:

"Don't be afraid. It's only a skull."

Syeira gasped and moved away. The bird stayed where it was.

"You *spoke*," said Syeira, her eyes wide.

"I did," replied the bird. Now she could see that it had a black band like a mask around its eyes. A naturalist would have identified it as a shrike, but Syeira was no naturalist.

It took a moment for Syeira to find her voice. "How did you learn to speak?" she managed finally.

"A lot of birds can speak," said the shrike. Its voice put Syeira in mind of a tiny file working on metal. "Parrots. Crows. Many of the starling family."

"But they don't really *speak*," said Syeira.

"True," admitted the shrike. "They just imitate. But all birds are capable of real speech. Real creativity. If they'd just nourish their heads right."

It flew to the bed of moss and perched on the skull.

"Speaking of heads," it said, "this is what the artists call a *memento mori*. A reminder of death. Probably some long-gone hermit or farmer. Now he just scares people. Not birds, though. You don't frighten me. Old calcium head."

The shrike seemed to speak as if it were at the end of its breath, forcing out each tiny phrase. Its breathing was recognizably a bird's, even if its sentences were human.

It pecked at the skull for a moment. "Yes, that's solid," it remarked. "*He* was no dream, anyway."

"Why should he be a dream?" asked Syeira.

"A lot of people are, in these parts," replied the shrike. It looked intently at Syeira, its eyes like small black pearls.

"A lot of people are *dreams*?"

The shrike nodded its tiny head. "In this valley the conditions are good for them. With the air so still and shimmering." Again it looked at Syeira, as if deliberating.

"Well," said Syeira shortly, "*I'm* not a dream."

The bird only studied her in silence. At length it said, "May I ask how old you are?"

Syeira guessed she was somewhere between ten and twelve, going by what people said, but she had never really given much thought to this question. A human's teeth are not such good indicators of age as a horse's.

"I don't know *exactly*," she replied.

"Hmm," said the shrike.

The novelty of a talking bird was starting to wear off for Syeira. She didn't like the way it kept looking at her.

"I think I'll be getting back to the horses," she said.

"Horses?" said the shrike.

Syeira immediately regretted giving away this information; even in the wilds of Broak they had to be careful. The shrike, clearly excited, hopped from the skull to the flattened log.

"You said horses," it pursued. "A roan mare and two colts. Wild horses from Arva. *Smart* horses."

Syeira stared. "How did you know that?"

"Shh! Keep your voice down," said the shrike, fluttering its wings. "This land isn't as empty as it looks." It glanced around in the jerky way of birds and then said, "I know about you and your horses because . . . I was sent to find you. I always know as much as I can. About my quarry."

"Your quarry?"

"Dreams. I hunt down dreams."

"You hunt down . . . ," Syeira began in disbelief, then caught herself. "Oh, you hunt down *dreams*," she said conversationally. She was determined to find out where this was going.

"I'm one of the few left in the world," affirmed the shrike.

"It's a very old office. Usually held by birds. We can cover more land than anybody else. But never mind that now." It flew to a branch three feet from Syeira's head so it could speak to her at eye level. "Someone in Swebban came to me. Someone who was wounded long ago, as a child, and dreams strange dreams because of it. Spoke to me of one dream in particular — of a girl and three horses. The horses were as I've described to you. At the instant of awakening, they rode away. Out of the dreamer's mind, into the world. Perhaps you don't know that this is how many dreams leave us. This is why they seem so vague and distant the next morning. It's surprising how ignorant some people are. Anyway, I was charged to find the dream of the horses. 'It was so *vivid*,' the dreamer said. Almost a vision. Of course I began my hunt at this valley. The dreams are as thick as marsh gas here."

"That is crazy," said Syeira calmly.

The shrike went on as if she had said nothing. "I thought you might be it. When I saw you. But I had to make sure. I couldn't risk returning with the wrong dream."

"I am *not* a dream," said Syeira; her voice had taken on an edge.

"Mm-hmm," said the shrike, but added in an undertone, "I've heard *that* before."

"I think I should go," said Syeira.

She turned, but before she could take a step, the shrike — raising its voice only slightly — said, "There are some simple tests."

Syeira turned back. "What do you mean, simple tests?"

"Simple tests to tell. If you're a dream or not," replied the shrike. "And maybe you're right: Maybe you're *not* a dream. I've made mistakes before. But wouldn't you prefer to hear the tests? Just to make sure? Then we can both rest easy."

Syeira folded her arms. This bird really did think she was an idiot. "What are the tests?" she asked curtly.

"Actually, I've already given you the first one," said the shrike. "I asked you how old you were. You said you didn't know. A common trait of dream people. They don't know when they came into this world. They don't know how long they've been here. How could they? They weren't born; they were *dreamed* into existence."

"You're wrong," protested Syeira. "I don't know how old I am because nobody ever told me. I never had a birthday."

The shrike waited until she was finished, and then said, "Second test."

"Look," said Syeira in exasperation, thrusting out her forearm and giving herself a pinch. "See that? It turns red. That means it's real. *I'm* real."

The shrike glanced at her arm. "Yes, that's a good pinch. You must be getting annoyed." Its small head moved again. "At least you didn't *spit* on me. That's what some dreams do. To demonstrate their brute . . . palpa-*bility*." It had to take a big breath to get this word out. "They also thump their chests. And grind their teeth. And kick trees." It flew to another branch, closer to the edge of the marsh, and Syeira moved toward it. "Must I explain how wrong-headed this is? It only proves that the world *accommodates* the dreamed one. *Of course* reality is hard, or red . . . when you expect it to be. The world is whatever it is — according to the *thoughts* in your mind. No, the tests are the only way to find out. If you're a dream or not. They're as old as my guild, and quite conclusive."

Syeira was about to say something in reply, but then shut her mouth tight and glared at the shrike. "All right," she said. "What's the second test?"

"A dream is a creation, not a creature," said the shrike, as if it were reciting a passage. "It is therefore alone. It often has no family. . . ."

Syeira seemed to take this as an insult. "I *had* a mother," she said coldly. "I had a mother, but she died."

"If I may finish," said the shrike patiently. "The dreamed one is alone. No mother. Often no father." When Syeira made no response, it continued: "The dream knows this deep down. So it attaches itself to anything around it. Animals, for instance."

"Well, then," said Syeira, "I guess Will Shanks was a dream, too, was he?"

And as she stood there, waiting for the shrike to reply to *that*, she suddenly wondered where Will Shanks was. It seemed so long ago that they had spoken. Now he was faint in her mind after her other adventures. She wished she had some of the devil's scratch left; that was a real link with him, something she could hold in her hand.

"Will Shanks," repeated the shrike, and for a second it seemed at a loss. Then it added quickly: "Yes, possibly. Maybe Grulla as well. And Marlow."

Syeira was now pale. "Who told you about them?"

"I have already explained that," said the shrike. "The details all come from the dreamer. The one who sent me to find you."

Syeira's hand shot up, as if she wanted to strike the bird. "Who *is* this dreamer?"

"I'm sorry," said the shrike, who was plainly getting irritated in its turn. "The rules of the guild forbid me from telling you beforehand. You must come and meet the dreamer. Face to face." It flew to a stump five feet out into the marsh; it seemed to be getting restless. "And when you do that, certain mysteries will become clear to you. The mysteries of your life."

Of all the things the shrike had said, this one made the biggest impression on Syeira. "What mysteries?" she asked.

The shrike, looking as if it had revealed a bit too much, remained silent. Syeira took a step into the marsh, and the bird flew farther out.

"What mysteries?" repeated Syeira sharply. "Come on, tell me. You're supposed to know all about me."

"I *don't* know all about you," countered the shrike. "The

dreamer knows all about you. To the dreamer, you are as transparent as water."

"Who *is* this dreamer?" said Syeira furiously. She was now ten feet out in the swamp, standing beside the shrike and suppressing an urge to squeeze it hard.

The shrike wasn't looking at her. It muttered something more about guild rules, then, glancing up, said in a low voice: "Listen. I have brought a token — a symbol, from the dreamer. Something that *might* demonstrate the truth to you. But I wasn't going to lug it out to the island." It seemed, after its wrangling with Syeira, to be losing some of its equanimity. "You must follow me and see it for yourself. But be *quiet*. You're pretty noisy for a dream."

With that, it flew across the marsh and disappeared into the trees. Syeira looked grim. She glanced back briefly, then stopped herself. *No, I'm* not *going back to check on the horses. Of course they are there. They're flesh and blood.* She could remember the pinkish muzzles of the colts, the smell of Arwin. *That* wasn't a dream.

But she was going to get to the bottom of this. Quickly she began moving across the marsh. The reed clumps and logs were thicker here, and she made good time. The pond scum breathed out heat and decay. *It's ridiculous*, she thought. *A dream*. A dragonfly suddenly appeared beside her, motionless, a thorn of burnished green suspended in midair. Its body was segmented and looked something like a sun-gilded pine needle that had been tightly tied at certain points with black thread. It dipped down barely an inch, moving to another invisible plane, then shot away. Syeira didn't want to look at it; that was the way things disappeared in dreams.

On the shore, she stopped and listened. She could not see where the shrike had gone; she could see nothing through the trees. The air was as still here as on the other side. She went ahead through the undergrowth, her heart beating in her ears.

"All right, bird," she said defiantly. "I'm here."

There was no answer. Suddenly she wondered if she should call to Arwin. The horses would hear her, wouldn't they? She stood still, peering ahead through the green shadows. There seemed to be a clearing up ahead. After a second she moved forward; she was pretty sure she could handle a *bird* by herself.

She came to the clearing, and there at the far end, showing up against a bramble bush, was something small and bright. Moving closer, she saw it was a butterfly — one of the large ones, with black stripes on its purple wings. She had never seen a butterfly so still. It seemed frozen against the bush, like a folded leaf caught under ice. Its wings were like flower petals, one torn and bent, the other outstretched. It must have been brilliant when alive, but its colors had faded with death. Syeira could see that its body had been impaled on a thorn. It was a strange, unnatural thing to see in a forest.

Syeira stared at it for a moment, her mouth dry, and then a familiar voice said behind her: "Do you like it?"

She turned, every muscle tensed to run. The shrike regarded her from ten feet away. Its voice had changed somehow — it was sharper now, more jagged, as if the file had speeded up.

"Another *memento mori*," it continued. "This one I did myself. While I was waiting for you. I have the artistic twitch, you see." It flew to a point just above the butterfly. "This is the last test, dream child," it said. "When you figure out what this stands for . . . you *wake up*."

Syeira took a step back and bumped into something. A hand went over her mouth — a large, gauntleted hand — and something sharp was pressed against her temple.

"No sound," said a man's voice from over her head. "No sound, or you die where you stand. Move forward."

Syeira's eyes were wide above the hand. She had no choice but to do as he said. The knife — for a knife it was — never moved from her temple.

"What of the horses?" said the voice — a dead, flat, *shorn* voice.

"Still there, patron," said the shrike, coming to rest on a twig. "But they'll start to get restless soon." It made an odd sound that just barely resembled a chuckle. "She fell for it, patron. Swam up all alone. I just popped the hook in."

Now, ahead of her through the trees, Syeira could see a horse in full armor. It had a spike coming out of its head, like a unicorn — part of the armored hood it wore. On its saddle was a large wicker basket. The man stopped beside the horse, the blade still on Syeira's head. The point pressed against her temple until she had to lean sideways.

"Get in the basket," the man ordered.

Syeira wanted to scream or bite, but she knew that either would be useless. After a moment the man lifted her with one hand and dropped her into the basket. Once more the knife was placed against her head.

"No noise, chicken," said the shrike from behind her. "Otherwise you'll end up as a work of art."

Syeira crouched down in the wicker basket, but before the lid was fastened she caught a glimpse of the man. He was tall — well over six feet — and wore a light kind of chain mail. He had no beard or eyebrows. His skin was faintly clouded and membranous, like the early stage of a cataract. Altogether he looked like one of those mummified men they dug up from the bogs of the Withers. Syeira knew who it was: She had seen him several times at Hulvere's castle. He came close to the basket, and his gaze was as charred and empty as a long-dead fire.

"The snare is set," said Ran.

11

In the City
of Mechanicals

That was the worst ride of Syeira's life. Scrunched inside the basket, jolted by the galloping horse, she could only hope that Arwin and the colts were on her trail. Only once did they stop: at nightfall, when Ran was joined by a small troupe of mounted soldiers. Syeira's basket was unhooked and she was moved to a fresh horse. Then the warlord and his escort were away again. Syeira didn't know it, but they were riding northeast, toward the sea. By dawn they had reached Swebban, the famed city of mechanicals.

With its smiths and armorers and shipbuilders and masons, Swebban was Ran's prize possession. He hadn't conquered it by force, but had gradually become its great patron until everybody there worked for him. His portrait, engraved by the chief silversmith, was on the city's coat of arms. Under his patronship, Swebban had gradually lost those mechanicals who made beautiful things, like town bells or fiddles or wonderful big clocks. They had dropped out of sight and become part of the hidden Swebban, the secret community of rebels that stretched all over Broak. Nobody spoke of these rebels, at least not openly, and to all appearances the city served only Ran. The reed weavers made baskets for the warboys. The clockmakers made sextants for Ran's ships. The Worshipful Company of Toymakers, one of the oldest guilds in Swebban, made the tiny metal soldiers that were used in planning campaigns. It was a noisy, dirty city and proud of it. Perhaps the worst part — or the best, if you were the mayor of Swebban — was the coal mines to the west of the harbor. There the grass was almost black and the workers wore hoods and handkerchiefs to keep the coal dust out. The mayor said that nobody was bothered by flies there. This was true, but it wasn't much consolation to the ponies who hauled the coal. They developed breathing problems very quickly and never lasted more than a couple of years.

Syeira *felt* the grimy strength of the city before she actually saw the place. From inside the basket she heard the clatter of iron-rimmed wheels and smelled smoke and charcoal. Once or twice she saw the glow of outdoor forges through the wicker. After a few twists and turns down the cobblestone streets, Ran and his escort dismounted. The basket was lifted off, unlatched, and tipped over. Syeira crawled out painfully to face two armed soldiers.

"March," they said, lowering their glaves.

She obeyed. They went down a long cobblestone path toward a large slate-roofed building. It might have been a stable once, for over the entrance was a bronze horsehead, but it wasn't being used as a stable now. From its two chimneys smoke poured out, and even outside Syeira could hear hammering and clanking. With the guards behind her, the girl passed through the double doors of the building and down a dingy corridor. The hammering and clanking grew louder. They came to another door, guarded by two soldiers, and then Syeira came to one of the strangest places she had ever seen.

It was the kind of workshop found only in Swebban. Two great forges glowed at either end of the long room. Behind each forge was an immense bellows, worked by a handle the size of a ship's tiller. Around the forges, half a dozen brawny workers were hammering metal that glowed as orange as a tropical sunset. Racks of tongs and hammers stood beside their anvils, and against the walls were troughs of water to cool the hot metal. The long worktables in the corner were strewn with wheels, belts, and clamps. Something that looked like a model of bat's wings — cloth stretched over a wooden frame — hung from a beam. Elsewhere, men bent over curious metal shapes, hammering and hacksawing. She crossed the room uneasily. The shapes seemed oddly familiar to Syeira. What were they making here?

Then, at the far end of the room, she saw.

It was a life-sized frame model of a horse, made out of thin iron rods. Only the head was complete; it had black molded nostrils, a mane of wire brush, and working ears. A man was turning a lever somewhere in the horse's flank and the ears were rotating around to face another angle — just as the ears of real horses did. Behind the horse, another man had a metal horse's leg (again life-sized) in a vise. He was using a file to shape the hock.

She walked at glavepoint to a small enclave at the far end of the room. There Ran stood with a burly, worried-looking man in a blacksmith's apron. The shrike was there, too, Syeira saw with disgust. The soldiers moved to her side and stopped her when they were ten feet away. Ran regarded her with his dead eyes. Every year, it seemed, his skin was being stretched tighter and tighter across his cheekbones. His gray hair had been cropped very short, but clumsily; he must have done it himself.

"So," he said, "this is the warrior who escaped from Black-lock Davy."

"Couldn't bear to see her shot, patron," put in the shrike. "Tender heart."

"Tender," repeated Ran in a bloodless voice. He had a strange, abstracted gaze and didn't seem to take in what he was looking at. Syeira remembered one of the stories about Ran — that he had dreamed nothing but nightmares since the age of ten. She wondered if the nightmares were always there, flickering in the corners of his mind, sending shadows across his vision.

"I want those horses," he said, looking at nothing.

"They'll come, lord," replied the shrike. "They'll come after the girl."

"They broke out of my compound," said Ran. "They swam away from my ship. Three horses and a girl. A *girl*." He spoke as if it were all beyond comprehension. Turning to Syeira, he said, "You are wondering where you are. This is the workshop of Bergomane the Chief Mechanical." He nodded slightly toward the man in the blacksmith's apron, who lowered his eyes and took a step backward. "You're a child," he continued. "Then you know all the fairy tales about flying mechanical horses — creatures of hammered metal that would fly when their riders turned a peg or worked a lever. That is what we build here." His lips drew taut in a mummy's smile. "Here we make the fairy tales come true."

On the wall behind him was a series of charcoal drawings of horses, done in the style of old anatomical books. The first showed a horse without its skin; the second a horse without its veins and outer muscles; and the third was just a skeleton.

"I do the same, patron," remarked the shrike. "In my own way. Make the fairy tales come true, that is."

Ran nodded, still looking at Syeira with his empty eyes. "The shrike is an artist," he said. "That is why I sent him. To get you."

"I just put together a little concoction," said the shrike. "Used what I knew — and what you gave me, dream child." It flew closer to Syeira and perched on a workbench. "No birthdays, eh? Nobody ever told you how old you are? Might as well be wearing a sign that says ORPHAN. And that's a nice blank slate to start with."

At that moment a noise could be heard over the hammering and hacksawing. A young soldier burst through the doors at the far end of the room. He came close to the group and knelt down.

"Well?" said Ran. He wasn't looking at the soldier.

It took a moment before the young man realized Ran was

speaking to him. "My lord," he said nervously, "three warboys were destroyed over the sea. Hit soon after they were sent up, like the other ones."

The din in the workshop had diminished noticeably; a lot of the men were furtively watching Ran. He was looking at some point between the man's head and the ceiling. After a fearful moment, the messenger added, "The pilots survived — with broken bones." He stopped and swallowed; Ran's eyes never moved. In desperation he breathed out hoarsely, "The sergeant found this on the waves."

He drew out a feather — a long feather, bigger than an eagle's or condor's. It was off-white, but it seemed to show up brilliantly in the dingy workshop. He held it up as if to fend off Ran. The warlord took it and studied it, running his fingers through the fledge. Then, his eyes on the feather, he said very softly, "The boy speaks of broken bones. Say something, Bergomane."

Bergomane, along with everybody else, had been looking at the feather. Now he started and looked around. A number of the workmen were watching him anxiously.

"They must be *light*," he mumbled. "So light. Otherwise they'd need wings fifty feet long . . ." His voice trailed off.

"Broken bones," said Ran. This often happened to him: Something in the conversation would lodge in his mind, some word or phrase, and for hours he would repeat it and work it into almost everything he said. He handed the feather to Bergomane. "This may come in handy. For your designs."

Bergomane took the feather. "Thank you, patron." He backed away, eyes down, and his men returned to their work.

"What will we do with the girl, patron?" said the shrike.

Ran turned to look at Syeira. "She likes horses. Let her stay here." He glanced at the soldiers. "Chain her to the forge: She can work the bellows."

As the soldiers moved to execute their task, the shrike said, "Patron. Excuse me for asking, but . . . does she need her *ears* to work the bellows?"

But Ran was thinking of something else. "Broken bones," he said meditatively. "Broken, *broken* bones."

"Of course, patron," said the shrike easily. "You know best."

∽☙∾

After a day by the forge, Syeira's skin was raw from the heat and her hands were blistered. Every minute or so she would pump the handle of the bellows to keep the coal fire going. As long as the fire was healthy, the mechanicals paid no attention to her. They had too much to do. Indeed, Syeira could see that they were working feverishly to realize Ran's vision. Bergomane, along with several assistants, would often wheel out a mechanical horse — usually a small one, no bigger than a miniature pony — and position it in the middle of the workshop. The trunk of the horse would be formed out of several overlapping sections, to allow greater movement. Generally it had two holes in its side, where the wings would go. Bergomane would turn a handle or work a lever, and the other men would stand back. The mechanical horse would move forward, working its legs jerkily. It rarely traveled more than a few yards. Getting the horses to fly seemed an impossibly remote prospect. Bergomane had small models, made of tin and balsa wood, that sometimes flew clunkily across the room; but usually these broke apart on landing.

Once, one of the mechanical horses — a large one without wings — actually started to buck. It clanked around in a circle, working its back like a very elderly bull and actually exhaling something sulfurous through its nostrils. The mechanicals backed away, looking surprised and pleased. After a minute the thing seemed to wind down, and the men approached it warily. Just then something inside it — some kind of propulsive charge — went off with a metallic bang. The creature shot across the floor, bucking wildly. For about a minute there was complete chaos in the workshop. The horse was skittering and kicking in a wide circle, smoke pouring out of its nostrils, its ears rotating crazily. Sparks flashed as its hooves struck metal. Racks of tools and metal rods crashed to the floor. The creature barely slowed down, even when one of its legs fell off. The mechanicals — who were now on top of their worktables — watched in silent awe. Finally there was another muffled explosion. The horse went about a foot in the air, and when it came down, it had separated at the seam between its trunk and hindquarters. A puff of smoke billowed from the opening. The head clunked on the floor and lay still. One of the creature's ears was pointing forward, the other backward.

For a moment there was complete silence in the workshop. Then Bergomane got down from his table and looked around balefully.

"Okay," he said. "Don't *anybody* say, 'Back to the drawing board.'"

So it went during the day. When night came, Syeira was unchained from the forge and taken to a small cell. Then she saw that the building *had* once been a stable; the cell was definitely an old horse stall, except that the open sections were now covered in thick cage wire. (One good thing about Swebban was that it had no dungeons — only workshops. When somebody had to be put in prison, any space was adapted for the purpose.) The cell had straw on the floor, but not enough to cover the stones. The first night, Syeira tested the cage wire for weak points, but it was the work of Swebban ironworkers — in other words, strong enough to hold a lion. She spent an uncomfortable night wondering where Arwin and the colts were, and in the morning was taken back to the bellows.

She could have survived all this had it not been for the shrike. The bird would go on endlessly about itself and its art. After a while Syeira didn't even look at it, and soon, to get her attention, it began talking of other things.

"Maybe you're wondering," said the shrike, "what happened to Blacklock Davy. *That* was interesting."

Syeira was lying in the semidarkness of her cell, her face turned away from the bird. When she made no sign, the shrike flew to the ledge of the stall above her.

"Well, the warship sailed here," it continued, "after the horses escaped. Davy had to tell the patron everything. But he forgot to mention how he had saved you all from getting shot. That part was supplied by the crossbowman in a later audience with Lord Ran. Naturally the patron was furious. You and your marvelous horses had made his army look like fools. Nothing better could be devised to inspire the rebels. Already talk was getting around on the docks — I think a few soldiers had been too disgusted with Davy to keep quiet. Well, the patron ordered Davy to find you and the horses. And the gypsy said *no*. Of course, you know what happens to somebody who says no to the patron."

Syeira was listening intently but wasn't going to let the shrike know that.

"Lost his ears," concluded the shrike. "Took five men to hold him down, but they did it."

Now Syeira sat up. "That's horrible!" she exclaimed.

"We can't close our eyes to violence," said the shrike. "Anyway, they put Davy in leg irons. Took him back to the ship. He's probably back in Thurckport now. In Lord Ran's dungeons, that is."

"I don't believe you," said Syeira savagely. "It's just one of your lies. Like that story about dreams."

"Oh, that wasn't entirely a lie," said the shrike, glad to be able to talk about its own artfulness again. "I'm sure the patron *has* dreamed of you. Irritations of all kinds make their way into his dreams. And didn't I say the mysteries of your life would be revealed? I was referring to the mysteries of death and fate. We all want to know how we will die, and —"

"Why did Davy stop us from getting shot?" Syeira interrupted angrily.

The shrike appeared to think for a while. "He wouldn't say. Not even after his ears were gone."

Syeira lay down, feeling sick and bewildered. She sensed that something had happened in the boat, when they'd almost shot her. *Did Arwin see it?* she wondered. *And where is Arwin, anyway?* Ran had counted on the horses coming after Syeira quickly. Capturing them in the wild would have taken far longer — if he had been able to do it at all. Maybe the horses were outside Swebban now, just biding their time. . . .

"If you don't believe me about Davy," said the shrike, in its most civilized tone, "I can bring you one of his ears. It's part of my most recent exhibit now, but if you want proof —"

"No!" said Syeira, horrified.

"It's the ear with the earring in it," continued the bird. "Very symbolic. Without his earring, a gypsy is vulnerable. Well, this is life: We're all marked for death. Children *must* understand this. I'm exploring this theme in my new —"

"Oh, shut up! *Shut up!*" yelled Syeira, in a rage. She closed her eyes tight and put her hands over her ears. The shrike kept on speaking, anyway: She could hear the tiny grinding hum of its voice. A moment later it flew down and perched close to her, still talking. Syeira wondered if she could be fast enough to grab the creature. She took her hands away just long enough to hear the bird assert: "You say that anybody could hang up pieces of dead things. But would anybody know what pieces to *leave out*?"

She was just about to lash out when the bird — perhaps guessing her intent — darted away. The minutes passed. There was no further sign of the shrike.

"*Finally,*" Syeira breathed. She vowed then to smuggle out a poker from around the forge so she could clobber the bird.

~◆~

The endless work on the forge continued. Often Syeira was not taken to her cell at night; the mechanicals, toiling away, forgot about her. Bergomane would sit at his worktable, poring over blueprints, or sometimes just staring with his hands under his chin. Usually his chief assistant, Cinnabar Jack, would be there, too. They rarely did any metalworking late at night, and so did not come near the forges. Syeira would sit beside the bellows as the fire slowly dwindled, watching and listening.

One night, Bergomane was slouched at one of the long work-tables, muttering and flipping through the pages of a thick leather-bound book. Cinnabar Jack was sitting not far away. In his hands he held a small winged horse made of tin and was turning it this way and that, squinting along its angles. Suddenly Bergomane let out a snort.

"This has gotta be the living end," he said, looking up from the book. "Hey, Jack! Want to know how to make a brass horse fly up and down? Lend an ear:

> *But when you list to riden anywhere,*
> *You moten twirl a pin, fixed in his ear . . .*
> *And when you come to where you list abide,*
> *Bid him descend, and twirl another pin . . .*
> *And he will down descend and do your will,*
> *And in that place he will abiden still."*

Bergomane raised his eyes from the book. "A'n't that beautiful, Jack? A'n't that a beautiful world them artists live in? No need to worry 'bout propulsion; no need to worry 'bout lift; no need to get your hands all greasy black with reality. All you do is *twirl a pin.*"

He pursed his lips and daintily twirled an imaginary pin, to imitate artists.

"Now, boss," said Cinnabar Jack, a chunky man with red hair, "how come you're reading that old stuff again? It just gets you upset."

Bergomane rose from his place noisily. "You're right, Jack, you're right." He closed the book, glared at its spine, and tossed it to the far end of the table. "Someday," he declared grimly, "the books will be written by mechanicals, *not* artists."

"Someday," Cinnabar Jack agreed.

Slowly, wearily, Bergomane went over to his own small, cluttered workbench in the corner. From a pigeonhole he took out the long white feather that Ran had given him. For a moment he studied it carefully.

"What I'd like to know," he said, "is how they *breathe* up there. There a'n't much air, high up."

Syeira stood up, clinking her chain. "Have you ever seen one?" she called eagerly.

"Quiet, you," said Cinnabar Jack, without much energy. Bergomane didn't even look up. He continued to twirl the feather around.

"We just hafta keep working on the alloys, boss," said Cinnabar Jack doggedly.

Bergomane shook his head. "We've been doing that for two years now. You know what we've learned? Bronze and iron are too heavy and tin is too bendy. *That's* what we've learned." He put the feather back in the pigeonhole. "No," he said wearily, "we're in right sticky, Jack. The laws of physics is agin us, and if physics is agin a guy, what can he do?"

"They said a man wouldn't never fly," countered Cinnabar Jack. "And then we made the warboys."

"That's different," said Bergomane. "The warboys is right orderly and lawful in their physics. But now I wish we'd never made 'em, Jack. Then we wouldn't be in the state we're in now."

He reached down beside his bench and withdrew a large piece of rolled parchment, which he began to tack up on the wall panel beside the bench. Syeira could see it easily from where she was. It was a charcoal drawing of a horse, standing in three-quarter profile. An aristocratic horse, too — curved neck, high carriage, cascading mane. It could have been any thoroughbred from any part of the world, except that it had *wings*. These were very long and broad, like an owl's, with many layers of feathers in the midsection. The wings were only half extended so that the artist could fit them into the picture. They looked amazingly strong. Where they joined the horse's body, just behind the shoulders, the connective tissue was as thick as a young beech tree. The artist had tried to show as much anatomical detail as possible, but he must have just guessed at some things. The horse seemed to have a few extra ligaments and muscles, because of the wings, but these had been drawn in dotted lines.

What Syeira noticed on the drawing were the wisps of fine hair around the horse's fetlocks. Some breeds of workhorse have this; it's called "feather." It made her think that the flying horse, for all its unearthly elegance, had some very humble blood in it.

Bergomane stepped back and regarded the drawing gloomily. "But look at this crazy animal, now," he said. "It breaks *all* the laws." Taking a piece of charcoal from his bench, he scrawled something at the bottom of the parchment. Syeira couldn't read it, but Cinnabar Jack could. It said, "No bloody marrow in the bones?"

"You see, Jack," Bergomane continued, "metal's grand for a lot of things, but not so good for others. Take smelling. A piece of metal can't smell you, and you can't smell it. When you give away a piece — I'm talking about even the most cunning crafted bit of metal — and then find it again after ten years, will it smell you and give you back the morning of ten years ago? It won't, Jack. But a horse will. If I had just a fleck of an idea 'bout how to do that, then maybe I could make a flying horse."

"The flying horses are *fighting* Ran, aren't they?" called Syeira excitedly. "They're fighting with the *rebels*."

Cinnabar Jack glared at her, but Bergomane, as if noticing her for the first time, put down his charcoal and came over to the forge. In the dim light of the workshop he looked faded and bent, a rust-stained ghost. For some reason he reminded Syeira of Will Shanks.

"You know why, kid?" he said in a low voice. "'Cause Ran made the mistake of sending soldiers into the White Mountains. The soldiers stumbled on the foaling grounds of them flying horses. Some fool sharpshooters brought down four mares. New chapter in the conflict."

"Boss," Cinnabar Jack warned, but Bergomane ignored him.

"So now Ran is fighting both men and flying horses," he continued. "By themselves, the men wouldna had no chance. But from the air, Ran is vulnerable; his big weaponry a'n't too agile when it comes to fighting straight up. Those horses are naught but flesh against iron, but when they strike, it's like a lightning storm."

He turned and looked past the forge to the small, cage-covered window that hung just above the bench. "Aye, you stumbled into a bit of history, kid — horses and mechanicals fighting together. And it wouldna come about 'cept for one man. Old and gray, but still the leader of the rebels. He made allies out of men and horses."

"Who?" asked Syeira.

"You're going back to your cell," said Cinnabar Jack, getting up from the table.

"No, tell me," pleaded Syeira. "*Who* made allies out of men and horses?"

"Shut up!" whispered Cinnabar Jack as he came close. "That bloody shrike might be here somewhere. Do you want to get us all killed?"

The shrike wasn't there, though — at least it never came to Syeira's cell that night. For the first time since she'd been taken prisoner, she got a decent night's sleep. But the bird appeared first thing next morning, and it had apparently decided to step up its attack on Syeira. It perched beside the forge and explained how each new development in art used a new language and that you had to learn the language before you could understand the art. To illustrate this, it gave many examples from its own work. Once or twice Syeira actually sat down and cried out in pain.

"Why does that bird *torment* me so?" she asked Cinnabar Jack, when the shrike had finally flown away.

This was perhaps the only topic that Cinnabar Jack would have discussed with a prisoner.

"It torments all of us," he said harshly. "It was raised that way."

"Raised?" echoed Syeira. She couldn't imagine the shrike being raised as if it were a pet.

"Listen and learn, kid," replied the man. "You know what a shrike is? Folks call it the butcher bird. It has this habit of sticking its food — dead shrews and bees and such like — on a thorn or sharp twig. Ran liked that idea, so he got himself a baby shrike for his menagerie. Put it in a cage by itself and then forgot about it." Cinnabar Jack raised his head cautiously, but there was nobody nearby except Bergomane, who was gloomily tapering a red-hot horse's ear on the anvil. "The keepers lined its cage with the usual stuff — old broadsheets and pamphlets and so on. But it turned out they used a lot of these quarterly screeds what deal with 'art today.' I'm not sure why; I guess in bulk that stuff is cheaper than straw. Anyway, that was all the bird had. It didn't have no sunshine, it didn't have no trees, it just had them . . . *articles* at the bottom of the cage. 'Course, it couldn't read the articles; it could only look at the pictures. But that was enough. After a while it began to think it was an *artist*."

Bergomane, who had heard most of the explanation, now paused with the glowing horse's ear between his tongs.

"You see where I'm at, kid," he said to Syeira. "I hafta make the fairy tales come true, and I got a bloody artist hanging around, making my life miserable."

Cinnabar Jack looked sympathetically at the other man. "Come on, now, boss," he said. "It could be worse."

"How?" Bergomane replied plaintively. He stared at his assistant, grimy and bewildered, the horse's ear starting to darken on the anvil. "How could it possibly be worse, Jack?"

Cinnabar Jack seemed at a loss for a moment. "Well," he said, a bit lamely, "imagine if the shrike coulda *read* them articles."

One evening, two soldiers came to get Syeira. She was unchained from the forge and marched out of the building. The street was quieter than the workshop, but she could still hear a muted roar from the small foundry out back, where Bergomane's mechanicals experimented with alloys. The soldiers marched her down the street to a thin tower, very much like the one Syeira had seen in Thurckport. Up a winding staircase they went, and then into a large, tapestry-draped room lit by several candelabra. At the end of the room, Ran stood before a window, looking out at the grimy dusk. The shrike was perched on the sill. The tapestries in the room were all dark red.

Ran turned and motioned for the guards to leave. "You will soon be reunited with your friends," he told Syeira.

Syeira's heart sank. She glanced around the room and saw, hanging in the corner, a latticework of barbed wire. Small, flesh-colored objects were attached to sharp points of the wire. Syeira quickly averted her eyes. She knew it was one of the shrike's works.

"They were caught in an iron-mesh net," Ran continued. "One of the many traps I set up around Swebban." He paused, considering Syeira. "You were in danger of becoming folk heroes, you and your Arva horses. Your story had got around. And yet I caught you as easily as rabbits in a snare. I will make sure *that* story gets around."

A hunted fox, exhausted and close to death, will sometimes turn and take a last stand against the pursuing hounds. Syeira was ready to turn.

"That tale about dreams," she said. "It was just a trick of the shrike's. But he *did* say something true about you; I know it."

Ran's eyes narrowed. "What are you talking about?"

Syeira's mouth was dry. "He said that the dreamer was wounded as a child. The dreamer was wounded and now dreams strange dreams because of it. That's true — and the strange dreams are all nightmares. I know *that's* true, because we've heard it in *Haysele*."

Ran glanced at the shrike, which hopped and fluttered uneasily on its perch.

"I didn't mean anything by it, patron," it said hurriedly. "I just threw it in to make the story real —"

"That's why you kill so much, isn't it?" pursued Syeira. "Because of your dreams?"

The room became absolutely quiet. Through the window they could hear the faint call of a night bird. The shrike watched Ran nervously.

"So," said Ran. His voice made the dry, rustling sound of a snake advancing on its prey. "They tell that story about me, do they? In *Haysele*?"

He spat out the word as if discharging a mouthful of poison. Syeira stood perfectly still. Ran was rubbing his forearms, and

Syeira remembered another story about him — that, as he grew older, the ghostly remnants of those he had killed drifted inside him in wisps, and when he walked, he could feel them all there, layered like dead leaves.

"Well," he said, his eyes flickering, "perhaps you should hear the *real* story."

"A wise suggestion, patron," interjected the shrike quickly. "Too much of the child in this one."

"You will die, anyway," Ran told Syeira. "Eventually you will die like all the others. But before you do, you shall know the truth."

It took a full minute for the warlord to collect himself. When he resumed, his voice was blank and lifeless. It took a while for Syeira to realize who the story was about.

"Many years ago," said Ran, "back when everybody slept more, there was an orphan. He was raised by a small group of lords and ladies called the Protectorate, who had great plans for him. One of the Protectorate had formerly been a general. This old general was a very cultured man and spent a lot of time thinking about dreams. People believe that dreams are born and die in the mind, but as the general discovered, this is untrue. They are born there, yes, but many of them pass out of the mind and enter the world. They are blown about like pollen or dust or spider larvae, and end up thousands of miles away from the dreamer. In vain do we try to remember these dreams — they are gone forever. The general came to believe that the right kind of landscape might trap these dreams. He amused himself, and the orphan, by talking about such a land. Then, as sometimes happens to explorers, he *discovered* the very land he had imagined. From some wanderer or wise man he learned that it was a real place, with coordinates in this world."

Now, frightening as it was, Syeira could not take her eyes off Ran. She sensed a change coming over him, even though he still spoke in his cold, empty voice.

Ran continued: "The general reported this place to the Protectorate and proposed that the boy be taken there. At first they harrumphed. Dreams were simply childishness, they said. They had enough childishness to deal with as it was. But the general argued what he truly believed: that dreams were a way to know yourself — and not just yourself. Know the dreams of others, said the general, and you will know everything about humankind — the bad and the good, the wishes evil and saintly. And would not this knowledge be very useful to one such as the boy, for whom everybody had great plans? Then they got to talking among themselves, the Protectorate, and looking at the boy. Finally they gave their consent, smiling.

"The voyage lasted weeks. There was a sea, then land, then another, smaller sea. A ferryman took the boy and the general across the inland sea. The ferryman was a hooded, silent man. He said nothing until the horizon showed two identical islands shrouded in mist. Then he turned to the general and asked why they sought the land of dreams. The general gave his answer: The boy was seeking knowledge from dreams. The ferryman said, '*All* dreams? *All* knowledge?' 'Yes,' said the general. For he was not thinking of the boy, but of himself — as a man hungry for secrets of the human soul. The ferryman said nothing, but the boy saw that he changed the tack of his small sailboat. One of the islands came closer; the other retreated into mist.

"When they landed, the ferryman said the boy must go on alone. The boy didn't want to; he couldn't see much beyond the fog on the shoreline. The general waved him on, saying that he must be brave and adventurous, since everybody had such great plans for him. All the while the ferryman stood silent at the tiller. And when, trembling, the boy finally stepped onto the shore, he blinked once and saw that the boat was suddenly far away, a speck on the horizon. Then he knew that he was in the land of dreams.

"The boy saw that the mist was clearing, and he began to

walk away from the shore. The landscape around him was very pleasant — rolling fields and brooks and hedgerows. Soon the sun was shining. The boy began to feel better. He hadn't walked very far before he came to a thatched stable by the road. The door was open. The boy stepped across the threshold and saw a horse standing in the shadows. He was excited: It could be any kind of horse — a talking horse, a flying horse, a magic horse. This was the land of dreams, after all. The horse, raising its head, turned and began walking toward him."

The shrike had hopped close to Syeira and was watching her intently.

"The boy moved forward, too," continued Ran. "But then he stopped, feeling suddenly frightened. The horse seemed unusually skinny, almost a skeleton. Because of the shadows, which seemed to move with the animal, the boy could not see its eyes. And — perhaps most unnerving of all — it walked in a strange jerky fashion, as if it were a huge puppet."

Syeira closed her eyes, and when she opened them, Ran had come a step closer to her.

"At that moment," he continued in the same monotone, "the door slammed shut behind the boy. The whole stable became dark. But the boy could feel the horse coming on, hear the soft crunch of its hooves on the straw. And when it was only inches away, a voice came out of the darkness — a terrible, cold, dead voice. 'Welcome,' said the horse. 'I am the gatekeeper of this island. By the end of your stay here you will know my name. Get on my back.'

"For a second the boy was frozen in terror, but then he stumbled backward and scrabbled at the door. It would not budge. The horse took another step forward; the boy cried out in fright. 'Ah,' said the creature. 'You thought this was the land of *good* dreams. No, you have chosen the nightmare island — or rather, *it* was chosen for *you*. And I tell you now that any child who comes here must stay until his childhood is gone. Get on my back.'

"The boy was huddled in the darkness, crying for the general. But the stable remained dark. At length the horse said evenly, 'You can stay there bawling forever, or you can get on my back and we shall begin the tour. If you want to get it over with, you had best pull yourself together. For I say again that you shall stay here until your childhood is gone, but no longer.'

"The boy had no choice but to get on the creature's back. Once he was on, the stable door opened. He saw that the landscape had changed completely. It was now black moors and withered trees and a lowering, stormy sky. The road stretched ahead toward a dark horizon.

" 'Let us be off,' said the horse.

"Later, the boy could not say how long he had spent in the land of nightmares. The question has no meaning, for time there is not like time here. The boy did not sleep; nobody sleeps in that country. He rode the horse all the time. It told him about the people and creatures he met . . ."

"Tell her, patron," interrupted the shrike eagerly. "Tell her about the viper's head. And the Hand of Glory. And the face of the drowned lady." When Ran remained silent, the bird swiveled its head toward Syeira. "That's what it's like there, girl. *Pieces* of nightmares, mainly. Fragments and figments. Because they have to travel a long way. They become tattered and torn. Blanched by daylight, muddied by —"

"The boy never ceased to tell the horse that he was ready to go home," resumed Ran, as if the shrike had never spoken. "He begged, he pleaded, but it only told him of the new horrors to come. And it seemed to the boy that something inside him, something more vital than his heart, was growing small and knotted. Soon he could not feel it anymore. The horse seemed to see inside him — or rather *smell* inside him. 'My, how you've grown,' it said. 'What you brought here to this land is gone, gone forever. And the one who brought you here, the explorer, the seeker of knowledge — he is gone, too. You are ready to go home.'

"Then the horse was off through the dark air — not trotting, but flying now. Looking down, the boy saw by the moonlight that they were flying over water, then land, then water again. After a long time the horse set down and then seemed to dissolve under him. The boy felt that something awful was happening again and closed his eyes.

"'You are going home, yes,' came the voice of the horse, 'but I should tell you that no one who has visited the land of night-mares can ever leave it completely. Waking or sleeping, you will often return to this place. What is my name?'

"The boy said it in his mind, for he couldn't bring himself to say it out loud: the Night Mare.

"'Good-bye,' said the creature. 'And pleasant dreams.'

"After a long moment the boy opened his eyes again. He was in his own bed in his own city, in the house of the Protectorate. He got out and looked through the window: It was still dark, but he could tell that dawn was coming.

"The servants were, strangely, not astonished to find him there. And that was when he found out that the journey he had taken had somehow skewed time. He was back on the morning he was to set off, with the general, for the very land whence he had just returned. The general, he found, had died in his sleep. The Protectorate was disappointed that the boy could not go to the land of dreams — no one was willing to take the general's place — but they did not remain disappointed for long. The very next day, the boy began learning the arts of war. He was ready now; he even chose his own hunting hawk. The Protectorate were pleased. The obstacle they had been struggling with had vanished. Now they could realize their great plans."

The shrike seemed restless. It hopped from the window to the floor and back to the window again. Ran turned and came close to Syeira; she backed up a few paces. "And you," he said, "no doubt you have other kinds of dreams. Of your horses, perhaps. The boy dreamed of the Night Mare and will always dream of its land. Tell me, is that fair?"

"No," said Syeira fearfully.

Very easily, as if he were reaching for the salt, Ran put out his hand and grabbed Syeira by the scruff of the neck. "I asked you if it was fair," he said.

"*No*," repeated Syeira, now terrified. "No, it's *not* fair."

Holding her like a rabbit, Ran carried the girl over to the window. The sun had set over the sea. "Somewhere out there," he said, "somewhere out there are . . . the *islands*." Pain and rage curled the edges of his voice. "And one day I shall set sail once again for the land of dreams. But not for the island where I was taken. No, I will be looking for the place I never reached, the island of . . . *good* dreams. It is there."

He held Syeira up with a shaking hand. "It *must* be there," he gasped.

"Yes," Syeira blurted, in a desperate attempt to prevent Ran from slamming her against the wall or throwing her out the window. "Yes, it is."

Still holding Syeira, Ran turned to face the shrike.

"The horses stay in the cage by the canal," he ordered, his voice still quivering. "I want everybody to see them. As for the girl, she returns to Thurckport tomorrow."

"Yes, patron," said the shrike.

"What —" Syeira choked; her jerkin constricted her throat so that she could barely speak. "What do you want with *me*?"

Ran closed his eyes and then opened them, wide. For a moment Syeira thought she would die right there, but the warlord simply let her fall. She backed away quickly without getting up.

"You may think that the island of nightmares is out of reach," said Ran. "Not so. It exists in my dungeons. People have seen the Hand of Glory there, and the viper's head, and the face of the drowned lady. You shall see them, too." He looked at the shrike. "What do you say, bird? Is that fair?"

"It is, patron," said the shrike. "*More* than fair."

12

The Found
Charm

That night, Syeira was left alone in her cell. Bergomane and Cinnabar Jack had long since gone, and the workshop was lit only by a single shielded lamp. For hours she lay awake, breathing in the straw smell from the floor. Nothing moved around her, not even mice. She was numb to her blistered hands, numb to the past, numb to the future. All she could do was wait until morning, when she would be taken aboard Ran's ship.

And while she lay there, as cold and inert as the iron in the shop, she gradually became aware of a sound outside. It was a bit like a far-off wind — or rather, a *troupe* of winds. There seemed to be many currents and streams, some rising and some falling, some darting away and some dipping close to the world. She sat up. Now she thought she heard shouts, too, but it was hard to tell — the workshop kept out the sounds of the living world.

She got to her feet and, on tiptoe, peered through the cage. The workshop was all cluttered shadows. The lamp — a perforated tin shell enclosing a candle — hung like a tiny constellation in one corner. Half-constructed horses cast strange silhouettes against the walls. She listened again. Yes, those *were* shouts. From somewhere deep inside the building she heard a distant bang, then a muffled tinkling. The wind sounds came to her again, and something in the workshop rattled faintly. What was going on?

Suddenly a figure moved into the lamplight and crouched beside the forge.

Syeira held her breath, squinting into the darkness. The figure had become one of the shadows. After ten seconds it moved again, this time in the direction of Syeira's cell. Something flashed dully in the figure's hand — a blade.

She crouched down behind the stall door. Through the wood of the stall she heard the wheezy, labored breathing of the figure. A man — and heavyset, judging by the way he moved. Very faintly, Syeira smelled something unpleasant, like a scab that hadn't quite healed. She began to back up against the far wall.

A dark shape appeared just above the edge of the stall. The figure was wearing a hood and a face kerchief — the garb of a Swebban coal miner. The blade flashed in the darkness, and Syeira heard a steady *shink shink*. A hackblade, she knew. She'd seen them in the shop — a knife with six inches of iron-cutting sawteeth on the back of the blade. This blade must have been a good one, for in less than a minute the man had sawed a foot-long vertical cut through the wire. He paused and coughed heavily. Then he began a horizontal cut, about a foot and a half above the stall ledge. This one went more slowly, for he had to reach up to saw.

Syeira couldn't bear it any longer. "Who are you?" she whispered hoarsely.

The figure made no reply. He kept sawing, grunting slightly with each stroke, until he had finished the horizontal cut. Then he began another vertical cut, parallel to the first one. Syeira, crouched at the back of the stall, heard his breathing grow heavier. When he had finished, he grabbed the wire with both hands and pulled it toward him, bending it down from the uncut bottom. A small window had opened in the cage. "Crawl . . . through," the man said in a raspy voice.

When Syeira hesitated, he added, "*Hurry!*"

Syeira hoisted herself up so that she stood on the stall ledge and then, grasping the mesh in front of her, gingerly lowered herself through. The man leaned against the stall; he seemed out of breath. After a moment Syeira stood on the ground before him — slightly scraped on one leg, but otherwise fine. Again she caught the sickly odor, and involuntarily she took a step back.

The man didn't seem to notice. Gesturing for her to follow, he moved in the direction he had come. They passed the forge, where a few coals glowed in the depths like dragon's eyes. The darkness grew thick around them, then lightened again when they came to another shielded lamp. They stopped at a window; the cage had been cut here as well. Syeira felt broken glass crunch under her sandals. Now she could hear the wind sounds better: Outside, the night billowed and flapped, as if caught in a thousand ribbed sails.

Just then she heard voices — rough, urgent voices. She crouched down. Heavy footsteps went past the window; Syeira could hear the clinking of armor. Soldiers. She looked at the hooded man, who had slumped against the wall.

"Who are you?" Syeira whispered again. In answer he reached up, drew back his hood, and pulled off the kerchief. In the dim light she saw a heavy mustache and straggly black locks, tinged with gray. Her breath caught.

Blacklock Davy closed his eyes for a long moment and then opened them.

"Yea," he said. "Do you know me, chobbin?"

Syeira stared at him. With all his hair she thankfully couldn't see the torn nubs where his ears had been. All she could say was, "They . . . they said you were back in Thurckport."

Davy grimaced. "Nay, I didn't reach there," he said. "And I have the boy Pouty to thank for that. He nabbed this hack-blade — from this very shop — and slipped it to me the first night at sea. I sawed through the irons in seven hours. Got overboard, but they shot Pouty dead on deck." He closed his eyes again. "I owe you, Pouty. You turned out to be a fighter." He shifted slightly so that he could look out the window. "I made it to shore and then came back here. Copped the garb so they wouldn't know me. I had some scores to settle."

Just then, from outside, came a distant explosion, followed by more shouts.

"What's happening?" asked Syeira, looking out the window.

"The ayrelings," said Davy. "They're attacking."

"*What's* attacking?"

"The winged horses," replied Davy. "They're toppling catapults and ripping apart roofs and kicking holes in the warships. Spreading fire, too — they've learned to carry firepans and flares." He got heavily to his feet. "The rebels have every man out fighting, and thanks to the ayrelings they've won the harbor. If we stay low, we can get out of this city. But we must move now, before the battle swallows us up."

"We can't leave Arwin and the colts!" Syeira exclaimed. "They're in a cage by the canal."

Davy laughed painfully. "So Ran got her, too, did he? The old bruiser. You did well to hook up with that one, little mouse ear."

And then his tone grew thicker. "I knew you. I saw *her* when you turned, and I knew you." He blinked, and tentatively, wonderingly, added: "Syeira."

Syeira gasped as if she had been struck. "How . . . how did you know my name?"

It is said that only after a mercenary has lost a certain amount of his own blood does he remember those he has wronged. Davy was remembering then. He leaned against the wall, wheezing into the moist edge of the kerchief. An old rawness or tenderness made it hard for him to breathe. He was standing in a river meadow of twelve years before, and beside him was a horse, an aging dun stallion, waiting to carry him away from the turmoil he had caused. From that night the horse would take away a single gentle smell, a human smell. Davy would leave a few songs, and something precious to sing the songs; and in a few seasons (he thought) he would be over it all. He didn't know then that a sliver had lodged inside him. It wouldn't come out until now.

" 'Tis a gypsy name," he said.

⌦⌫

He said he would tell me everything. . . . Syeira's head was spinning as she stumbled after Davy. The gypsy would say nothing more until they were safely out of the city; already he seemed to regret what he had let slip. They moved down a back street that was shuttered and empty. The sounds of the flying horses filled the sky above her, but on the ground there was only shouting and the clanging of metal. Away in the east they saw the glow of a fire. Again and again Syeira saw flaming projectiles shot into the sky. Most of them went out quickly, but several fell with the bright liquid arcs of shooting stars. She didn't see any flying horses: only milky streaks high up, like the seethe of a distant sea.

But as they reached the canal, the battle spilled close to them — spectacularly.

From above them came yells and a sudden, smashing noise, as if two ships in a high wind had plowed into each other. Instinctively Syeira crouched down. Something was flung from overhead, and Syeira realized with a shock that it was a man. He flew above them toward the canal, turning over and over, the wind whistling through his mail shirt. Bits of metal rained down around Syeira; she winced and put both her hands on her head. The man hit the water with a final, swallowing sound — not so much a splash, but rather the abrupt *whoosh* that red-hot iron makes when it is immersed. Something else clattered to the ground in front of them and wobbled briefly before coming to rest. It was a wheel from a catapult.

"*That's* what it's like to be hit by an ayreling," said Davy, turning to look above and behind them. "That catapult must have been up on a roof. The army did have ones what could shoot big nets into the air, but they was sabotaged by the rebels."

They continued their desperate rush along the canal. At one point they had to duck behind a cistern while a group of soldiers passed, dragging another catapult. When they came out, Syeira saw the iron-mesh cages at once. There were no guards; the soldiers had probably joined the battle against the winged horses. But Ran's menagerie was all there. Leopards, lions, and wolves, spooked by the battle, paced and glowered in their cages.

In the middle cage, snorting and stamping, were the horses. They were clearly unnerved by the presence of Davy and laid their ears flat back at him.

"It's all right, Arwin!" said Syeira, as she came close. "He's going to get you *out*." Then, as if seized by doubt, she turned to Davy and said, "Aren't you?"

Davy said nothing; he was already sawing away with his hackblade. The spaces in the cage were just big enough to get the blade through. He sawed downward from eye level — slowly at first, then more rapidly as he was able to bring his strength into play. From thirty feet away, two leopards watched him with lashing tails. Syeira was glad the animals were there, surrounding the middle cage. Nobody who passed by would be able to see their escape.

Slowly Davy worked away with his blade. In a few minutes he had cut five feet down to the bottom. "Here, lady," he said tightly, pressing the cut edge inward. "Take it in your teeth and pull." Arwin caught on at once and yanked hard on the wire. A space opened up big enough for a horse's head. The colts came to help, and the wire was curled like hot lead over a blacksmith's anvil.

"You lads first," said Davy. As first one colt, then the other, inched out, he kept on cutting. As Arwin squeezed through the hole, the caged animals let out a chorus of growls and hisses, but the horses ignored them. They stood still while the humans got up — Syeira on Arwin, and Davy on one of the colts. (The colt had flinched under Davy's hand, but Arwin had calmed him with a breath and a touch.) Then they all moved south along the canal. High above them the sky seemed to have turned into a huge dark river, swollen and foam-flecked, ready to leap its banks at any moment. As she rode, Syeira would now and then hear a set of wingbeats detach itself from the muted roar. She would look up, but she could only see flurries of white in the darkness.

They were in the old part of Swebban now, galloping past crumbling customs towers and guardhouses and decrepit cottages. The clash and roar of battle continued around them. The path became dirt, then cobblestones again. Suddenly a wall loomed ahead, and the path veered off to the right, away from the canal. The horses wheeled and clattered along the route until it widened and Syeira saw sky. Ahead of them was a wall and an archway, topped by a torchlit parapet. The way out of the city, she knew. But blocking the path was a broken catapult, a mass of wheels and beams and springs. The horses came to a stop, half rearing, as if pressed back by an invisible wave. They seemed unreasonably spooked by the shadowed jumble: In the torchlight it looked like some small angular monster that had died while kneeling.

Davy slipped off his colt, swearing, and took a hold of the splintered frame. Just then the torchlight around him flickered. Syeira raised her eyes but saw only the archway and the blackness beyond. "Hurry, Davy!" she called. Davy thrust the frame to the side, kicked away a wheel, and returned to his colt. At that moment a voice rang out.

"Stay where you are!" it thundered.

It was Ran's voice. He stood over the archway, a loaded crossbow in his hand.

Davy froze beside his colt, clutching the mane to keep the horse from surging ahead.

"I will shoot the first one who moves forward," said Ran.

Davy's voice was thick with hatred. "You can't shoot us all," he called.

"No," replied Ran calmly. "But I can shoot one before you get out. Maybe two. I've always been fast with this thing."

Syeira could only keep still and pray that none of the horses would do anything rash. Davy had turned to face Ran, and his hand made a slight movement at his side. The girl didn't look at him: She knew he'd got his hackblade out and now cradled it against his forearm.

"Unluckily you are in advance of the rebels," said Ran. "My men and I are scattered through the old town, waiting for them." He raised the crossbow slightly. "I have sent the shrike to bring reinforcements; they are less than a minute away. So come, test your luck. Try me."

Above them they heard the river of wingbeats in the air. Davy's hand was motionless; the knife blade rested in his fingers.

"Your empire is dying, Ran," said Davy. "Killed by horses."

The crossbow turned slightly in Davy's direction. "You didn't know, gypsy," said the warlord. "You haven't heard. The world of horses is finished."

The colts were amazingly still, with only the skin on their flanks twitching. Arwin stood with her head high and her ears flat back. Syeira's breath came in small gasps.

"The world of horses is finished," repeated Ran, "and the world of iron has begun. I knew that years ago. In fact, I brought it about."

"I didn't see any of your iron horses up in the sky," spat Davy. He was edging, inch by inch, one foot away from the other, to get a better stance.

"They will be," answered Ran. "Once the sky is empty."

At that moment, one of the colts twitched a hoof. Ran's head turned, and Davy saw his chance. In a gesture too fast to follow, he raised his knife. It was a desperate move: Ran was thirty feet away, and the hackblade made a clumsy throwing knife. Maybe he had simply hoped to knock Ran's hand, trigger the harmless release of the arrow. In any case, the warlord was too fast for him. Syeira heard the harsh elastic sound of the crossbow releasing, and Davy spun around.

"No!" she screamed.

All of the horses exploded into action at once. Davy staggered, looking as if he had just drawn a long, painful breath. The fledge of the arrow showed as a small white blur on his chest. One of the colts went down on his knees behind the gypsy. Syeira scrambled off Arwin and tried to ease Davy onto the horse's back. He was unmanageable in her hands, but the colt went way down and then up, very neatly, so that Davy collapsed onto his back. In a second Syeira was behind him, trying to keep him upright.

They were too late. Ran already had a second arrow ready; Syeira could see it glinting in the torchlight. "Who's next?" he roared.

Syeira's colt was puffing and snorting under the weight on his back. Ran's crossbow swung toward Arwin.

"You've caused me enough trouble," he said.

At that moment, from high above, they heard a stallion's savage neigh.

It happened in an instant. Something raced down behind Ran like an angry sea bursting through a dam. He was punched forward, as if hit by a jousting lance. Over the parapet he tumbled, the crossbow falling from his hand. Above them the darkness became a squall of white, as though somebody had emptied a huge sack of ashes into a high wind. Syeira's hair was lifted by the updraft of twenty-foot wings. The colts ducked, their legs splaying, but already the flying horse was gone. It made one extraordinary move that nobody saw: To get between two buildings it turned slightly sideways, as a swallow would to enter a crack in a barn. Then it was three hundred feet up in the night sky.

Ran lay crumpled and still on the cobblestones. The horses swerved around him as they galloped out of the city.

Slowly the noise of battle faded. On either side of the canal, fields stretched out in the darkness. Syeira tried desperately to hold Davy upright, and the colt kept throwing its neck back to keep him on. Blood or saliva dripped onto the girl's hand. She herself almost fell off more than once, and the other colt, sensing this, came close and kept pace with his brother.

The horses drew up by a great oak tree, and the colt sunk down to the ground. Syeira slipped off, and Davy sagged slowly onto the dark earth. His entire body seemed to be stiff, but his eyes blinked slowly.

"Hold on, Davy," said Syeira frantically. She stared at the fledge of the arrow, then at Arwin. "Help me take the arrow out!" she cried. "*Help me!*"

But Arwin couldn't help; she only lowered her head and raised it again, showing the whites of her eyes. Davy's hand moved spasmodically toward the pocket of his jerkin. Syeira, desperately hoping he had something there to help — medicine, magic, anything — scrabbled at the pocket. Her fingers touched the broken glass of a bottle. A faint smell came to her nostrils. Even in her shock she recognized the Sleight. But now she only smelled it as a human would — so faint as to be barely noticeable.

Davy was looking at the night before him with a long, calm stare. The horses drew back, snorting and pawing. It was strange and unnerving for them, to smell death in the midst of the vivid, shimmering Sleight.

For Syeira, the Sleight was as muted as an autumn flower. She looked at Davy and knew he was dead.

She slumped there on her haunches, head back, like a runner

who had just finished an exhausting race. Her hand with the touch of Sleight rested palm up on her leg. Her eyes were closed tight, as if against smoke, but the tears streamed down her cheeks.

"He was going to *tell* me," she choked.

When dawn came, Syeira could be seen digging in the earth with a heavy stick. From her movements she might have been a tiny, arthritic old woman. Soon she had dug a shallow pit, and with much tugging she managed to place Davy in his grave. Then she covered it with earth and bracken and a small log. For a long time she lay facedown beside the grave, unable to get up. The horses moved around her uneasily, the smell of death and the Sleight mingling in their nostrils. Eventually the girl raised herself to her hands and knees and looked at the earth. She felt as sick as a victim of fire or flaying, but she just stood up and got on Arwin's back. They began trotting along the canal again.

Gradually the canal left them, slanting off to the west. Clouds came, and some drizzle. Once they had to hide while a group of soldiers passed, but the men seemed intent on hurrying back to Swebban and did not notice them. They rested at night by an old mill, then continued on the next day. Syeira noticed nothing around her. Once she looked up to see that the day had declined into twilight. Soon they heard a river in the distance — the Hawkey.

The sound of water was the only thing to make an impression on Syeira's numbed mind. She watched as the horses came close to the river. *It must have been around here*, she thought, *that Davy first captured Arwin*. Oak trees lined the shore, not quite thick enough to make a forest, but thick enough to give cover.

There were a lot of birds here, singing in the twilight.

They trotted along the shore. The trees stood apart from one another like lawn statues, carved and self-sufficient, holding in the air the way resting whales hold in the calm upper ocean. A few white birches showed against the gray umber of oak and elm. Arwin had stopped to look out across the Hawkey, perhaps wondering if it would be a good place to cross, when the colts suddenly turned and raised their noses. Arwin, after a moment, did the same.

Somebody was coming behind them.

Syeira knew it couldn't be soldiers: The horses, while tense, didn't seem inclined to run. The birdsong grew quieter. Syeira peered through the trees but couldn't see anything.

After a moment they saw him emerge from the twilight. His face was in shadow, but what Syeira noticed were the items on his belt — bits of goat horn and flint, horse brasses, bright crescent moons, and shoots that looked freshly plucked. She had seen these things in stables all over Haysele. She slipped off the mare, for she knew who it was.

"The Stablecharm Man," she said.

He might have been an old farmer, except that he seemed to carry a lot of the night with him. His face was grained like old wood, his brow silvered and a bit skeptical. From his look he might have just retired and was now walking (for the first time) the road beyond his fields, noting everything with a stolid, practical interest. But he wasn't a retired farmer: There was all that dusk around him. Syeira suddenly felt the night above her not as weight, but as air. She looked up. A few dim constellations had drawn together and grown quiet, like horses feeding in a meadow.

"Evening, all," said the Stablecharm Man. At the sound of his voice the birdsong died away completely. He turned to the river for a moment, listening.

"Now, that's a sweet sound," he said. "I'll just get a drink."

THE BLUE ROAN CHILD · 247

Taking a mug from the bag he carried, he made his way to the riverbank, where he knelt down creakily and scooped up some water. "That's good," he said, after taking a sip. "Nice and clear here. Not like down south."

Syeira had come close and was watching him raptly. The horses stood behind her, ears forward and nostrils flaring.

"You're wondering if they're on your trail," said the Stablecharm Man, without looking up. "They a'n't. Ran is dead. Or let's say he's dreaming the dreams that were always denied him. I don't know what happened to his black pet there, the shrike. Maybe it went back to being a bird? I hope so."

Two sparrows had alighted in a tree nearby and started up the singing again. "Stalwarts," said the Stablecharm Man. He took another sip and watched them, his eyes crinkling. "Take the rest of the night off, men," he called.

Syeira didn't take her eyes from him. "Davy is dead," she said, her mouth trembling.

Without a word the Stablecharm Man shook out his mug and put it back in his bag. After a moment Syeira said, "Did you know him?"

"I'd heard of him," replied the Stablecharm Man. "Heard about his many torts and felonies. Then I met the man. Wounded and sick he was, and mad to get into Swebban. Said he had scores to settle. I gave him what I had for his ails, but he wouldn't stay out of Swebban. Fell out that he chose the night of the big attack."

"The ayrelings," said Syeira, remembering Davy's word for the winged horses.

The other nodded, his face grave. "Aye, the ayrelings. A dozen of 'em are dead in the streets of Swebban, their wings all bent and shivered, like saplings after a windstorm." He straightened with an effort. "But they won in the end. Ran is dead and the army is in chaos. We mechanicals captured the city, and —"

"We?" said Syeira in surprise. "You're a rebel?"

He nodded. "I'm a Swebban man, originally. Always hated what it had become."

Syeira remembered her conversation with Bergomane. "You're their *leader*!" she exclaimed. "Bergomane told me about you."

"Bergomane and I were once friends," replied the man. "Maybe we can be still." He shook his head. "He knew his job was hopeless. Nobody can make a flying horse; that takes a whole universe. The real ones have air pockets in some of their bones, so they're lighter than ordinary horses. Something about their lungs, too — helps 'em breathe higher up." He looked at the colts, which had come a step closer. "Years ago I planted Bayard trees in their foaling grounds, in the White Mountains. I was the only one who knew the horses were there. But then Ran invaded their country, and they had to learn right quick how to dodge arrows and cata- pults. Just like the rest of us." His glance shifted to Syeira. "Some of us mechanicals were fighting Ran, too — and losing. I saw that horses and humans could help one another. We did the ground raids and the sabotage, and they worked the high mischief. Some of us doctored the ayrelings when they got hurt. That took a bit of learning: Mechanicals are better at fixing *things* than creatures."

He looked around at them all. "Well, it's over now. I guess you're keen to get going. I came to see the Arva horses I'd heard about; all of Swebban knows how you swam away from Ran's warship. And also . . ."

He scanned the trees on the shore.

"Also, I never know what I'm going to pick up along this river at twilight," he concluded. "Found a lot of nice pieces that way."

But there was one more question that Syeira wanted answered. "What's going to happen to Broak," she asked, "now that Ran is dead?"

"That's partly why I'm out here wandering," replied the Stablecharm Man. "We're at the rebuilding stage, and for that I need harps and water clocks and those model universes with real comets inside 'em." He chuckled. "Leastways, I need the folks who can *make* them things. They went into hiding years ago, and now I aim to find 'em out and get 'em working again. Maybe I can even get 'em to spread through Stormsythe and into Thurckport. Magic can crumble an empire that's already crumbling, and these lads can fashion wonders. I tried to make a working universe myself once, and believe me, it a'n't everybody who's got the touch."

He slung his bag over his shoulder.

"So that's it," he said. "Now for a little charmwork."

He began walking along the river, picking his way carefully, and Syeira fell into step with him. The girl noticed that he was often glancing up and around, at the twilight, at the trees.

"Do you *find* charms?" she said.

The man nodded. "Sometimes. Or I should say, they find *me*. I just have to give 'em to the people they was meant for." He resettled his bag. "Bit of a chore, that part of it. But my old job had its own bedevilments."

"What was your old job?" said Syeira.

"Clockmaker," he replied. "Wanted to catch time and lay it out on my workbench. Hopeless as Bergomane's enterprise."

The dusk deepened. They passed a tree with strange smoky foliage, as if a nebula from the heavens had been brought down to earth and stained blue green. The horses kept up with the humans with no effort. The colts walked as they always walked, seeming to find quiet swells in the night to carry them along. Arwin laid down each foot lightly but without show, just as a great queen lays down a winning hand of cards. She walked as if she knew her troubles were over.

At length the Stablecharm Man stopped and looked across the river. Syeira could tell from the sound of the water that it was much shallower here.

"You can probably walk across now," said the Stablecharm Man. "No need to swim this one, brothers," he added, looking at the colts.

There was silence for a moment. Syeira looked at Arwin and remembered the night of their escape, remembered the pure arrow of emotion that had gone through her when she had smelled the colts. Would the mare let her remain with them? It occurred to the girl that Davy's Sleight, its content and essence, was now lost — except in the mind of Arwin. The mare would hold it there for the rest of her life.

"I'm going with them," she said to the Stablecharm Man. "I *think* they'll have me."

"Good," said the Stablecharm Man. "Then I'll have another friend in Arva. I already know a few gypsies there — and hacklers."

Gypsies and hacklers. Syeira remembered what Will Shanks had said about their trading secrets. Looking out over the river, she suddenly knew that Arva held something else besides vast empty spaces. It was a place of secret wisdom, a place to win and share lore, a place of brotherhood.

"I hope I'll see Will Shanks in Arva," she murmured. "He said hacklers go there at the end of their lives."

The Stablecharm Man nodded. "Arva is a big place, but it's funny how old friends find each other there. You may even run into Grulla and Marlow in those parts, sometime. I'm sure they'll get very curious about your new life among the hacklers and gypsies."

Beside them an aspen rustled in the breeze; the foliage was like an immense cluster of dusk-colored butterflies, all fluttering in place.

"Now," said the Stablecharm Man in a more businesslike voice, "I've got a charm for you."

Syeira grew quiet. She had been wondering if she could ask for something.

"At least I *hope* it's here," continued the man. "It comes and goes." He looked up into the trees and gave a soft whistle.

Out of the dusk came a brief flicker of light. Syeira thought for a moment it was a shooting star, but it flew to the tree beside her. She looked up through the foliage.

A tiny yellow bird was perched there.

For a second she couldn't breathe: The moment had grown all soft and twisty, as it does in dreams. The bird cocked its head at her and then broke into a song. Syeira stretched her hands high up on the trunk. The foliage had grown blurred in her eyes, but the bird's song was clear and sharp. She knew the song — knew it from somewhere far away, but also from somewhere near. For a moment it seemed to knit together two sections of time. She sank down at the foot of the tree, her shoulders shaking.

"It's my *bird*," she said, her voice clenching and unclenching as she wept. "It's my bird and I thought he was *dead*." She blinked at the Stablecharm Man. "How . . . where did you get it?"

"I didn't get it," replied the Stablecharm Man. "It's not one of my own. It came to me; I'm passing it on to you."

"But . . . it's my mother's bird, I *know* it," said Syeira. "From the river stable. When I was little . . ."

"Maybe," said the Stablecharm Man kindly. "I just know it was meant for you." He listened for a moment. "'Sakes, that's a *ballad* the man's singing. I've never heard birdsong like that." He looked at the bird for a long moment, wondering, curious. To the gypsies, certain birds were the most magical creatures in the world, even more magical than Arva horses. Well, this girl had one now.

Syeira had stood up again and was watching the bird. "Will he come with me?" she said. "With us?"

"I'll wager so," said the Stablecharm Man. "He seems to be at loose ends right now. I think he's come from pretty far away." He gave the bird one last look. He didn't know where it had come from — there was a lot to know in his line of work — but he was quite certain it had once belonged to Blacklock Davy. That was a gypsy song it was singing, he was sure. He gave a half-smile. Things had ended as they should: The daughter had been given the father's bird. "Well, time to go," he said. "I've done what I came for. Good-bye, friends. We'll meet again when the world begins to spin the other way and all the old songs come back to us. If that a'n't happening already."

Syeira got up on Arwin's back, never taking her eyes off the bird. When Arwin turned, the Stablecharm Man came into view and she said, "Thank you."

The man nodded. "You're right about hacklers going to Arva at the end of their lives. They also go there at the beginning. And I think you got a head start on the others, with all you know now."

Syeira smiled at him. She noticed that the charms on his belt still gleamed, even though the light was almost gone.

As the horses entered the water, the bird flew across to the other side to wait for them. Syeira could hear it singing out of the darkness. She would have plenty of time to listen to it where she was going. And when death and loss had finally left her, she would understand its song. Ghosts would come to her then, as they had come to her in the hold of Marlow's ship; and she would know that she was a roan herself, a mixture of sun and shadow — a cordial like the dawn, as the old horse books say. But all this lay on the other side of the river. On that last night in Broak, she saw only the dark waters before her. She heard only birdsong in the summer twilight.

And she didn't know that the bird would be with her only till autumn — that year and the years to come. An older gypsy would have understood this from its song. It was one of those birds that goes elsewhere in the winter.

ACKNOWLEDGMENTS

When I began this book, I knew nothing about horses, and so writing it has been a long and enjoyable education. For some scholarly lore I am indebted to John H. Pryor's classic article "Transportation of Horses by Sea During the Era of the Crusades," in *The Mariner's Mirror* of 1982. Also useful was Caroll Gillmor's paper, "Practical Chivalry: the Training of Horses for Tournaments and Warfare," in *Studies in Medieval and Renaissance History* (1992). I learned about "horsemen's oils" — aromatics used to control horses — in the fascinating books of George Ewart Evans, notably *The Pattern Under the Plough* and *Horse Power and Magic*. Other books that proved helpful were Stephen Budiansky's *The Nature of Horses* and Desmond Morris's *Horsewatching*.

In rendering the invention I call the warboy, I drew on several sources, notably Jim Woodman's book *Nazca: Journey to the Sun*. Woodman believed that the Nazca people of ancient Peru had developed primitive hot-air balloons, and to test his hypothesis he assembled a team to build and fly one.

I am grateful to the following people for reading and commenting on the manuscript (or portions thereof): Jennifer Watson, Fiona Marshall, Theresa Grant, Michèle Leslie, Dave Beedell, and my brother Scott. Thanks are also due to Maguy Robert and Cécile Roy, who granted me a leave of absence from my job in order to finish the book.

About the Author

Jamieson Findlay began his writing career as a science journalist. One day, ready for a change, he sat down to write a story. That story eventually became *The Blue Roan Child*, his beautiful first novel. He lives in Ottawa, Canada, and is at work on another book for young readers.

Heartland™

Share Every Moment...